The Legends of Glencyndal

Jo Sutton

Published by New Generation Publishing in 2018

Copyright © Jo Sutton 2018

First Edition

The author asserts the moral right under the Copyright, Designs and Patents Act 1988 to be identified as the author of this work.

Paperback ISBN: 978-1-78955-328-4
Hardback ISBN: 978-1-78955-329-1

All Rights reserved. No part of this publication may be reproduced, stored in a retrieval system or transmitted, in any form or by any means without the prior consent of the author, nor be otherwise circulated in any form of binding or cover other than that which it is published and without a similar condition being imposed on the subsequent purchaser.

www.newgeneration-publishing.com

Acknowledgements

Once again I would like to thank my family and friends for all their encouragement and support.

A special thank you, too, to Linda Harris and Jacqueline Abromeit for their hard work on my behalf and to New Generation Publishing for their guidance and patience.

Jo Sutton 2018

Also by Jo Sutton

In the *Henrietta Trout* series:

Golden Shifter — Book One
The Mythic Encounter — Book Two
The Island of Shrouds — Book Three
Death at Stonehenge — Book Four

and:

The Apothecary's Daughter

Contents

Part One – Frame One
The House of Secrets

Chapter 1	Arrivals	1
Chapter 2	Paintings and Things	6
Chapter 3	Enter a Dragon	10
Chapter 4	Where are you?	14
Chapter 5	Inside the Castle	18
Chapter 6	Charlie	23
Chapter 7	Annabella	26
Chapter 8	The Dragon Slayer	30
Chapter 9	The Mind Barrier	38
Chapter 10	Making Plans	43
Chapter 11	The Foothills of Ondraedan	46
Chapter 12	The Night can be Treacherous	49
Chapter 13	Ferlian Forest	56
Chapter 14	And then came a Bear	62
Chapter 15	Weapons	67
Chapter 16	A New Friend	69
Chapter 17	Bestim	75
Chapter 18	I have seen them	77
Chapter 19	The Bravery of Pitzic	81
Chapter 20	A Night of Crudelis	88
Chapter 21	Reunion	92
Chapter 22	The Escape	96
Chapter 23	One has to die	101

Chapter 24	Back to the Forest	106
Chapter 25	Beweglic	113
Chapter 26	The Banshee's Reward	118
Chapter 27	Bella's Journey	123
Chapter 28	A King's Story	128
Chapter 29	I want to go home	135
Chapter 30	The return of the Master	138
Chapter 31	Sorting	143

Part Two – More Frames
Shadows and Graves

Chapter 32	Caught!	149
Chapter 33	Friends or Foes?	152
Chapter 34	What do you want?	156
Chapter 35	Through Caddy Copse	159
Chapter 36	Equal Shares	162
Chapter 37	What do you know?	167
Chapter 38	Urthslean Speaks	172
Chapter 39	White Elephants and Bric-a-Brac	178
Chapter 40	Tea	182
Chapter 41	Shadows in Time	186
Chapter 42	Even the best laid Plans	190
Chapter 43	Jigsaw Pieces	197
Chapter 44	Life at Sea	202
Chapter 45	Unwelcome Visitors	208
Chapter 46	Tea with Geschwind	214
Chapter 47	The Reverend Wood's Diary	219
Chapter 48	Graves	223
Chapter 49	It's here!	225
Chapter 50	The Storm	230

Chapter 51	Charlie	236
Chapter 52	The Bells are Tolling	244
Chapter 53	Why?	247
Chapter 54	The Damage	250
Chapter 55	Is this just a story?	252
Chapter 56	A Cup of Tea	255
Chapter 57	Ends and Beginnings	259
Chapter 58	Cream teas always help	265

Part One

Frame One

The House of Secrets

Chapter One
Arrivals

The car scrunched to a halt. "Well, we're here!" announced Mr Ferriston. "Out you get!"

That was easier said than done. Tom and Charlie were surrounded by odd packages which their mother had decided would travel best in the back of the car. After much struggling and huffing, they emerged to stand on the gravel path outside their new home.

"Wow!" exclaimed Tom. "It's just like my painting, y'know, the one I did last week at school."

Charlie said nothing.

"You've seen quite a few photos of it lately, they probably gave you the idea," said his father. "And we did bring you here once as a little boy."

"Did I come?" asked Charlie.

"No," answered his mother, as she placed her free arm around his shoulder. Her other one was clutching the teapot close to her. "Tom was only two and a bit. You weren't born then."

"Well," said one of the removal men, "we ought to get a move on, the weather doesn't look that good, it looks like rain's coming. We've got to be up in Scunthorpe tonight, some folk are moving down south tomorrow. So, are you going to open up, squire?" he added, looking at Tom's dad.

Mr Ferriston laughed. "I'm no squire," he said, "but you're right, we'd best get things moving before it rains."

He produced a large, hefty key, for as the removal man said, the weather didn't look that good.

"As soon as we get in," said Mrs Ferriston. "I'll put the kettle on and we'll all have a cup of tea."

"That sounds a great idea," replied the first removal man. He was already lifting some chairs down from the van.

They all began traipsing back and forth carrying items from the van into the house whilst Mrs Ferriston made a welcome cup of tea, in fact by the time they had finished she had made several welcome cups of tea, and they had all learnt a great deal more about 'Green Willow'.

"The original house was a farm," explained Mr Ferriston. "It is believed to date from the 15th Century. It was given to my ancestor in payment of a gambling debt."

"Blimey," interrupted a removal man, as he heaved another box into the hallway. "Are you landed gentry then? If we'd known that we might have charged you more for your removal."

Mr Ferriston laughed. "We'd hardly have been living in an end-terraced house if we'd been landed gentry, would we?"

They nodded.

"It was known as Buckshill Farm, and, over the years, various ancestors of mine added the two wings and more land. In fact, it originally had a hundred acres. Some of my ancient relatives were not very good business men, and so, later on, much of the land had to be sold off to pay for their debts. Now there's only nine acres left, and at some time, in the 19th Century, they changed its name to Green Willow."

"Nine acres is enough surely," said one of the men, as he manoeuvred another box into the house.

Mr Ferriston agreed.

The first removal man gave him a long hard look. "So, you and your family must know all about the rumours... some of your ancestors must have lived here during all the troubles."

"What rumours?" asked Mrs Ferriston. This was the first she had heard of such things.

Mr Ferriston just laughed. "It's just rumours that's all. Nothing more."

"Well," said the removal man, "you wouldn't get my wife living near Chepham, that's for sure."

"What rumours?" persisted Mrs Ferriston.

Mr Ferriston frowned at the man. "Many years ago the area had a reputation for its witches and warlocks. Lots of strange things were supposed to happen here. I think it was just a way of getting tourists to come and to bring in trade. Nothing more."

"If you say so," said the man, "but there were some funny goings-on, so they say. Some even said that the village disappeared from time to time. Couldn't be found."

There was an awkward silence.

"That's Sussex roads for you," said Mr Ferriston, trying to make light of the man's comment. "And besides, that was all a long time ago. We're in the 1970s now, these are modern times. No one believes that rubbish nowadays."

Another pause.

"Well, we must be going," said the other man suddenly. "We need to start our journey up to Scunthorpe. Good luck!"

They were quickly on their way.

Tom and Charlie burst into the kitchen. "Do you know, Mum," said Tom. "There are eleven bedrooms in this house as well as masses of smaller rooms. What are we going to use them for?"

"Haven't you been listening to your father and me when we've been explaining all this at home?" she asked.

Both boys shook their heads. Tom grinned.

"Tell us again then?" he said.

"Pleeeease," added Charlie.

"Your dad and I are going to turn this into a small hotel, and run it on behalf of all the family. We'll need all those bedrooms for guests. Now go and put your things into your room and sort out all the cupboards and drawers. I don't expect to find a mess when I come up to check."

The two boys shot out of the kitchen and up the oak staircase to their room at the front of the house.

"I don't like it here," announced Charlie, as he sat down on his bed. "It's creepy. All this dark wood on the walls, and pictures of old people, it's horrible. I'd much rather be back in West Lee, in our old house, where we knew everyone and I had lots of friends."

He looked as if he might cry.

Tom came and sat by him. He couldn't believe that they had moved when he was half way through the top juniors, and he, too, was missing his friends, but this was the moment when he knew he had to be the big brother. After all Charlie was only just eight and he was ten. He put his arm around Charlie, who now had large tears running down his cheeks.

"Dad even said we might have to have separate bedrooms, Tom," he sobbed. "I don't want that. You don't want that either, do you?"

Tom hadn't even thought about it. They'd always shared, and he decided that there was no point in thinking about it when his brother was so upset.

"Of course, we'll share, Charlie," he said kindly. "Crumbs this is such a huge bedroom. It must be three times the size of our little one in our old house. No, of course we'll share."

They sat there in silence for a while.

"This hotel thing…" said Charlie, wiping his eyes. Tom nodded. "…Do you think some of the guests have already arrived and Mum and Dad haven't told us?"

Tom looked down at his little brother. "No there aren't any guests yet," he answered warily. "Why do you ask?"

"Then who's that little girl I saw in the corridor this afternoon?" he asked.

Chapter Two
Paintings and Things

Tom felt a cold shiver run down his back. His little brother was prone to a great imagination. They sometimes played amazing games when they were fighting aliens, or walking the plank, in reality they had never even left their bedroom, but this was different. He could see by the look on Charlie's face that, whatever Charlie saw, he really believed that a girl was in the house. He had intended to tell Charlie about some of the things which his father had said last week about his ancestors, especially his great-grandfather, which Tom really didn't like hearing, but now that Charlie believed he had seen a girl, well, he decided he would have to play a waiting game. Too much information all at once, Mum would say.

"I'll go downstairs and ask Mum and Dad," he said, in a matter-of-fact way.

"No," replied Charlie, standing up. "Let's go and search together. She was only little, about five I think. Let's just go and see."

Tom hesitated. "Okay," he said. "But we stick together, not like those crazy films when people split up and go searching in different directions. Understand?"

Charlie nodded. He picked up his cricket bat.

"Why on earth are you bringing that?" asked Tom, staring at him in amazement.

"She might have a big brother," he answered, grinning.

"So have you," returned Tom, and strode from the room.

"Wait for me!" replied Charlie.

Together they made their way out into the gallery, from where they could look over the bannister down into the great hall, then they passed their parents' bedroom and turned left. This really was a great sprawling house. Another short corridor was immediately on their right and led past four smaller rooms. On the left was a bathroom, and a large walk-in cupboard. A broken chair lay in the bath, and the room smelt very soapy and damp. The boys tried the taps on the wash basin, they were old and squeaky. At the end of the corridor was a long, dirty window which overlooked a large patio in the back garden. In the distance they could see fields which lay beyond their land and woodland. Beyond that, way into the horizon, was a silver sliver of sea.

"So, where's this girl?" asked Tom.

"She was here," replied Charlie. "I'm sure of it. She saw me and ran into this room."

He pointed to the corner room which looked out onto the garden. The heavy oak door was closed.

Tom knocked on the door. "Just in case," he explained to Charlie. There was no answer.

He turned the handle. It was hard to move, the door was well and truly stuck and, in the end, they both had to push hard to open it.

"There's no way a small girl could open this on her own," he said. "She must have had help, or perhaps she wasn't there?" he added, looking down at Charlie.

"I'm not making it up," retorted Charlie. "There definitely was a girl here, and when she saw me she rushed into this room."

"It could have been a trick of the light," suggested Tom. The look on Charlie's face told him that in no way did his brother believe that.

They glanced around the room, and Tom peered out of the window. There was an old-fashioned metal fire escape just outside, but he reasoned that the girl did not come into the house that way because the window was covered with cobwebs which hadn't been disturbed for years. A large black spider ran silently down the window frame as though daring him to come closer. In one corner of the room there were several old paintings stacked together as though someone was preparing to move them out.

"Let's search the rest of the rooms up here," he said kindly. "You never know, she might have slipped back into one of those."

Charlie just nodded.

The gallery ran around three sides of the great entrance hall. It allowed access to all the other bedrooms and cupboards. At the back of one such cupboard was a door which led straight to a stone spiral staircase. The boys decided not to climb it but to leave it for another day, at the moment they were more concerned with finding this girl, whoever she was. In the end Charlie had to agree it was probably a trick of the light, all they found was dust, old furniture, bits of candles in jam jars, mouse dirt and several spiders.

"Let's go back to that first room," said Tom, seeing the disappointed look on Charlie's face. "Let's see what those paintings and things are about."

Tom was really good at art. He enjoyed going to art galleries much to his friends' amusement. His other great love was running. He had been the fastest boy in his old school.

Altogether there were about twenty paintings. At first the boys just rummaged through them, but then they decided to take them back to their bedroom to sort them out properly. The dust in this little room was causing them to sneeze so much, and they weren't that fond of the spiders. Tom counted five large ones looking down at them from the ceiling. It took some time to carry all the paintings along the corridors, but eventually they were there, and both boys felt a sense of achievement.

They began to go through them when suddenly Charlie said, "Look, Tom, look. It's like your castle."

Tom stared at it. Charlie was right. As far as he was concerned, it was identical to the painting which he had done at school last week. It definitely was his castle.

Chapter Three
Enter a Dragon

"What on earth have you boys been doing?"

Their mother stood in the bedroom doorway, staring at all the clutter in amazement.

"You were supposed to be sorting out your cases and putting everything away," she exclaimed. "Instead you seem to have acquired an enormous number of old paintings and some jam jars, and you're covered in dust!"

"Look," said Tom. Charlie held up the painting of the castle, which they had found, as if he was an auctioneer displaying an antique, whilst Tom delved into his school folder and produced his own painting. "There – see."

"See what?" replied his mother.

"It's my painting," replied Tom, almost shouting in frustration.

"What's going on?" his father suddenly joined them. "What's the problem?"

Tom explained it all again, and then added, "And then there's the dragon!"

Even Charlie looked surprised at this last comment.

"What dragon?" asked his father.

"Come and see," replied Tom.

They all went downstairs to the front of the house. The large, heavy, double oak doors stood shut. With some difficulty Tom pulled them open and pointed to the ornate decorations. The doors were covered with medieval ironwork. Leaves, flowers, and mythical creatures, such as strange birds and lions, but there in the left-hand corner was a different beast. Carved into the wood was a dragon which appeared to be slowly crawling up the ironwork. Its face was turned towards the outside and its eyes seemed to be able to follow anyone who was looking at it. It was menacing.

Tom ran back to his room and reappeared very quickly clutching his own painting.

"There!" he said triumphantly. "It's my dragon!" He remembered how one of the girls in his class had said that it was the most evil-looking dragon she had ever seen. Not that she had seen that many, he'd retorted.

Mrs Ferriston shivered. "It's getting quite cold, Jack," she said to her husband. "Let's go back in and close the doors."

They stood in the hallway.

"I agree," said his father. "It is funny that you should paint a picture of a castle like the other one, but they're not that similar. Yours reminds me of Bodiam Castle but the painting you've found doesn't look quite like that, it has turrets and a drawbridge, and as for your dragon, well, all dragons look the same to me, Tom. I don't think there's anything strange or odd about it."

"The kitchen's warm," Tom's mother gave a shudder, she remembered the words of one of the removal men. "And I've made a beef casserole which should be ready now. Come on, let's go and eat, we can talk about it after some food!"

"A good idea, Sue," he said. "Let's go and eat. Moving house makes me very hungry!"

Charlie was off to the kitchen like a shot. Mr Ferriston put his arm around Tom's shoulder.

They chatted about the new house over the meal.

"You see," said their father. "Green Willow is a very old house. We Ferristons have owned it for over four hundred years. It's now become a bit of a liability because there are so many covenants attached to it, which means it cannot be sold whilst a Ferriston still lives. Costers, our solicitors, have worked hard for us over many years. We're a long living family and your great-aunts and uncles have entrusted us to look after the house and to make it viable."

"What does that mean?" asked Charlie.

"It's got to pay its way," replied his mother. "It's come at a good time for us, what with your father being made redundant, and my qualifications in catering, we should be able to make it work. I feel guilty that we haven't been able to talk much about it to you both, especially you, Tom, but, as you know, things have been a bit difficult."

Tom nodded. He knew how upset and worried his parents had been when his dad had learnt that he had lost his job; even so, he still hated leaving his old school and friends.

"But you won't get rid of the paintings, will you?" he asked.

"Well," replied his father. "I don't think we could, even if we wanted to. Costers said that nothing was to be removed from the house, everything must remain, not necessarily in the same place, but all the furniture must stay in the house, and that, I suppose, must include the paintings."

"Good," replied Tom.

"Did the people before us," asked Charlie, as he took another helping of the casserole, "did they have a little girl?"

"No," replied his father. "Why do you ask?"

Tom gave him a gentle kick under the table.

"Oh, nothing," replied his little brother, giving him a kick back.

"Now," said their mother. "It's been a hard day. At least your beds are ready, so it's time to go up. I'll come up with you tonight, just to make sure that there is some hot water and everything is alright, but, Tom, those paintings cannot stay in your bedroom for ever. Tomorrow you and Charlie must take them back to that end room. Understood?"

Tom nodded. He knew those paintings were important, why he couldn't say, it was just instinct. He decided that, before they all went back to that room full of spiders, he was going to have a good look at all of them. There must have been some reason why they were kept together, and why Charlie's 'little girl' hid in that room, because he was beginning to believe Charlie's story. There was something definitely odd about this house.

Chapter Four
Where are you?

The next morning dawned bright but cold and showery. Cold March winds were driving early icy April showers towards them. Apart from the banging and rattling of the old radiators, it was difficult to believe that this house had any central heating.

"I'd hoped to get out in the garden, I wanted to explore it," complained Charlie. "But Mum says it's too wet, and she says we're to put all these paintings back first anyway."

Tom nodded. He wanted to have a good look at all of them.

"Dad doesn't think that the painting of the castle looks like mine, but I think it does," he muttered. "Let's have a good look at it."

Charlie dragged it from the pile. It was a good metre long and almost a metre in width.

The castle was set on a high rocky mound with a moat and a drawbridge. It towered over the small village which nestled close by. A gnarled and twisted oak tree stood in the foreground. It was a wintery scene, so its bare branches seemed to be reaching out from the painting, as if enticing the watchers to step forward. Much of the ground was covered in snow. They stared at it for some time, and both shivered, it was a cold and harsh painting.

Tom asked Charlie to hold it up.

"I don't think I like it as much as yours," said Charlie. "Look how dark the sky is becoming, and I don't like holding it."

"What do you mean?" asked Tom. "What's wrong with holding it?"

"It's cold and it's getting heavier," replied his brother.

"Don't be silly, Charlie," replied Tom. "The sky can't be changing, it's not moving. This is how it was painted, and this is how it was when we first saw it."

"I don't think so," Charlie shook his head. "I think some of the clouds have moved since yesterday. And what's this on the floor? It looks like snow." Charlie propped the painting up against the wall.

Tom laughed, though he didn't sound too sure. "I'll get my picture out and we'll compare them," he said.

Turning to get his own painting he suddenly heard a gurgle and felt a blast of cold air. He turned back just in time to see a large black hand curl around Charlie and drag him into the painting. All the colours seemed to be exploding into large bubbles of paint which were quickly filling their bedroom.

"Charlie!" he shouted.

The painting grew larger.

"Charlie, where are you?" he repeated. "Stop messing about! Charlie!"

"Come quickly!" said a voice. "Come now! There's no time to lose if you want to see your brother alive again!"

Tom looked around. He felt as if he was drowning in white paint. It turned into a blizzard. Outside had become inside, the whole painting now dominated his bedroom. Someone threw a heavy cloak around his shoulders.

"Come," said the voice again. "Follow me."

"No!" shouted Tom. He couldn't see for the snow being driven into his face. "Where's my brother? I must find him. What have you done with him? Charlie! Where are you? Answer me."

"He can't," said the voice. "He's been taken. If you want to save him then you must come with me into the castle. We must get within its walls before the Solanum realise that you are here."

"I don't understand," replied Tom, trying to wipe the snow from his eyes. "What has taken him? Where is he?"

The wind was howling and the snow felt like little shards of glass hitting his face. It was hard to stand upright. A deep growling was coming towards them, and the sky began to fill with dark shapes twisting and turning as bolts of lightning bit into the ground.

"If you want to see your brother alive again," said the voice with more urgency, "then you must come with me to the castle."

"I can't even see you," shouted Tom angrily.

"I am right beside you," said the voice. "You just have to look."

Tom almost fell over in surprise, for there by his side stood a stocky man no bigger than himself. He had on a deep mustard-coloured cloak and long brown boots.

"Okay," said Tom, his voice shook as he tried to control his fear. "But you had better be able to help me find my brother or I shall go straight back and tell my dad."

The little man laughed. "Where will you go back to, Tom?" he asked.

Tom looked behind to the place where he knew his bedroom should be. The room had gone, all that was there was an unending blizzard.

"Come," said the man again. "We must get within the castle walls before the Solanum attack. They cannot reach us there."

Tom followed.

It was only a short journey of about two hundred metres, but it was very hard and full of danger. They slipped and slid their way up the slope to the castle. All the time the wind roared and pulled at their clothes. Tom felt as if the skin on his face was being slowly peeled away.

Invisible hands kept clutching at him, pulling him down to the ground. The little man constantly helped him to his feet. If it had not been for his strength, Tom felt that he would surely have been dragged away. He kept thinking of Charlie. Where was he? What sort of evil had taken his brother? How was he going to find him in this strange place? How were they going to get home?

The journey across the drawbridge was hard. Exposed as it was, the dark shapes gathered in force. Their aim seemed to be to drag Tom into the icy waters of the moat.

'Nothing is going to stop me finding, Charlie,' thought Tom angrily. He pushed his way towards the gates which swung open as they approached. Eager hands pulled them through into the courtyard.

"Close the gates!" someone shouted. "Bring down the portcullis!"

A great bloodcurdling scream tore through the sky. Tom looked up. The black shapes had disappeared and a pale blue sky appeared above their heads, then all was quiet.

Chapter Five
Inside the Castle

"Follow me," commanded the little man.

"No," replied Tom firmly. "You said if I followed you I would see my brother again. So, where's Charlie? What is this place? It's just not possible that I've…" He stopped.

It was obvious that this little man was someone of authority as the gasp which rose from the group, which now surrounded them, was very audible. To everyone's surprise the little man did not argue but smiled.

"Follow me please, Tom," he said quietly. "We can change into some dry clothes, have something to eat, and then I will explain everything to you, especially what has happened to your younger brother, Charlie. Come."

Tom gave a grunt and followed. He was trying desperately to look brave but inside he was trembling. Who were these people? Where was he?

The walls of the castle were very thick, so thick in fact that they contained whole rooms. Tom had never given any thought to such things in his own painting. Down through the walls they sped, all the time their way being lit by a golden light which seemed to come from the little man's hand. Suddenly they entered a large room which Tom quickly realised was the castle kitchen. People were busy working at the kitchen stoves, baking cakes, loaves and pies, but when they saw his guide they stopped and bowed.

"Get on! Get on! Don't stop," said the little man, waving at them.

They immediately went back to their work.

"Dry, clean clothes are waiting for you in that side room," he said. "Come back in here when you are ready. Poco will help you."

An even smaller young man, with long pointed ears, came and bowed before Tom.

"Follow me please, Tom," he said, and pointed to a doorway.

Tom looked for his guide, but he had already left. "Where did he go?" he asked in panic.

Poco laughed. "Geschwind moves very quickly, but then, he is the Grand Master of all Magicians," he added, as though this was common knowledge.

"The Grand Master of what?" asked Tom. "What did you call him? Gesh…?"

"He is the Grand Master of all Magicians," replied Poco, laughing. "His name is Geschwind… Gesh… wind," he added slowly.

He handed Tom a small pile of clothes. "Change into these dry clothes and when you are ready come back here for some food," and with that he ushered Tom into the side room.

They had given him a dark blue shirt, knee-length trousers and knee-length boots. The clothes fitted him perfectly and were surprisingly warm and comfortable. He left his wet clothes on a stool and made his way back to the kitchen.

"Welcome to Glencyndal. My name is Poco," explained the young man, then seeing the look on Tom's face he grinned and waggled his ears. "I'm an elf," he added simply.

"An elf," repeated Tom, in a matter-of-fact tone. 'Why not?' he thought with an air of resignation. 'After all, a few moments ago I was in my bedroom looking at a painting of a castle, and now I seem to be inside it.'

Poco brought him a bowl of the stew which was being cooked in large pots.

"Thanks," said Tom. "Have you seen my brother?"

"No," replied Poco and left.

Geschwind suddenly appeared and sat down opposite Tom. He too was presented with a bowl of the stew. Tom took the opportunity to have a careful look at his guide.

He was about the same height as Tom but, because he was thick-set and broad-shouldered, he gave the impression of being much bigger. Tom could see by his hands that he was a person of great strength. His eyes were of the palest blue, but they weren't cold, no far from it, they were full of kindness and humour. Above them arched magnificent shaggy eyebrows, like mountains of white frost. His snow-white hair curled and tumbled its way down and over his shoulders, and his moustache seemed to melt into his long beard which straggled down to his waist. His clothes were a motley collection of dark greens, of autumn shades and mustard yellows, he looked as though he had just stepped out of a much earlier time.

'But then,' thought Tom. 'No one here looks a bit like anyone from my world, but dressed like this, I doubt if any of my friends would recognise me either.'

He felt that attack was the best way to hide his fear. "Where's Charlie?" he demanded. "What have you done to him?"

Geschwind paused, his spoon was halfway towards his mouth. "I don't know, but I have a good idea, and I have done nothing to your brother. Those are the answers to both your questions, Tom."

"Those aren't good answers!" retorted Tom. He thumped the table hard with his fist, making their bowls rock. "The only reason I've followed you is to find Charlie." He was almost in tears with frustration. He started to calm down. "Now, please, where is he?"

All the chefs and cooks looked up from their work. They were not happy at hearing their Grand Master being spoken to in such a manner.

Geschwind answered quietly. "I understand your anger and your fears more than you can imagine. Everyone here, including myself, has lost a dear one to the Solanum. This time, however, they have ventured out into your world. This has not happened for many, many years. Dreadful though it may seem, it also gives us hope that they have been forced to take such action."

"I'm sorry," replied Tom. "I'm sorry for all your troubles, but I am here for my brother and I intend to find him with or without your help. So where do I go to reach this Solanum or what's-his-name?" He stood up to leave.

"Sit down," commanded Geschwind. A flick of his wrist caused Tom to do as bid.

"Listen carefully," said the magician. "The Solanum is not a person but an evil group of the followers of Skadmeer the Destroyer. They are led by three commanders, Teracind the Claw, Slaf the False One, and Nhiamar the Bringer of Nightmares. It is my belief that Teracind the Claw has abducted your brother, perhaps he even thought it was you, I don't know, but this I do know, if it was Teracind, then your brother will be guarded by the dragon Bestim, and you cannot fight him on your own. Do you understand?"

Tom sighed and looked about him. "Why should all that be difficult to understand?" he answered sarcastically. "I've just stepped into a painting, I've met an elf, a magician, and I've walked into a castle which looks just like one I painted at school. So, let's throw a dragon in for fun, I expect you're going to tell me it's the same as the one on the front door, the same as my other painting, aren't you?"

Geschwind looked at him long and hard. "Yes, you are right," he answered quietly.

The room became suddenly silent. Everyone was looking at Tom, waiting for his reaction. As for Tom, he wasn't sure where to look. It was all becoming a great fog in his brain, this couldn't be real. Names such as Teracind and Bestim didn't exist in the normal world, but then he remembered that final scream of terror from Charlie.

"Okay," he said. "So, who's going to help me fight this dragon?"

Chapter Six
Charlie

Charlie thought he was going to die. The black gunge, which seemed to be all around him, was dragging him further away from safety, away from his bedroom, away from Tom. He let out a scream of terror but it came to nothing. The gunge was stifling all sound but its own. It roared and growled about him, plucking at his clothes, filling up his ears, and pulling at his arms, so he was forced to go wherever it wanted. He tried closing his eyes tightly hoping that it was some kind of hallucination, or even a bad dream, but it wasn't.

Gradually, he opened them to see that he was being hurled forwards over the top of a dark forest. It wasn't a comfortable journey. Whatever it was, the thing carrying him made erratic movements and didn't seem to care if Charlie crashed into the tops of trees. The forest gave way to a mountainous region, and Charlie's feelings of panic began to grow. What if this thing dropped him? What if he fell down into one of the gorges below? He tried to call out again, but no sound came, and just as he was about give up, he saw the front of a large castle set into a mountainside looming out of the mist. He was unceremoniously dropped at the entrance and lay there, unable to stand because he was shaking so much. At that moment their new house, which he had hated, was the best place in the world. If only he could return there. Something or someone grabbed hold of him and whisked him into a large dark hall. There at the very end, on a tall granite throne, sat a monstrous figure.

Teracind the Claw, towered over the scene. He didn't bother to descend from his throne but looked scornfully down at this poor, trembling child.

"You are not the Master of Urthslean," he hissed. It was a statement of fact not a question.

Charlie just shook his head.

"Answer me properly, little man child," boomed Teracind. "What is your name?"

Suddenly Charlie's mouth felt very dry. It took him a while before he was able to answer.

"Charlie, my name is Charlie Ferriston."

It seemed a lifetime before Teracind spoke, during which Charlie ventured to look at this monster. It must have been at least twice the height of his father. On the end of each finger he had a twisted talon. Charlie couldn't see his feet because he wore a long black robe, but he was aware of Teracind's teeth, which were enormous, and shone white against his deep purple skin.

Teracind lifted his head and roared in anger. Charlie fell to the ground in terror.

"You fools," he shouted to no one in particular. "You have brought me the wrong child. Take him away, give him to Bestim. Get rid of him. Kill him."

Little dark green shapes came running out from the walls of the hall ready to snatch Charlie. They were not much bigger than Charlie himself, but they too had large claws and enormous yellow eyes.

Suddenly Teracind stood, "Stop!" he bellowed. And everyone froze.

"Put him in the cave with the other one," he smiled, which was even more terrifying. His great teeth loomed large towards Charlie. "He will act as bait for the so-called Master of Urthslean. Yes, that will seal his fate for ever."

The little people quickly gathered Charlie up before Teracind could change his mind or seek revenge for their mistake.

Once again Charlie felt himself lifted up, but this time there was no roaring or erratic flying. He was taken to a large cave on the far side of the mountain. The little people bundled him inside and left. From the cave's entrance he could see way into the distance. Mountains and yet more mountains stretching endlessly to the horizon. He was alone. He curled up in the entrance and began to sob.

"I wouldn't stay there if I were you," said a voice from the back of the cave.

Charlie leapt up and spun round. No one was there.

"Come back here with me. It's safer. You don't want to be there when Bestim gets back."

"Where are you?" he asked. His voice shook with fear.

"Here," said the voice. "Come on, come here."

Charlie stood and made his way towards the sound. From out of the shadows stepped a figure. It was a girl.

Chapter Seven
Annabella

She looked as if she had been burrowing in the ground. Her clothes were filthy and ragged, she had no shoes, and her long dark hair was tangled and knotted. Charlie saw that she carried a hefty stone in one hand. He looked at it warily which made her laugh. He would never forget that first laugh, it made him feel good.

"Who are you?" he mumbled, wiping at his tears with the back of his hand. "Annabella," she answered, tossing away the stone and holding out her other hand to greet him. "And who are you?"

"Charlie," he replied. "Charlie Ferriston. Where are we?"

"Come," she said, and led him further into the cave.

Charlie imagined that the cave would be darker the deeper they ventured in, but it suddenly seemed to be lit by a great light. Looking up he could see a large hole in the roof of the cavern where the sunlight poured in. Annabella had obviously been there for some time, because she had made herself a comfy corner with a bed of rushes, and had tried to brighten up her surroundings with strange-shaped stones which she had placed on rocky ledges. A simple oil lamp even sat in one corner. She collected some water, from the side of one of the walls, which she let trickle into a small stone cup.

"Sit down," she said gently. "My friends call me Bella, you may do that too. Drink this, it will make you feel better."

Charlie accepted the drink and gulped it down, which was not easy as he couldn't stop his hands from shaking. "Where are we?" he asked again. "Why am I here?"

"Where do you come from, Charlie?" she asked.

"West Lee," he answered, but then corrected himself. "No not any more. Two days ago we moved into Sussex and now we live at Green Willow. Are you the girl I saw in the house? Were you kidnapped too?"

"No," replied Bella. "I've never ventured into the land of Sussex. So how did you get here, Charlie?"

So, Charlie told her everything; the removal day, Tom's drawings, the paintings, once he had started he couldn't stop. At the end he held out the stone cup for another drink and Bella poured one out. At last his hand was steady.

When he mentioned the great purple monster, Bella gave a sharp intake of breath.

"So, you saw him, you saw Teracind?" she asked in awe.

"I don't know who it was," replied Charlie. "It didn't give a name but kept saying I was the wrong one, I'm pleased to say."

"Teracind, the Claw, he is the right hand of Skadmeer and the Solanum," she replied, as if that was the answer to everything. "Why do you think he said you were the wrong one?"

"He said I would be bait for the Master of something or other," replied Charlie, he started trembling again. "I can't really remember. To be honest I wasn't listening, I was too scared, and all I want is to go home, to be with Mum and Dad, and Tom."

"Tom?" interrupted Bella. "Who is this Tom?"

"My big brother," replied Charlie. "The one I was telling you about who can paint really well. He's about your age I would think."

Bella smiled but said nothing.

"Who's Bestim?" asked Charlie, knowing that he wasn't going to like the answer.

"Well," began Bella. A large roar interrupted her reply. "Here he comes, you can see for yourself."

She hastily pulled Charlie over to one side of the cave as a blast of hot air and flames shot past them.

"He's a dragon," she continued with a sigh. "He is our guard, we are his prisoners. I have tried many ways of trying to escape but I haven't been successful. If it wasn't for the bear…"

"The bear!" echoed Charlie in horror. "A dragon AND a bear?"

Bella chuckled. "The bear is my friend," she said. "I think I would have perished without his help. He brings me food from time to time and bulrushes for my bed, but at great cost to himself. If Bestim sees him it is terrible, as the bear is no match for this dragon. It is large and ugly and—"

"I know," interrupted Charlie. "It will be Tom's dragon. It will be like the dragon on the great doors to Green Willow. I've seen it."

Bella looked at him in surprise.

"So, what does your bear look like?" he asked.

Another roar and a blast of hot air made them both shrink against the cool wet walls of the cave.

"Does Bestim come deeper into this cave?" asked Charlie anxiously, before she could answer his first question.

"He tries," replied Bella, "but he can't. He's far too big. My bear can only come when Bestim is out hunting, which isn't that often as the Crudelis usually bring the dragon his food here."

"The Crudelis?"

"The little people who brought you here," she answered. "I was captured by them on the orders of the Solanum."

Charlie looked at her. What on earth could she have done that these creatures needed to kidnap her? "And your bear?" he asked.

"When he stands tall he is easily more than twelve feet in height," she said with a hint of pride. "When he comes here, he is too large to enter the cavern, so he leaves any gifts outside on the ledge for me to collect."

"What sort of a bear is he?" asked Charlie, puzzled at the idea of having a giant tame bear.

"Well," she answered. "He is a golden bear with a broad brown stripe down his back. He has deep green eyes and enormous feet, but he is still not strong enough to defeat Bestim on his own."

"Perhaps this Master, whoever he is, might help the bear to defeat Bestim," suggested Charlie. "Then we can both go back to our own homes."

Bella looked at him and smiled.

Chapter Eight
The Dragon Slayer

"This is not going to be easy, Tom," said Geschwind. "You can't just ask for a group of volunteers and go charging off to fight a dragon like they do in story books. This needs careful planning."

His next comment surprised Tom.

"Tell me all you know about your family, your ancestors."

"Why?" asked Tom. "I just want to find Charlie and then go home."

"It's very important, Tom," replied the Magician.

Tom sighed. "Well," he said. "There's not much to tell really. Most of what I know I've only learnt recently. I know that when great-grandfather Ferriston died he was more than one hundred years old. I was told that he'd lived in Green Willow all his life and that he had people come in to look after him. I've discovered our family has owned Green Willow for more than four hundred years and that they were Iron-masters. Dad said that when the iron industry began to fail in Sussex, then our family turned to sheep farming and a bit of smuggling on the side. According to Dad, no one visited great-grandfather because he was evil. That's about it really, but what has this to do with finding Charlie?"

"He was not evil," interrupted the Magician. "Foolish, perhaps, but not evil."

"But everyone in the family knows that he murdered my great-grandmother!" replied Tom. He was beginning to feel frustrated by all this delay. "That's evil."

Those within earshot looked up from their work in horror.

Geschwind spoke gently. "Was he sent to prison?"

Tom shook his head. "Dad says, that there wasn't enough evidence."

"There is so much more," said Geschwind calmly. "So much, including the coming of Dark Forces into your home. There are other tasks which must be undertaken first before you will be ready to do battle with these. Trust me, Tom, and I will help you to clear your family's name and to find Charlie." He paused as if to emphasise this last sentence and stared straight into Tom's eyes before adding, "This I promise."

Tom took a deep breath. "Am I in some horrible dream? Are you really a Master Magician?"

Geschwind laughed. "This is no dream, Tom. I am the Grand Master of Magicians. I can trace my ancestry back to the true magicians of the First Age, the Guardians of the earth's treasures." He rose from the table, and carefully wiping the crumbs from his beard, he said, "Come my friend, we must meet Lusinga."

"But Charlie…" began Tom.

"Do not worry," replied the Magician. "He is safe all the while you are alive!"

The brightness and size of the Great Hall took Tom by surprise. He had never considered the interior of the castle when he had painted his version at school. The Hall was very long and flanked on either side by slender, fluted, pastel-shaded pillars. Rich, red, heavy curtaining was draped around its grey stone walls. It was full of little people of all shapes, sizes and the countless colours of the rainbow, who broke into spontaneous applause as they entered. Two very thin men with extremely pointed noses ushered them in, and they bowed so low that Tom was sure their noses touched the ground.

At the end of the hall, at the top of a small flight of steps, stood the elegant figure of Lusinga. All bowed as she stepped forward to greet Tom.

"Welcome, Dragon Slayer," she said.

For some reason, which Tom could never explain, he felt the need to kneel before her. In contrast to all the colours around, Lusinga was dressed in a simple white gown, her long golden hair cascading down her back, she was beautiful.

"Welcome to the Castle of Campandella." Her voice was soft and echoed on a whisper towards him. "We are of the faery folk, Tom, and have lived on this earth since before the beginnings of time. We have travelled through many countries and many times. It is here we will make our last stand against the Solanum."

Tom's mind was in such a turmoil that he couldn't have replied even if he had wanted to. He still half believed that he would soon wake up, to find all of this to be nothing more than a strange dream.

'What,' he thought, 'on earth was she talking about? Did she really say 'faery folk'? No, it wasn't possible, and yet…'

Lusinga was still talking. "Gioco has real pixie blood in his veins." She indicated a sturdy man, about the same height as Tom, with bright red hair and long pointed ears. He smiled.

"Whilst Pitzic comes from elfin stock." Another little man came forward and bowed low to them.

Tom gazed at them both. 'Well,' he thought, 'they certainly don't look like any pixies or elves I've ever seen in books. The one called Pitzic looks as though he'd make a good scrum half.'

"Those of the faery folk who follow the Solanum are led by Skadmeer, the Evil One. Skadmeer controls all that comes from the Dark Side. Teracind, the Claw, is one of his most important generals. It is he who commanded the

Green Ones, the Crudelis, to capture your brother. They thought they were kidnapping you. Over time, some of your ancestors have been able to help us in our battle against these creatures," continued Lusinga.

"How did they do that?" asked Tom fearfully.

Geschwind interrupted. "Your family's destiny and that of our land of Glencyndal are entwined, Tom. It was the House itself which called you here."

"You mean 'Green Willow'?"

Geschwind nodded. "Yours is a parallel world to ours. There is a time fault which runs through the House. Events are happening even now which are causing the fault to shift again. Our worlds exist together and should never ever have to meet or cross one another."

"Are you saying," Tom spoke in measured tones, "that this has happened before and that the house has some sort of magical powers?"

"Yes," replied Geschwind. "Yes, to both of your questions. I harnessed its powers to reach you, which is why you painted—"

"The house and this castle," interrupted Tom excitedly. "I told my mum and dad this but they didn't believe me. Charlie did though, I'm sure he did."

"The keys to Glencyndal are concealed in some of the paintings, Tom," said Geschwind. "It is because of my stupidity that they have been placed in danger, it is—"

"No," said Lusinga. "That is not true, Geschwind. You were not to blame. Many of your ancestors, Tom, have tried to help us in the past. Some have been more successful than others. If Geschwind is correct, and he's seldom wrong," she smiled, "then you are surely the Master of Urthslean, and this gives us much hope."

Geschwind nodded to Pitzic who gave a short bow before handing a blue velvet cloth to the magician.

"You must have this," said Geschwind. From the folds of the cloth he produced a dull, ancient scabbard covered in strange patterns and designs, the hilt of a sword jutted out. "This is Urthslean. It is yours." He held it out and presented it to Tom.

Tom recoiled. It was too much. At that moment the whole castle gave a sudden lurch. Cries of fear could be heard in the corridors from those who sheltered nightly within its walls. Tom could hear parents comforting their children, and then all was still, all was quiet once more.

"It is the time fault, Tom," Geschwind frowned. "They have been more frequent of late and are beginning to slip beyond my control."

Tom stared at the sword, the horrible reality of having to kill something raged in his head.

Geschwind answered his thoughts. "Bestim is not an animal, Tom, he is pure evil. Urthslean was forged by your ancestors many, many years ago for this very purpose. They knew such a time would come, when one would be called to destroy the Dark Forces, to kill Bestim. You are that one, Tom. You are the Dragon Slayer."

"I know, I know," Tom clenched his fists. He was tired, and at this moment he just wanted to go home with Charlie. "You keep telling me all these things but no one really says why. Why me? All I ever wanted was to find Charlie. Now you're saying that you want me to find out the truth about my great-grandparents, and I've got to kill a dragon, just because of a carving on the door. It's not fair. I didn't ask to come here. You're the magician. You do it. I just want to find my brother, and leave."

Everyone in the Hall gave a gasp. Tom was aware of a quiet humming sound coming from somewhere.

Geschwind gave a little cough.

"All the paintings which you have found in 'Green Willow' were created many years ago by Jonathan Ferriston, one of your ancestors. Not all are portholes into Glencyndal, but some were created using very special paint. These are the keys, and much of what has happened to you and your family is because Jonathan found them and used them."

"Then it's his fault," interrupted Tom. "Let him kill the dragon."

Geschwind smiled sadly. "If a fault lies anywhere, it is with me and the House," he murmured.

Tom began to interrupt again but the Magician held up his hand for silence.

"Your family has been remarkably careless in their handling of money—" he said.

"My dad says that," interrupted Tom again.

Geschwind smiled. "Your great-grandfather was no exception, Tom. He mixed with some very dangerous people who flattered and encouraged him in his silly habit of gambling. Just like Jonathan, he fell deeper into debt. It was under their influence that your great-grandfather began to carve the dragon. Even as he worked on it, he felt its life force struggling to be free. He nearly destroyed it, this creature of great evil, but others far stronger than him persuaded him to place it on your doors.

"They tried to buy the special paintings from him, knowing that they were portholes to other places, but it was your great-grandmother who prevented this from happening at great cost."

"How…?" began Tom. He could hear that humming sound again. The little people were becoming restless. "How did my great-grandmother die?" he whispered.

"There was a terrible accident, Tom, but first we must dispose of the dragon, Bestim, and release the others, including your brother. Whilst Bestim lives he is capable of calling the Evil Ones to your home. The carving on your door is becoming more powerful," answered Geschwind.

"Are they already there?" asked Tom, thinking of the little girl whom Charlie believed had been in the room with the paintings.

Geschwind looked puzzled. "No, I don't think so. With each new owner the Evil Ones must receive a fresh invitation into the home. None of the Crudelis have ventured into your world for many years now. It is possible, I suppose," he wrinkled up his nose. "No… they cannot enter unless you allow them in, or the dragon, Bestim, calls them. They will try anything to reach the magic paints, the keys to other worlds."

The castle gave another lurch and the little people cried out in fear. Geschwind clasped his hands over his ears, frowning as though in great pain.

"What is it?" Tom moved quickly towards him.

Geschwind's eyes were closed and his breathing heavy and measured. Gioco was by his side. After a while he looked up and smiled, his blue eyes clouded in pain and sadness.

"It is nothing," he said. "It will pass. I must not relent but concentrate on my purpose. Forgive me, a moment's doubt nearly broke through my thoughts."

Tom didn't understand Geschwind's words but he suddenly felt a new feeling of confidence. "I would like to hold Urthslean," he said quietly.

Without a word the Magician handed Urthslean to Tom. A sigh filled the Great Hall as Tom slowly and deliberately withdrew the sword from the scabbard where it had lain dormant for hundreds of years. As Tom held it high he could hear a beautiful flute-like melody whispering around his head, it filled the Hall and the corridors of the castle from the highest turret to the lowest cellar. The ponies in their stables snorted and whinnied in expectation. The Song of Urthslean filled the air once more. Tom made little thrusts and cuts and, as the blade moved through the air, so slivers of light traced its path.

The song finished, though for a while the final note seemed reluctant to leave. As it quietly faded, so Tom gently replaced the blade and the lights disappeared.

"I didn't expect that," he said softly. "It feels right. It's not as heavy as I imagined."

"It was made for you," replied Geschwind. "Your early ancestors were fine blacksmiths and iron-masters. They knew that one day it would be needed. We have waited so long for this moment, Tom. You are the Dragon Slayer."

"I hope so," Tom smiled. "I just hope you're right, Geschwind, that's all."

The humming sound returned but this time it was much stronger as all the little people rose into the air, their wings beating as fast as any humming bird. They were all cheering Tom, the Master of Urthslean.

Far above the heights of Mount Ondraedan, green lights hovered in a dance of defiance. Someone or something was laughing, scornful of the little people's new-found resolve.

Bestim sniffed the air and threw giant flames of anger across the canyon. Deep in the cave Charlie blocked his ears to deaden the noise, whilst Bella smiled quietly in her sleep. She felt certain that someone was coming to rescue them.

Chapter Nine
The Mind Barrier

Despite everything that had happened, Tom slept well that night. Perhaps it was the tankard of Hunitwede which he had enjoyed with Pitzic, or perhaps it was the way Gioco seemed to be able to calm all fears by his own happiness. He felt guilty knowing that he had slept so well, and that Charlie had probably had a fearful night.

He knew he was still somewhere in the castle, which was in the painting, which was in his bedroom. He now knew what it must be like to be the smallest Russian doll! He made to leave his room to go to breakfast but a whistle called him back. Urthslean was rattling in its scabbard.

"Oh no," he sighed. "Have I got to drag you around everywhere with me? You'll weigh a ton around my waist."

He was, however, surprised to find that it was as light as a feather, in fact he soon forgot he was wearing a sword. It was as if he and Urthslean had become one. He still worried about his parents, but both Geschwind and Gioco had assured him that time was on a different plane in Glencyndal, and that all the time he was alive, Charlie was safe. He definitely had no plans on dying at this moment.

He made his way to Geschwind's quarters. Little people kept bowing to him as he passed by, wishing him luck and a safe journey. A single "Come!" answered his knock on the study door.

He entered a large, oak-panelled room lined with books, oh, so many books. A large old map hung on one wall, he didn't recognise the shape of the country. In the wide bay window was a huge desk piled high with twisted scrolls, scraps of paper and even more dusty looking books. It was flanked by another similar desk. In contrast this was quite clear, except for writing paper and some beautiful snowy white quills paired with dark green ink labelled Dragon's Blood. Altogether eight quills were poised for action, no hand guided them, they were all being controlled by Geschwind's thoughts.

"Good morning, Geschwind," whispered Tom, gently closing the door behind him. The magician merely nodded as one of the quills faltered, causing a blot to appear on the paper. He shot a fearsome look at the offending quill which quivered and the blot disappeared.

"Sorry," said Tom, the quill blushed bright pink.

"Concentrate," snapped Geschwind to the quills, they immediately shot upright. "We have eight different messages to send to the far corners of our land. Lives may depend upon these arriving in time."

Eight different messages were being sent in eight different languages all by Geschwind's thoughts.

"Keep up! Keep up!" roared the magician to the little quill who had blushed pink.

The room was silent, the only sound punctuating the stillness was the scratching of the quills. Finally, Geschwind sighed and the quills collapsed by their pages.

"Sometimes it is safer to send messages by conventional means rather than use magic," he said.

He didn't seem to notice Tom's eyebrows shoot up at the word 'conventional'. Nothing was remotely conventional in this room. Full of books, scrolls, half dead potted plants, clay pipes, and a moth-eaten teddy bear lounging in an armchair looking as if it was following his every movement. No nothing was conventional here.

What really caught Tom's eye was the line of tiny model elephants which stood on the wide windowsill which ran around the bay window. They were beautifully made. He carefully picked up one and nearly dropped it when a clear deep voice said, "Please put me down."

Geschwind laughed. "They are not toys, Tom. These are my messengers. Watch. I need eight messengers to fly to the Far Corners."

Immediately all the elephants stood to attention. There was quite a bit of noise as they were all made of metal, and there was a great deal of trumpeting.

Eight elephants rose and settled on his desk. Wings sprouted from their sides. These, plus the careful use of their ears, would ensure quick getaways and soft landings. They gently rolled their trunks around the scrolls, and, on his command, rose as one, flying through the window with ease. Straight through it without breaking the glass or even causing a crack, and disappeared into the sky. Geschwind turned to the remaining herd.

"Change!" he commanded again. With a whirr and a click, the metal plates covering the elephants moved and remodelled themselves as lions.

"Nothing can be traced," muttered Geschwind to an amazed Tom.

"Wow!" exclaimed Tom. "How did they do that? How on earth did they fly through that window? And now these others have changed shape! How many shapes can they do? It's amazing!"

"It's just magic, Tom," replied the Magician simply.

"And after they have delivered these messages, will they change too?" asked Tom.

"No," replied Geschwind. "Though," he added ominously, "such is the danger, not all will return."

"Can we go now?" asked Tom, impatient to leave. "I must find my brother."

"Yes, of course," answered the Magician. "Once on the journey I will explain all you need to know about the Solanum." Suddenly Geschwind gave a grunt and fell to his knees.

"What is it?" asked Tom. Twice Tom had seen the Magician struggling in pain. Grand Master or not, he could not hide this. He helped the Magician to a chair.

"I have thrown a Mind Barrier around Glencyndal," he answered simply, as if it were an everyday occurrence.

"A Mind Barrier!" echoed Tom in amazement. "What on earth is that?"

"My thoughts have conjured up an invisible wall around the entire kingdom. It has not been without a price," Geschwind sighed. "Some of my dearest friends have had to lose their memories of other lands and relatives, but this was the only way I could protect them. I shall make certain that these memories are returned to them as soon as the Crudelis are defeated. Over time the Barrier has been breached, once by Beweglic and at least twice by the actions of your ancestors, and each time the Solanum has grown stronger."

It didn't surprise Tom in this strange world that the little teddy bear had climbed down from his chair and was now sitting by the side of Geschwind as though trying to comfort him.

The Magician continued. "Each time the Solanum try to break my thoughts, it is like a knife that twists and probes about in my brain. They know you are here."

"This explains why Gioco could not remember what lies beyond Glencyndal," said Tom. "He became quite distressed when I asked him last night."

Geschwind nodded. "It is safer for him not to know."

"It's amazing," said Tom in admiration. "It's real magic."

"Yes, it is," smiled Geschwind, his eyes suddenly lighting up with laughter, then he added grimly, "Others would do well to remember that we Gnomes were appointed as the Guardians of Earth's Treasures. We take our duties very seriously. It is very dangerous to underestimate our strength."

"We must leave, Geschwind," said Tom urgently. "My brother needs me."

"You are right," replied the Magician standing up quickly. "Come let's saddle up the ponies!"

Chapter Ten
Making Plans

Charlie looked for Bella, she seemed to have disappeared. For one horrible moment he thought she had left him here in this dark cave on his own. Surely she wasn't a ghost as well? She couldn't be like that other girl back in the house, he had spoken to her, she'd given him water and food. He began to panic, when he became aware of muttering coming from the cave entrance. Bella was there, she was talking to someone.

"Come, Charlie," she called when she heard his movements. "Come and meet my Bear!"

Charlie moved cautiously forwards keeping one hand on the damp wall of the cave, it seemed to give him some support and helped keep his balance.

"This is my Bear!" announced Bella proudly.

The sudden light after the darkness of the cave momentarily blinded Charlie. He could only gasp when he saw the Bear. It was enormous. The ledge outside the cave entrance was not very wide, it was part of a narrow path which circled around a crater. A crater which could well be all that was left of a small extinct volcano. The Bear was standing on the other side of the crater, almost opposite them, and next to a strangely shaped rock.

"This is Charlie!" called Bella. "He is my friend."

The Bear grunted. "I have food for you," he called. "I cannot come around the ledge as some parts have disintegrated since my last visit. I will throw this across to you. I hope your friend can catch!"

With that he hurled a large fish across the chasm which hit Charlie hard in the face and caused him to fall over.

Bella laughed and grabbed hold of the salmon before it slithered off Charlie and fell down the crater.

"Thank you, Bear," she called. "Where is Bestim?"

The dragon was nowhere to be seen.

"He has been summoned by Skadmeer and Teracind. Beware, they are all in a very bad mood. Keep well out of their way, especially you, Charlie," replied the Bear.

"What has made them so angry?" asked Bella.

The Bear looked about him, he seemed to sense that the Crudelis were on the move.

"It appears that Teracind has confessed that the Crudelis brought back the wrong person. They were supposed to bring the Dragon Slayer, so that Skadmeer could dispose of him. Instead they brought back Charlie. Skadmeer is very annoyed by this. Keep well into the cave, Charlie."

Charlie nodded. "Is the Dragon Slayer my brother?" he called out to the Bear.

The Bear was anxious to be away. "What is your full name, Charlie?" he asked.

"My name is Charlie Ferriston," he answered. "We've just moved into our new house, into Green Willow."

The Bear grunted. "Get back into the cave," he suddenly ordered. An unpleasant looking creature appeared by the strange stone. It was green and had three talons on each hand and upward slanting eyes. The Bear seized it before it could do anything and hurled it into the chasm. "The Crudelis are returning," he shouted. "Go!"

Bella and Charlie needed no second telling. They ran, clutching their precious fish, deep into the cave. Outside they could hear the screams of the Crudelis as the Bear fought his way from the crater and back down the mountainside.

After they had both regained their breath, Charlie said, "Will your Bear be alright?"

She nodded. "They are no match for him in the daylight, it is night time when they are at their most dangerous."

"I thought that they were just black shapes," said Charlie. "I didn't realise that they look like real people and that they are green."

"At night they become dark," she replied. "They can take on shapeless forms, and they turn into carnivores, but in the daytime they are green and, despite their large eyes, have poor vision. They used to be Faery folk like me, but they have lost so much because they chose to follow Skadmeer."

"Faery folk!" exclaimed Charlie. "You're not a faery, are you?"

"I am," she giggled, with that she removed her cloak and unfurled a beautiful set of pale blue wings.

Charlie was just about to ask why she didn't just fly away, escape from the cave, when he saw that one wing was in tatters. It had been deliberately shredded.

"Oh no," he uttered. "Why, I mean how?"

Bella held his hand. "Do not look so sad, Charlie. They will mend in time. The Crudelis did this on the orders of Skadmeer so that I cannot escape. At least I am alive."

"Then," said Charlie, very firmly. "It's about time we made some plans to get you, and me, out of here. We both need to get home, and if Tom is the Dragon Slayer we must think of a way to help him when he comes."

Bella clapped her hands in delight and small blue stars rose from her tiny wings.

Chapter Eleven
The Foothills of Ondraedan

"The others are waiting for you in the courtyard," said Gioco, as they made their way from Geschwind's study.

There in the centre stood Pitzic, the dark swarthy elf whom Tom had met earlier. Though small he obviously had immense strength, and there was an air of quiet confidence about him. Equally small but very slight, with fine features and short fluffy hair, was Kurz, a faery being from an ancient and well-trusted family.

"Bring the ponies," announced Gioco, in a matter-of-fact voice.

Two young elves disappeared only to emerge seconds later leading five beautiful chestnut ponies. In fact, Tom thought he could see ripples of red running across their backs. The outstanding image, however, was that all the ponies had golden tails and manes. They were amazing.

"They are exceptionally strong," said Geschwind.

"They look incredible," answered Tom.

He patted Urthslean and was rewarded by a hum. He noticed that whilst the others also carried swords, Geschwind had none.

'But with a mind like his,' thought Tom, 'who needs a sword?'

Lusinga entered the courtyard. Much to Tom's embarrassment, she came forward and rubbed noses with him. It was the normal way of greeting for the little people.

"We all wish you a safe journey," she said. "May you destroy Bestim and bring your brother back to safety. The death of the dragon will do much to weaken Skadmeer's powers."

"Thank you," replied Tom.

Whilst he was trying to work out how to mount his pony, Tom saw Lusinga and Geschwind talking in quiet tones. He felt certain that he heard her say, "Please bring her back safely, Geschwind." He decided to ask the magician about it later, at the moment he was too busy trying to sit on the pony without falling off.

The Master Magician leapt onto the nearest pony, which also happened to be the smallest and shouted, somewhat dramatically, "To horse!"

The little pony was completely enveloped under the Magician's long, green cloak and shied with fright, almost unseating him. Gioco moved forward and grabbed its head.

"No, Geschwind," he said, trying hard not to laugh. "You must ride Thencan." He pointed to one of the largest ponies.

"Urrumph!" snorted Geschwind as he changed steeds.

"He might be the Grand Master of magicians," muttered Pitzic quietly to Tom, trying hard not to smile, "But he's no horseman!"

The smallest pony shook itself from top to tail, and immediately, Kurz, as light as a feather, leapt on to his back.

"Tom, your pony is called Treo," said Gioco. "He has been especially chosen for you."

Tom leant forwards and whispered in the pony's ear. At once Treo began to paw the ground, his tail swished from side to side, he was alert and ready to leave.

"Come!" commanded Geschwind, and the five ponies and riders clattered over the cobbles and out across the drawbridge to begin their long journey to Ferlian Forest which skirted the foothills of Mount Ondraedan. Frozen snow still covered the ground.

To start with, the little people came out of their homes to cheer them on their way, but gradually the houses and cottages became fewer and fewer, and the cheers grew fainter and fainter, until at last the friends were riding across a vast open plain clear of snow. Their journey had begun.

Chapter Twelve
The Night can be Treacherous

At first the plain appeared almost welcoming. The grass was of the deepest green, and here and there were clumps of beautiful strange wild flowers. Gioco told Tom that the secrets of Hunitwede, the delicious drink he had had the previous night, lay within the petals of some of these plants. The butterflies were particularly plentiful, and even settled on the travellers' hands as they rode by.

Suddenly it all ended.

The grassland became coarse and patchy, and as they reached the top of a steep incline, they found their way barred by a sea of thistles, brambles, weeds and giant thorn bushes. Far in the distance lay Ferlian Forest, and glowering above it towered Mount Ondraedan. Kurz's little pony snorted nervously, whilst Gioco bent forward and whispered into the ear of his pony, Swivan. After a moment staring at this sea of thorns he looked up.

"Give your pony its head," he commanded. "Swivan will lead us swiftly through this part."

Sure enough Swivan plunged into the thicket, Kurz followed quickly on Calan, the smallest in the group, then came Tom on Treo, Pitzic on Barus and finally Geschwind on the mighty Thencan. Somehow, by following Swivan, the ponies began to thread their way through the tangles. No one spoke, everyone knew how important it was to find a safe path, then after some time, Gioco signalled to Geschwind, and they changed places. This next section needed the skills of Thencan, for out of sight, beneath the thick mesh of the weeds were the hidden holes, the boggy patches waiting to ensnare the unlucky traveller. The air smelt foul, like bad eggs, or rotten meat, only much worse. As each mud bubble burst so the stench increased. Several times Thencan paused as he and Geschwind worked together to find the safest route through this sinister landscape.

Tom looked at Pitzic. "What is this place? Why is it so dreadful?"

Pitzic answered warily. "It is full of the traps laid by the Crudelis, and the mountain, too, is also trying to warn us to stay away."

"Warning us?" repeated Tom, gripping his reins tightly. "Do you mean it's trying to help us, y'know, that sort of warning?"

"No," replied Pitzic with a grin, "I'm afraid not, Tom. It's more of a 'KEEP AWAY' sort of warning."

At last they broke through to an open patch of thin grass. It was a small rise, and once again Ferlian Forest straddled the horizon.

"We must rest here awhile," said Gioco. "The ponies are tired, and I think Tom is too. We must not forget, even though he is our Dragon Slayer, he is still a human boy."

"How thoughtless of me," replied Geschwind. "I was so eager to reach the Forest before nightfall, I forgot about your discomforts, Tom. Now what shall we eat?"

Tom had no idea how the little men conjured up such a meal so quickly and when he asked they just grinned and said it was, "Just Magic!"

Whilst they were enjoying their feast he noticed that Kurz kept wriggling his shoulders and seemed uneasy.

"Is Kurz in pain?" Tom asked quietly.

Gioco grinned. "No, he's a bit uncomfortable, that's all."

"Why?" asked Tom.

"It's his wings, they're beginning to itch which means he'll have to fly soon," replied Gioco.

By now the others were listening.

"Fly!" Tom's eyebrows shot up. "I didn't know he had wings. Can he really do that?"

"All true faeries can fly if they want to," said Pitzic. He had finished his meal and was lying back, his arms behind his head, completely relaxed and gazing up at the sky.

"Doesn't he want to?" asked Tom in amazement, for he knew, that given the chance of wings, he would be airborne every minute of the day.

"He doesn't like it," replied Gioco, smiling at Kurz kindly.

Kurz scowled.

"He's afraid of heights," said Pitzic in a teasing tone. The others laughed.

"I'm not, I'm not," retorted Kurz angrily. He looked at Tom.

"They just get in the way sometimes," he explained. "They're growing and I must exercise them otherwise they will ache."

"Like muscle cramps," said Tom, trying to be helpful.

"I don't know," answered Kurz. "But I expect so." He turned to Geschwind. "I will have to fly soon."

"I understand," replied the Great Magician. "You must do what you must do. I wish to speak with Tom."

The others moved away as Geschwind beckoned Tom to come closer.

"You and I need to go through that dreadful forest, Tom," he said. "It is a wicked place and to reach your brother it is essential that we succeed. The last time I tried I failed, but this time you are with me and I sense that we will win through, O Dragon Slayer."

"Why did you attempt it before?" asked Tom.

Geschwind sighed. "Lusinga, our great lady, has not only lost her husband to the Crudelis, but also her daughter Annabella. I gave my word that I would try again to rescue that little one. To have you with me, the Dragon Slayer, is something I have always dreamed of. Together we can rescue your brother and Annabella, if, that is, she still lives. The death of Bestim, the dragon, will bring about the downfall of many of the Solanum, including, I hope, Beweglic, the dark leader."

Tom remained silent for some time. Then he said, "Would you still have helped me even if this Annabella had not been captured? Would you still have helped me to save my brother?"

Geschwind took his hand and held it tight. "You have my word that I would still have been with you," he said.

Pitzic overheard their conversation. "I will follow you, Tom, into the gates of hell if need be. I will never let you down."

Suddenly this difficult moment was interrupted by a quiet rippling sound, a waterfall of gentle notes tumbling and cascading through the air. Tom turned to see Kurz rise from Calan's back and up into the sky above them. The delicate wings hummed and glistened in the pale light.

"That's beautiful," he whispered, as Kurz slowly descended to the ground.

"Ah," Kurz sighed, wriggling his shoulders and gently folding his wings. "That feels much better. Afraid of heights indeed." He looked scornfully at Pitzic and they both burst into laughter, for in reality he and Pitzic were the best of friends.

"Did you see anything?" asked Geschwind.

"There are no Crudelis," he replied.

They pressed on and the ponies quickened their pace. No one wanted to be on the plain at nightfall…

At last they stopped. They had reached the edge of a deep, dark place, for towering before them stood the trees of Ferlian. Nothing stirred, not a twig nor a leaf nodded. It just stood there waiting, dark, sombre and dead. There was a sullen arrogance about it.

"A place of dread," whispered Geschwind.

The atmosphere seemed to affect everyone because no one spoke for several minutes. It was as if they were transfixed by this line of lifeless trees before them. Even the ponies were nervous, they snorted and shifted uneasily.

At last Gioco spoke. "This is where we must part ways, Tom," he said, turning in his saddle to look at him. "Pitzic and Kurz will remain here with your ponies and await your return. I must travel swiftly back to Campandella to inform Lusinga that you have safely completed this first part of your journey."

"Don't go now, Gioco," pleaded Kurz rising from his saddle, his wings fluttering anxiously.

"No, Gioco," added Geschwind. "Wait until morning. Stay and camp with us tonight and begin your return journey at first light tomorrow."

"That would be sensible," muttered Pitzic.

Gioco hesitated as the others dismounted and began calming down their ponies, patting them, rubbing them and whispering gentle sounds into their ears.

"You know," continued Pitzic, "that at night the plain is full of weird folk and Crudelis, who just enjoy tormenting and hurting their victims. Stay with us until the morning."

Gioco nodded. "You are right," he said. "So, let me help set up camp."

Tom was sure that no scout had ever made a camp like this one. Within minutes, no seconds, they were standing inside a small wooden hut lit only by oil lamps. It appeared to Tom that by sheer concentration of will power they caused this to materialise out of nothing. They were in fact combining their magical powers to produce a force field which for practical purposes they shaped as a hut. It seemed to rise out of the ground and to grow around them, the side walls first, then the roof and finally the base shot under their feet. There was very little noise, though Tom was conscious of a tingling feeling in the back of his neck. The ponies took it all in their stride as Kurz quickly unsaddled them, and made them comfortable in a corner of the room. He and Pitzic had saved their own powers in readiness for later.

"We have no doors or windows," observed Tom.

"That is to keep THEM out," replied Pitzic.

"Don't worry, Tom," said Gioco, placing his hand on Tom's shoulder. "When the time comes you will know what to do. You are the Dragon Slayer. Together we will rescue your brother and, if she is still alive, we will find Lusinga's daughter."

'I have to find, Charlie,' thought Tom. 'I just have to.'

That night they dined well and drank Hunitwede, and the little men did their best to keep a lighter mood by telling stories of Kurz's famous fishing trip when he caught a Muzzy. These fish were well known for their ability to talk, and it complained and moaned so much about being caught, that in the end Kurz threw it back to get some peace and quiet.

Sleep did not come easily to the group. Tom could hear strange scratching and moaning sounds outside their cabin. At times it sounded as if someone was slowly running their nails down a blackboard, at others as if a hundred rats were scurrying across the roof. The hut groaned and creaked but remained firm.

The ponies stamped their hooves and whinnied nervously. It was reassuring to know that they were safely stabled within the hut. Tom's hand felt for his sword, for

Urthslean. He gave it a little pat and was rewarded by a quiet hum.

"Don't worry."

It was Kurz, who was lying at the left side of Tom. "The Crudelis are angry because they cannot break through the magic of Geschwind and Gioco. They are just trying to frighten us but they won't succeed."

Another cackle split the air. It was as if someone was gargling with venom.

"You have nothing to fear tonight, Tom," continued Kurz. "Sleep well. You will need all your strength, my friend, for the battle which lies ahead of you."

It was the longest speech that Kurz had ever made to Tom and he was grateful for it.

"Thank you, Kurz," he whispered.

Tom pulled his blanket up over his ears to block out the sounds.

'Oh, Charlie,' he thought. 'I'm coming. Please stay safe until I can reach you.'

Chapter Thirteen
Ferlian Forest

The morning dawned a steely grey, stillness lay in the air. No dawn chorus issued from the Forest, no blackbirds to herald the new day, no thrushes to be heard breakfasting on snails. The sparse grass was wet with dew, and an early mist still hovered over the ground.

Tom ached and itched all over from lying on the straw the whole night. The hut had long since been dismantled and everyone looked tired and weary after such a restless night, a night shattered by hideous sounds of screeching, howling and moaning. Kurz was silently and carefully stretching his wings, Pitzic seemed deep in thought, only Gioco and Geschwind were locked in earnest conversation. Tom strapped Urthslean to his side, he was beginning to develop the habit of talking to his sword as though it could understand him.

"Now," he whispered. "If we can kill off this dragon, then I can save Charlie, and we can go home. I might even find out more about my strange ancestors. Who knows?" The sword hummed quietly.

"Goodbye. May truth conquer all," it was Gioco. He was leaving.

There was a great deal of shaking of hands and rubbing noses. Pitzic gripped his friend's hand firmly and nodded, no words were necessary.

Gioco turned to Tom. "Take this," he said, placing a small leather bag in Tom's hands. "It is full of useful odds and ends which we pixies take with us whenever we travel. I'm sure you won't need it but, just in case you become separated from Geschwind at any time, it could prove useful. Good luck, Tom. Our thoughts will be with you."

They gently rubbed noses. The thought that he might lose Geschwind filled Tom with dread.

Gioco mounted Swivan and left.

The others watched him in silence until he was only a speck on the horizon. The quiet weighed heavily, everything was still, nothing stirred, just a great emptiness filled the air. Suddenly the rasping cackle of a hooded crow passing along the fringe of the Forest broke through their thoughts.

With a deep sigh, Geschwind turned to the others. "Well now, Kurz, we will leave our ponies here with you. I feel sure that there is enough of our people's power here in the atmosphere, for you to form a protective barrier for possibly two more nights. If after that time we have not returned then you, Kurz, must fly with all haste to Campandella to warn the others. Pitzic, you know what you must do."

Pitzic nodded, Kurz started to protest, but Geschwind held up his hand.

"No," he said, "I forbid you to change the plans. You have your tasks. You will return without us, Kurz, and you must take the ponies with you. If Pitzic should fail, you must be ready with others to rescue Tom."

"And Charlie," interrupted Tom.

Geschwind did not answer.

"And Charlie?" persisted Tom.

"No one is going to fail," muttered Pitzic. What thoughts the others had they kept to themselves.

"We must leave," announced Geschwind abruptly.

This was the defining moment, their forces would be split and everything rested on the success of this mission. Tom knew that the well-being of his family was somehow linked to the outcome, but above all he began to realise that the life of Charlie, his younger brother, depended on their success.

Nothing moved. There was no breeze, no rustle of leaves. Ferlian just stood there in front of them, silent and forbidding, waiting to envelop them within its darkness. Without a word they crossed the twenty metres or so to its edge, and with a final wave to their friends they plunged into the Forest and were immediately engulfed in an eerie, luminous and unnatural green light.

Strange misshapened branches clung crazily to distorted twisted trees, whilst creeping plants slithered and snaked their way up and down the trunks. Many fungi huddled around the largest trees, and vile-smelling yellow and purple flowers grew wherever space allowed. No birds sang, no bees hummed, in fact not a single insect nor animal appeared to exist. Were they the only living creatures in this forest? If so, who or what had caused the tracks which led off of their pathway?

Tom began to pay more attention to his surroundings and hoped he would not meet with anything or anyone, though deep down he knew that the sight of a green face would be no surprise. They pressed on in silence, Geschwind leading the way along the narrow path which oozed brown, sticky mud. They had to be careful where they trod, as what would seem like harmless muddy puddles proved so deep, that they sank, without warning, almost to their knees. Only once did Geschwind speak, and that was to warn Tom to keep away from the strange flowers which not only had an evil smell but were also poisonous to the touch.

"Look," said Tom suddenly. There were a few large beetle-like creatures amongst the rotting wood. "They're as big as my hand, like giant stag beetles, the sort we have at home, except they're a bright green colour."

"Don't let them get near," warned Geschwind, without looking round. "Keep close, they spit venom and can give a nasty nip with those antlers."

Tom sighed, was there nothing pleasant in this forest?

They twisted and turned with the path, sometimes to travel upwards and at others to slide and slither down into deep humid gullies. He tried hard to memorise their path just in case… but it was no use, he knew he'd have to trust his instincts. At last he could go no further.

"Geschwind," he panted. "Couldn't we just stop for a while, for a short rest?"

"Soon, Tom, soon," came the reply, but still Geschwind did not turn around. "There's a small patch of grass where sunlight streams in. We can stop there in the open. We must not stop in Ferlian."

Tom was beginning to gasp with exhaustion. He was wet through, his shirt stuck to his back, sweat was dripping down his face and running down the back of his neck. He had never felt so uncomfortable in all his life. It seemed an eternity, but it was probably only ten minutes, when they suddenly broke through into the sunshine and fresh air. They both sank wearily to the ground. Was it Tom's imagination or was Geschwind ageing? His white hair now appeared a matted dingy grey, his skin looked tired and he now had a definite stoop.

"Let us have some refreshment, Tom," said the magician, producing an ice-cold drink.

"How old is Ferlian Forest?" asked Tom, trying hard not to stare at Geschwind's altered features.

"It has grown as the power of the Crudelis has increased. As they became bolder so the plain began to dwindle, and slowly this evil Forest has twisted its way into existence. It is growing and stretching over the plain, forcing the grasslands to retreat. Unless we can stop it, it may even reach the borders of our villages one day."

"These Crudelis," said Tom. "They are controlled by the Solanum, but the Solanum is also controlled by this person called Skadmeer. Is that right?"

"Skadmeer is the leader of the Solanum, but he is no ordinary person," replied Geschwind.

"As far as I can tell," interrupted Tom. "There aren't any 'ordinary' people in this land."

Despite his pain, this last remark caused Geschwind to smile. "I think you may be right," he said, and laughed.

"So, who controls Bestim, the dragon which I have to kill?" asked Tom. Urthslean gave a small hum.

"Teracind, the Claw, the leader of Skadmeer's troops," replied Geschwind.

"All I want to do is to rescue my brother," said Tom. "I don't really care about all these others. I just want to save Charlie."

"I understand…" began Geschwind. He suddenly clutched his head, his face was riddled in pain.

"Is it the Thought Barrier?" asked Tom anxiously.

Geschwind nodded. "As we approach Bestim, my powers will be under a fearsome attack from the Solanum. They have realised that you have come to kill their dragon. It will weaken their hold on Green Willow, and their hopes of travelling into a parallel time." He closed his eyes and gradually Tom saw his face change from one in great pain to one of calmness.

Geschwind smiled. "The barrier has been restored," he said quietly "Our people, yours and mine, are safe again."

"I don't understand," replied Tom.

The Magician straightened his robes before replying. "Think of the Thought Barrier as a giant bubble. It floats over the whole of Glencyndal. I keep it intact with my mind, but it is under constant attack from the Crudelis and the whole Solanum. As we approach Bestim these attacks will increase and, each time, I must repair the damage before the Barrier is breached by the Dark Forces."

Tom looked at Geschwind in awe and amazement.

Chapter Fourteen
And then came a Bear

They reluctantly left the glade and plunged once more into the Forest. Immediately the humidity and stench engulfed them.

Suddenly, with no warning, a long green tentacle shot out from the side of a rotting tree. In one movement it wrapped itself around Tom's legs and slammed him into the muddy path.

"Geschwind!" His shout was muffled by the mud.

A second snake-like vine swiftly whipped itself around his left arm. Urthslean came into his right hand, and with remarkable ease Tom swung the sword at the vine around his legs. There was a shriek as the vine was sliced in two, the severed section lay writhing and flapping on the path, whilst the other retreated back to the parent plant. Geschwind spun round and drove a volley of searing light through the tentacles binding Tom's arm. That was the last movement Geschwind made, for above them came a triumphant shriek and, with a flurry of roots and tentacles, the Magician was suddenly enveloped in a mass of green. Geschwind was lifted off his feet and hauled into the branches above.

"Tom!" he shouted in desperation as his whole body was smothered by this giant monster.

Without thinking of his own safety, Tom leapt onto the tree, which because of its gnarled and warty bark was easy to climb. He stood firmly on the branch where all the parasitic tentacles were rooted. Grasping Urthslean with both hands, he raised it high above his head. His mighty shout, the battle cry of the Dragon Slayer, could be heard throughout the Forest as he brought the blade crashing down upon this octopus-like plant. It let out a terrifying scream before releasing its grip on Geschwind, who fell crashing to the forest floor. The sweeping force of Tom's sword caused him to topple headlong from the branch and down onto the boggy path. Together they lay on the slimy ground, stunned by the fall. A tangle of dead and dying vines were still entwined around Geschwind, whilst others were twisting and twitching in the mud, their eerie screeching and moaning drowned out all other sounds.

The attack had been so sudden, so full of ferocity and venom that Tom was panting, his heart pounding against his ribs.

He heaved himself to his feet and began hacking at the foul and festering limbs which lay scattered around. All the time he kept calling Geschwind's name.

The Magician seemed to be unconscious. Tom felt sharp stabbing pains in his arms and legs. The plants were spitting at them. Very slowly the Magician began to stir.

"Leave me, Tom," he whispered. "Save yourself. I will follow."

"No!" shouted Tom. "Get up, Geschwind. Please get up!" His voice was half pleading, half demanding. "We must go together. You must help me find my brother."

With that he pulled Geschwind to his feet, and began to drag him along the path with a new-found strength and vigour. The plants could do no more, they could not follow, but they could wait for Tom's return.

The humidity and heat were taking their toll, once again Tom's clothes were sticking to his body, sweat ran down his forehead, into his eyes, and dripped off the end of his nose. He felt encased in a bubble of moist heat. He became aware that the soft forest floor was gradually giving way to small stones and pebbles. Trees dwindled, the air became cooler, and in a matter of minutes they were standing on the lower slopes of Mount Ondraedan. The land rose steeply before them.

"Thank you, Tom," sighed Geschwind, as he leant against a boulder. "Thank you. The poison in those plants tried to prevent me from maintaining the Thought Barrier. I have to keep our people safe." He paused. "Now let me look at your wounds." He dabbed some soothing ointment on the sores which were already beginning to form on Tom's skin. The plants' minute darts were creating spots which had begun to itch and smell, but within seconds the ointment started to heal them and they quickly disappeared altogether.

Tom looked at Geschwind. His friend's face was drawn and tired. The cold air sweeping down from the mountainside only added to their problems. One minute they had been so hot. Now it was bitterly cold. He began to realise the meaning of Geschwind's earlier words, 'As we approach Bestim so the attacks on the Thought Barrier will increase'. The strength seemed to be draining out of the Magician. How could a dragon have such powers? How could plants be so terrifying? What was Geschwind fighting in his mind?

"It's not just Bestim, Tom," said Geschwind, as if reading his thoughts. "The whole Solanum is working through this monster." His next words brought a chill to Tom's heart. "They want you, but not me."

"Why?" he asked, trying to control his fear. "Why me?"

"They know you have come to kill Bestim, and with his death so much of their power will be lost," replied the Magician.

"And are they still attacking the Thought Barrier?" asked Tom.

Geschwind closed his eyes tightly and frowned. "I can see fighting in the far reaches of our kingdom. A whole village has been massacred, many have been taken prisoner. It is in the north… the Barrier has been breached in the north."

He gripped Tom's shoulder. "I must attend to it."

"You're not going to leave me, are you?" asked Tom, horrified by such a thought.

Geschwind smiled gently. "I will not leave you, Tom," he whispered. "You are as much part of my destiny as Bestim is yours. No, I will not leave you, but the Barrier is sapping my energies. It is becoming increasingly harder to maintain the force field and, at the same time, to protect us. I can probably only sustain this for two more days and then…" He broke off.

Tom thought of Charlie, and felt the first pangs of real fear creep through his bones, almost paralysing his ability to think. Then he thought of his parents, somehow he had to rescue Charlie, somehow he had to make right the wrongs which his ancestors had forced upon these little people. The terror which now stalked the land of Glencyndal had been caused by his family… he was the Dragon Slayer.

"Come on, Geschwind," he heard himself saying. "We'll be alright. We won a battle back there against that overgrown clump of ivy. Urthslean will help us." He patted the hilt of his sword which gave a hum of appreciation.

The Magician shook his shoulders and stood tall and straight. "You're right, Tom. We must be positive. We must go."

"But which way?" asked Tom, gazing up at the formidable path.

"Why this way, of course," said Geschwind, looking up at the mountain path.

"Of course," replied Tom grimly, and so they began the climb.

They slipped and slithered their way up the mountainside. Sometimes the path disappeared altogether and they had to pick their way over rocks and across dry gullies, but it was always upwards. The coldness in the air, and the biting wind tore at them each time they turned a new corner. Sometimes the wind was so strong that it drowned out all sounds. They were well above the tree tops of Ferlian Forest but, try as he might, Tom could not see into the distance for everything was shrouded in a green mist. It felt as though they were the only two living beings in this world.

They pressed on wearily, the wind shrieking in their ears pulling them this way and that, the path forcing them to the very edge of precipices, over jagged rocks and down into hollows. It was whilst Tom was climbing out of one of the hollows that he became aware of a gradual rumbling under his feet. The mountain was waking. At first these grumblings caused small stones to fall and become dislodged but then several rocks suddenly cascaded down the slope towards them. Geschwind and Tom both dodged to one side out of harm's way.

Geschwind, his mind still grappling with the Thought Barrier, stumbled and fell into a solitary shrub. As Tom turned to help him he suddenly came face to face with a giant golden bear. It had been lying in the hollow behind a bush, sleeping.

Chapter Fifteen
Weapons

Charlie glanced at Bella. She looked tired, but then they both were, they had been working hard all day.

"So how many have we made?" he asked.

"Probably more than fifty," she answered, proudly looking at all the water bombs. "I'll count them."

"But it's not enough, is it?" said Charlie sadly. "He's a big dragon. We're not going to dampen his flames that much, are we?"

"Fifty-three," said Bella firmly. "No, we won't, but we can certainly give him something to think about. After all, a gnat is very small but it can easily get your attention when it strikes, and we will strike Bestim, Charlie!"

She looked so determined that Charlie broke out in laughter. They gave each other a big hug, and wiped away their tears.

"Tom will come," said Charlie firmly. "I know he will. He's my big brother, he won't leave me."

"We must make more," Bella looked about the cave. "We have very little cloth left, but if we are careful, we might make another twenty or so."

"That would be good," said Charlie. He gave her a long hard look. "Your Bear hasn't been here for a few days. Why's that?"

Bella shook her head. "I do hope he's all right," she said, "but he can't come whilst the dragon remains outside. It's as though Bestim senses that someone is coming, and won't leave us alone."

Charlie nodded. "I think he knows that Tom is on his way. Yes, my brother's coming!"

Chapter Sixteen
A New Friend

It was an enormous golden Bear with slanting eyes of yellow-green, and a face full of anger. It did not seem at all strange to Tom when the bear lowered its head towards him, just like a snake, and hissed in cold tones, "And where might you think you're going?"

Instead of cowering away, Tom stood his ground and shouted, "Get out of the way! Our business is with Bestim. Go on, move aside!"

The Bear drew himself up to his full towering height of around three metres, his head swayed from side to side and his eyes narrowed as he surveyed this arrogant, young and foolish boy. Only now did Tom see that his body was covered in scars and weeping sores from recent battles, and patches of fur were also missing.

"Your business is with me now!" it thundered.

He raised a powerful arm and prepared to strike Tom down who stepped back to give himself room to draw Urthslean, but then lost his footing on the loose gravel. Immediately Geschwind flung himself between the two of them, and by sheer will power held the Bear's arm in mid-air.

"Stop!" shouted the Magician. "We are on a mission to rescue Bella and Tom's young brother, Charlie."

This had a strange effect upon the Bear, he faltered, made little moaning noises and slowly dropped down onto all fours.

"Ah," he sighed. "She is guarded night and day by Bestim and the Crudelis. A young boy is with her. You will find her in the cave beyond this mountain." He turned to Tom. "Forgive me, great warrior, I thought you were a friend of the Solanum. I did not see your companion, I did not realise you had the Great Magician with you."

"I thought you must be a friend of Bestim too," said Tom, much relieved that they didn't have to fight, and secretly proud to be called 'great warrior'.

Tom tried to shake the Bear's paw but it was gigantic in comparison to his small hand; they turned to Geschwind whose face was racked with pain.

"I am pleased we have met, Bear," he said quietly. "I must rest for a while. There are many battles raging in my head, and I need to concentrate my energies. May we share your shelter here under this bush?"

The Bear nodded and pulled aside the branches of the bush to reveal his hollow, a small sheltered space between some rocks, hidden from view. It offered them some protection from the biting winds.

Geschwind sank down, closed his eyes and fell into a deep and troubled sleep. The others had no idea of the nightmares he was fighting in his mind. Though he remained there in body, all his magical powers were being employed in the defence of his people. Young and old were calling for his help. Nhiamar, the Tormentor and Bringer of Nightmares, was relishing in his task of showing Geschwind the agonies of the little people. Teracind, the Claw, was leading armies of Green Ones, of Crudelis, into villages, burning homes and destroying all in their path.

"Come, Rowana, come Treysta. Come my sisters. I need you, our people need you. We must drive the hordes from our lands so that I may repair the damage now in the north. Come with speed to me!"

Tom and the Bear had no knowledge of this turmoil. Though Tom guessed that Geschwind was trying to repair the Thought Barrier, he had no idea of the battles which the Magician was waging, he assumed that Geschwind was still wholly with them. It would be much later before Tom met with Rowana and Treysta.

"Where do you come from?" asked the Bear. "You do not look like one of the Little People."

"I'm not. You're right, Bear." Tom smiled. 'How do you explain to a Bear that you've just moved house?' he thought. He decided not to bother. He sighed. "I'm the Dragon Slayer," he said.

The Bear wrinkled his nose, his top lip curled upwards. Tom thought he was going to snarl but then realised that the Bear was trying to smile. He just said, "I see. And who is the boy who is imprisoned with Bella?"

"He's my brother, Charlie," replied Tom very firmly. "I am going to rescue him."

The Bear snorted. "I see," was all he would answer.

They sat in silence for a few moments but then the Bear stood, and said, "I must go and find food. Keep watch." He left before Tom could say anything.

Tom began to gather a few dry twigs to be ready to light a fire for the night and to cook their food. Whilst he was waiting he decided to make his way to a ledge where he had an amazing view over the top of Ferlian Forest, way, way, below. He was full of apprehension. Even if they completed their mission, he knew that they would have to make the return journey within the allotted time. He must not fail.

It was some time later when a voice in his ear made him visibly jump. It was the Bear.

"I thought you were keeping a careful watch," he admonished gently.

"You're so quiet Bear," replied Tom, relieved at the return of his new friend.

"The Crudelis can also move quietly if they wish," grunted the Bear. "Now let us eat." In his large paws he held two fish which he'd caught in his favourite mountain stream about a mile away.

"I prefer mine in its natural state," he added, as he began to tear at one with his enormous teeth.

Tom had already lit his fire. He had found an orange-coloured stone in the bag which Gioco had given him. It was labelled, 'Fyrstan, place amongst firewood BUT use with care'. Just by placing it among the twigs had been enough to start the fire. He was really hungry. It seemed to take an age as he slowly turned the fish over the fire. He would share this one with Geschwind, who was beginning to stir.

"Are you alright?" he asked anxiously, kneeling beside him.

With a wave of his hand Geschwind dismissed Tom's fears. "Do not worry about me, Tom," he answered almost falling asleep again.

"I would like to come with you both," said the Bear, crunching the last of his fish.

"Oh yes," replied Tom eagerly. "I think we could do with all the help we can get. Don't you agree, Geschwind?" Geschwind snorted.

After their meal the Bear explained what lay ahead of them. It became clear that the Bear had already encountered the dragon, hence some of the sores and wounds on his body.

"We must travel on and upwards for some distance," he said. "The air becomes quite thin and the mountain is high. Any exertions can make you feel extremely weary, so be warned, save your strength as much as possible, especially you, Tom. We climb up until we pass the jagged rock, shaped by the wind into the likeness of a man's head. Once we have edged around and under his chin we will be standing on the rim of a crater, and there, on the far side, you will be able to see the lair of Bestim, most contemptible of all dragons."

"We need to see this lair before we make our plans," said Tom, and Geschwind agreed.

They put out their fire and tried to hide any evidence of having been there. As soon as the flames disappeared the Fyrstan became icy cold. It was going to be a much easier journey now as the Bear insisted on carrying Geschwind on his massive back. The Magician did not seem at all embarrassed by this piggy-back, on the contrary he looked as if he was enjoying it. "I can concentrate on the Barrier," he whispered to Tom by way of explanation.

Secretly Tom believed Geschwind just enjoyed having a ride and not having to walk.

The path was dangerous, at times it ran perilously close to the edge of the mountain, any slip would send them plunging down a sheer drop. It became difficult for Tom to keep his footing as small stones skidded from beneath his feet. He fell and scraped his knees on jagged rocks many times, and all the while the bitter wind battered his face and tore through his clothes. After more than an hour of this tortuous climb the Bear, who was leading, paused.

"Look up there, Tom," he said quietly. Tom's eyes followed his pointing arm, and there silhouetted against the setting sun was the strangely shaped large rock.

"That's Skull Rock, the one I was telling you about," continued the Bear. "The wind has moulded it into the shape of a man's head. You get a better view as you get closer, away from this sunlight."

"I can see what you mean," replied Tom, shielding his eyes as he looked up.

The last part of the climb had been really steep and hard going and Tom was grateful for any stop, however brief it might be.

The outline of a man's head became even more obvious as they continued to climb. It had an exaggerated forehead and a very flat top making it resemble the head of an angry giant. The whole profile, from the bottom of the chin to the top of its forehead, must have been about twelve metres. It was huge.

"Quiet now," whispered the Bear, as he shifted Geschwind's weight on his shoulders. "As we near the rock we come very close to Bestim's lair, and echoes have a nasty habit of tripping you up around here." The others nodded in agreement.

Once behind the rock and out of sight from the dragon's lair, the Bear gently lowered Geschwind to the ground and signalled Tom to follow him silently. Slowly they began to inch their way forwards and round to the other side of Skull Rock. Tom was thankful that they were crawling on their hands and knees, for he had not been prepared for the view on this side. The mountainside suddenly disappeared before them. They were on a high narrow ledge looking down into a deep crater, a huge, yawning bowl-shaped, bottomless hole. He crept forward to see further, but it was no use, a thick swirling green mist carpeted the bottom. The Bear pulled him back, just in time, signalling him to be silent and still. Tom looked across the crater.

There, close to the cave's entrance, sat Bestim.

Chapter Seventeen
Bestim

There was no doubt about it, this was the dragon of nightmares, the one his ancestor had carved on the front door of Green Willow, the one he had painted at school. The only difference was that this one was alive and massive. Its body was probably the size of a double-decker bus, but this did not take account of its sinewy neck and head, and its powerful, twitching tail. There seemed to be a real intelligence in those yellow slanted eyes, a cunning and an evilness both arrogant and bold. Obviously restless, it kept rearing up, sniffing the air as if sensing their presence. Each time its front legs came down, a thunderous thud echoed around the whole crater, followed by a bone-grinding roar. Every rock shook. Beside the dragon lay a chasm of a hole, but there was no sign of Charlie or Bella. Tom was transfixed. How was it that his ancestors were supposed to have created this Monster? How on earth was he going to kill it? He needed to get a better look but the Bear tugged at his sleeve signalling that they should make their way back to Geschwind. This wasn't easy as they had to crawl silently backwards for some distance, there was so little room or cover on this side of the rim.

"Well?" asked Geschwind, in a hoarse whisper, on their return. "Did you see Charlie or Bella?" They shook their heads.

"Come on," said Tom, clutching at Urthslean. "Let's go and fight him now. He's a great ugly brute, but let's get it over with. I want to see my brother."

"Steady." The Bear shook his head and gently laid a giant paw on Tom's arm. "You don't really mean that, do you? It would be foolish, and you don't strike me as foolish. We must make careful plans before attempting to fight Bestim. It will soon be nightfall and we must, at least, be able to see where we are going and what we are doing. One false step on that treacherous ledge could prove fatal."

"Yes, you're right, of course, Bear," replied Tom reluctantly. "Let's find a place to sleep for tonight. We'll attack tomorrow at first light."

"Good," said Geschwind. "There's no way we could even consider fighting the dragon tonight, plus the light is fading fast. I will be of better use to you tomorrow. Of this I am sure."

"You have done enough, friend," replied the deep voice of the Bear. Tom was surprised by his tenderness. The Bear seemed to sense this and, as if to cover his own embarrassment, he quickly directed Tom and Geschwind back a little further and into a small cave. The Bear settled down across the opening to give them some warmth and protection during the coming night.

Chapter Eighteen
I have seen them

They watched in silence as their two friends disappeared into Ferlian Forest. Not a thing stirred, even the ponies seemed transfixed as Tom and Geschwind were swallowed up in the treeline. A great feeling of loneliness swept over them.

Kurz looked hard at Pitzic. "I think the next two days will be very long and arduous," he said, as he quietly began to groom Calan.

"Yes," Pitzic nodded in agreement. "We should have gone with them." He looked worried.

"Geschwind told us to stay here," replied Kurz firmly. "You must definitely remain here for Tom, in case anything goes wrong. I believe we will have the time of a full moon should they fail, which means they only have the two days to complete their mission. Geschwind's powers will be difficult to sustain beyond that." He paused and patted his pony as if reassuring himself. "Failure is something I do not wish to contemplate."

"How does Geschwind use his powers to keep the Crudelis at bay?" asked Pitzic.

Kurz shrugged his shoulders. "I don't know," he said. "All I know, all I want to know, is that somehow he can and he does. This Forest area is the weakest part of our Kingdom and the most dangerous for all of us. The Crudelis have only been able to find this fault because of the presence of Bestim."

"It's very dangerous for Tom and Geschwind then," muttered Pitzic, as he began to brush his pony's tail.

"It is their mission, their destiny," Kurz stepped back from Calan. Stretching his wings, he slowly rose and hovered over the ground.

"When the time comes, if it does," asked Pitzic, "shall we go together into the Forest to bring them both back?"

"No," came Kurz's answer. "We gave our word. If Geschwind's powers fail then you must leave him and bring back Tom safely. You may not even be able to find Charlie in time. It is Tom you must save. It is Tom who is the Master of Urthslean. I will return to warn the others. Then we will return for Charlie, and do all we can to save him. The Crudelis will try to break through the time fault, to enter Green Willow and beyond. We must keep our promise."

The ponies became restless and began snorting as if anxious about something.

"Can you see anything?" asked Pitzic.

"No," replied Kurz. He fully opened his wings and flew towards the trees.

"Be careful!" called his friend.

Pitzic held on firmly to the ponies' reins, they were very restless. He could hear scrabbling and scratching coming from the undergrowth, as if a thousand birds were foraging amongst the fallen leaves all at the same moment.

"What can you see?" he called, as Kurz hovered about two metres from the edge of the Forest. Suddenly Kurz recoiled. "Come back, Kurz," he shouted. "Come back at once!"

His voice seemed to wake Kurz from a terrifying trance. He flew back instantly, as a hideous cackling broke out amongst the trees. Gradually it died away.

"What happened?" asked Pitzic. "What did you see?"

Kurz's whole body was trembling as he tried to calm himself.

"I have seen them," he whispered, "standing there, in the darkest fringes of the Forest. They've been watching us all the time. I have never seen them so close before. Oh, Pitzic they are hideous."

"What do they look like?" asked Pitzic impatiently. He handed Kurz a tankard of Hunitwede.

Kurz gulped it back before replying. "They are squat, even shorter than me. Less than a metre high. Their bodies are covered in broken, rotting scales the colour of a murky swamp. From where I flew I could even smell them. Oh, but those eyes..." he broke off and buried his face in his hands as though to block out the memory, but Pitzic was curious, he wanted to know.

"Tell me," he insisted. "Tell me about the eyes."

"They're large, yellow and dull, set in faces that are lifeless." Kurz began to sob as he continued. "Oh, Pitzic, it's as though they are dead inside their own bodies. It is not pity they want, their eyes seem to tell me that I will become one of them. If the Solanum win, if Bestim is not destroyed, they will come for me and for all those I love and—"

"Stop it! Stop it at once" Pitzic shook his friend roughly by the shoulders. "This is what Geschwind is protecting us from. We cannot, we must not give in so easily. Kurz, think! We are here to help Tom and his young brother, to help Geschwind and to rescue little Bella, to kill Bestim! Think, Kurz! Think!"

Kurz looked up and managed a weak smile, "Is that all?"

The very hopelessness of the situation made them both grin and then burst into laughter.

"Oh well," said Kurz, still smiling. "That's not so bad then, is it?"

Pitzic laughed. "Nothing like a good laugh to lift your spirits, as my dear Grandmama used to say."

Kurz took another drink, rose into the air and sat quietly hovering over Pitzic's head. He closed his eyes and took deep breaths, as though trying to calm his own thoughts.

"It's alright, Pitzic," he said. "I'm calmer now. There are some very clever Mind Controllers with the Crudelis, for a moment they caught me unawares."

"Geschwind is greater than all of them," replied Pitzic firmly.

"Geschwind is greater than all of them," repeated Kurz.

Chapter Nineteen
The Bravery of Pitzic

As the afternoon drew on, so Pitzic began thinking.

He put his ideas to Kurz. "Do you think we'll be able to build a protective barrier tonight? Perhaps one of us should then remain outside as a guard?"

"No," replied Kurz firmly. "We must wait and see. We must make sure that we don't do anything that could cause problems for Geschwind, or Tom."

He looked up, birds were gathering to make their way home. Home was as far away from the Forest as they could fly. No birds ever roosted in there.

"The sun is dipping, we must be on our guard, Pitzic," he said.

Throughout the day they had used no magic. It was important to save as much power as possible for the night. As the sun began to sink, so a waxing moon filled the sky. Gathering in the ponies, they began to plan their force field in their minds. Slowly, very slowly a hut began to form around them. Kurz nearly faltered as dark shapes began to flit across the face of the Forest. At first, he thought the movement came from the trees themselves, then with a jolt he realised that the Crudelis were gathering to attack. With a mighty effort he redoubled his energies and as the last wall came into sight they could just make out several squat shapes rushing from the Forest to attack them.

The Crudelis howled in anger and despair, beating their claws against the outside walls as the two friends stood inside with swords clenched firmly in their hands, watching, listening and waiting. Though their hut swayed and trembled from the onslaught, it did not give way. Whistling and snorting with fear the ponies shifted, and stamped the ground, and it took great strength for the little men to keep all four ponies tethered together.

Suddenly... silence. All was still.

"I think they've gone," whispered Kurz thankfully. "We must try to sleep, to get some rest. We still have another night to face after this one."

They lay down wearily and fell into a fitful sleep. How long, Pitzic could never remember, but when he woke in the inky blackness he could feel slimy, slithering claws clutching at him. He seized his sword and leapt to his feet. Where was Kurz? Where were the ponies? What had become of the hut? A thousand questions burst into his head and crowded in on his reasoning.

"Kurz!" he shouted. "Kurz! Answer me, where are you?"

His desperate calls were echoed by a harsh, rasping voice mocking him. He sensed rather than saw some movement about him. He called again.

"Kurz! Kurz! Where are you? Answer me! Please!"

He heard a quiet moan by his feet and with terror pounding in his heart, he knelt down and felt the limp body of Kurz lying on the ground. No time to find the ponies, he must defend his friend. Again many thoughts raged through his head as he stood astride his friend's body, wielding his sword left and right and cutting down all who dared to approach him.

Why had their force field crumpled? Did this mean that Geschwind and Tom had failed? Was Kurz dead? Would dawn never come? Why must it be so dark, where was the moon?

As if in answer to his last question, the clouds, which had hidden the moon, slowly rolled away and he began to make out the dark, squat shapes of the Crudelis. There were about a dozen of them, they were all over the ponies, digging and tearing with their claws. In one movement, Pitzic cut clean through the arm of a Crudelis just as it was about to rip out the throat of Calan. Another pony reared up, terrified. It was Treo. Flailing the air with his hooves, he twisted and brought them crashing down on the head of a Crudelis who was preparing to attack Pitzic. Barus and Thencan were fighting for their lives.

The onslaught from the Crudelis increased. No time for any more thoughts save those of survival. The smell of blood and slime burnt into Pitzic's nostrils. He wanted to be sick. He felt something dig into Kurz's body, and turned in time to make out a dark shape trying to drag him away. With a great effort he swung his sword down and felt a jolt as it dug into the scaly flesh. His heart hammered in his lungs, which felt as if they might burst at any minute. Terrible screams tore through the darkness until he thought his ears could stand no more. A fickle moon decided to disappear behind the dark clouds. Pitzic just had time to realise that no other Crudelis had joined this raiding party. Suddenly he was knocked down and thought all was lost but then, with a grunt and a whinny, Treo came to his aid once more.

The light was not good, there were too many shapes and shadows. If only he could see more, if only these incessant shrieks would stop. Slowly he began to realise that the attacks were lessening, and his heart gave a surge of joy, for there on the horizon came the first gentle, grey whispers of a new dawn. Crudelis began to scurry back into the Forest dragging their dead with them, and Pitzic was left to survey the horrors of the night.

There was no more force field, their hut lay in ruins. Treo was twitching in agony on the ground, whilst the other three ponies, though badly wounded, were still alive and huddled fearfully together. Pitzic looked down at Kurz, dreading what he might see. Kurz's face was smeared with blood, there was a large unpleasant lump on the side of his face, one wing was in tatters, and his right arm had been badly mauled, but, he was alive.

"Kurz," sobbed Pitzic, as he knelt beside him. "You're alive. Can you hear me? Can you speak?"

The tiny figure of his friend groaned.

"Save yourself, Pitzic… warn the others… Tom and Geschwind must be dead. Leave me." He fell unconscious.

Gently Pitzic set about cleaning his friend's wounds and making him comfortable. After a while he managed to stop the bleeding, and so decided to let Kurz sleep whilst he turned his attention to the ponies.

Quietly he calmed them down, found them some food and all the time praised them for their bravery that night, but Treo began shivering. Slowly the little pony sank onto his front legs before keeling over on to his side, he had terrible gashes across his flanks. Huge teeth marks could be seen on his neck and one eye had been badly gouged. Pitzic pulled a small flagon from his pocket and sat cross-legged by Treo's head. He was becoming ominously quiet and Pitzic knew that death could not be far away.

"I was saving this flagon for myself or Kurz," he said quietly to the pony. "But it seems that at this moment your needs are greater than ours. I will never forget that you saved my life. You were well chosen for our Dragon Slayer." With that he gently rubbed all the pony's wounds with the Elfin's sacred Healing Balm. "There," he said. "This will give you the time and perhaps a chance to recover."

Secretly he doubted if any of them would be given the time to recover.

Throughout the morning he repaired the damage of the night, looked after his friend, and watched over Treo. It was well into the afternoon before he made his fateful decision.

As was his custom he made his choice quickly and without emotion. He reasoned that Geschwind's power, and that of the faery folk must be very weak, otherwise why would their force field have crumbled in that way? Perhaps, he hoped, there would be enough positive energy left in the atmosphere to create a force field just to protect Kurz for the night. He and the ponies, even Treo, would have to take their chances outside.

All day long, whilst he had been caring for Kurz and the ponies, there had been a strange green glow in the sky and terrible sounds had reached his ears from the Forest and the mountain beyond. Great shrieks and moans as if a whole army was at war.

'Perhaps,' he thought, 'these sounds mean that they are still alive and battling. I must keep faith and wait at least until tomorrow morning.'

With some difficulty he created a small hut, just big enough to cover Kurz. It took enormous concentration and he gave it a flat top so that he could use it as a vantage point. In this way he would stand higher than the Crudelis, and he felt this would give greater protection for Kurz, then he tethered the ponies closely together, so that they would not become separated in the dark.

Gently he stroked Barus's head as he whispered. "You will need all your strength tonight, Barus. I sense we will have a battle like no other on our hands."

Barus softly nudged at his shoulder.

Then he made a solemn promise to himself and to them, that should everything seem hopeless, he would cut them free to give them a chance to escape. He sat cross-legged by them and calmly waited for the dark to come.

When night finally came the sky didn't blacken at all, the strange green glow grew stronger and cast terrifying shadows everywhere, shadows which moved and swayed, teasing his senses before disappearing into the darker recesses of the night. As he waited he thought he heard the howling of wolves and tried hard to pinpoint the origin of the sounds, but then a sick horror swept through his body as he realised that it was the wailing of the Banshee, the restless spirit foretelling death.

Whose death? Was it his?

For a brief moment, fear took charge of his reasoning. It was all he could do to stop himself from running away, anywhere, just anywhere away from this hideous wailing.

Suddenly he realised that he was surrounded by Crudelis, they had crept up whilst he had been off guard, and cursed himself for listening to the Banshee. The ponies stamped, shifted and moved closer together. Treo, though still very weak, pawed the ground and turned to face the enemy. Barus and Thencan, the two largest ponies, moved quickly so that Treo and Calan were protected and sandwiched between them. They were prepared to fight to the death.

In one quick movement Pitzic jumped onto the top of the hut to begin the defence of his friend. So much depended on this moment that every nerve in his body felt as though it was at screaming point. Slowly, very slowly, Pitzic began to swing his sword back and forth around his head, uttering strange high-pitched sounds as he did so. This stopped the Crudelis, they hesitated, unsure of themselves.

This was completely different from the previous night, they had never met a war-like elf before. It was as if they were bewitched by Pitzic's peculiar singing, but before they could attack, he tore into them, swinging his sword from side to side. Too late, he had killed four of them whilst their wits were still befuddled, and with shame Pitzic knew that he had enjoyed the killing and made a fateful hesitation. Immediately claws sank into his back and arms. He swung again and again, always singing his strange battle cry, as a warrior might have done in days of old. The smell was evil.

His clothes were soaked in a green spongy mess, the life-blood of the Crudelis, his own blood, too, poured freely from his wounds. How long he fought he didn't know, but he fought with a fury seldom witnessed but long remembered on those frosty story-telling nights by young and old. It was as if the days of the Old Magic had returned and there was a great warrior standing in the midst of wickedness, fighting for all that was true and just. A great legend had been born.

Such was the wail of the Banshee that it seemed to tear through the heavy blood-stained air as if it was a flimsy curtain. Looking to their leader, the Crudelis froze in fear. At his signal they turned as one and scurried back to the protection of their forest. Suddenly all was still.

Pitzic found himself standing alone.

Chapter Twenty
A Night of Crudelis

Throughout the night the Crudelis tried in vain to reach Tom, but they could not pass Geschwind nor the Bear. Tom slept soundly, mainly due to the craft of Geschwind. The Magician had placed a slumber-mode on him and, as Tom had no idea that this had been done, he was able to enjoy a good night's sleep.

The Bear smiled. "He will need all the rest he can get if he is to fight Bestim tomorrow."

Geschwind nodded.

"Are you sure," asked the Bear, as he settled himself down in the cave's entrance, "that this boy is the Dragon Slayer? He is very young, and surely you must know that Bestim is a monster. What chance will Tom have? He will be scorched to a cinder by this dragon."

The evening was becoming decidedly chilly, and Geschwind pulled his cloak tightly about him. He looked at the sleeping figure of Tom and gave a long sigh.

"Many years ago, before the pulse of time throbbed, we faeries lived in harmony with one another, travelling between lands and dimensions as freely as the air itself. There were no wars, no battles, it was seamless, a perpetual co-existence of kindness and well-being. Oh yes, there were little skirmishes, little disagreements, but they were of no consequence, you understand?"

The Bear nodded. "I remember," he said, looking fearfully out of the cave. It was getting darker and he was aware that the Crudelis would soon be hunting.

"And so it was for thousands of millennia, until Man came and invented time. They took our homes, the Dunnlins, and built upon them, they even renamed them and many denied our existence. The Dunnlins became known as hills, forts, downs and even mountains, and with the birth of time and boundaries there came much greed and a desire to conquer other lands and people. Tom's ancestors came to live on the Dunnlin which had always been home to Glencyndal. Of course, we were in a different dimension and there was no need to meet, but these people were different."

The Bear quietly began scratching his back against the rock wall. It was as if he had heard all this before but felt it impolite to interrupt the wizard.

"They were blacksmiths and worked with the treasures of the earth, producing wonderful tools and weapons for others. They knew about the Old Magic, and realised that the land was not theirs to own but to keep in trust for others. The first weapon they fashioned was Urthslean, the sword which Tom now wears. This they planted in the hillside to protect the land and their homes from evil spirits. Gradually it was forgotten and left to rust until many years ago, when I rescued it and restored it to its original glory. On the blade they had engraved 'I am Urthslean, who sings only for the Dragon Slayer'. When Tom held it for the first time Urthslean sang, and I knew he must be the one."

"That's all very well," grunted the Bear, "but he still looks very young and puny to me." He sat up straight and whispered. "I think we have visitors."

Strangely the Crudelis did not all attack at once, which would have easily overwhelmed them. They seemed to prefer little sorties, five or six of them would launch an attack about every fifteen minutes, like cats playing with a mouse before deciding when and where to make the final blow. Geschwind saw that their plan was to exhaust them and not to kill them, to keep him occupied and distracted whilst others continued to attack the Thought Barrier in the North. The Crudelis would have loved to go in for the kill, but they had their orders from Skadmeer. Geschwind's end was to be a piece of theatre, something to be enjoyed and savoured over many years, something to create great fear throughout all Glencyndal.

All night they came. They bit and tore at the Bear. They wrapped themselves around his arms and dug deep with their talons and tried to gouge out his eyes to finish the job they had started weeks ago. From Geschwind's fingers snaked bolts of luminous blue-green light bringing each creature down, and hurling it into darkness. Not once did the Bear falter, not a single Crudelis managed to break into the cave where Tom slept soundly, wrapped in Geschwind's slumber-mode. Hour after hour they came and then, at last, as they sensed the coming of dawn, the attacks ceased and all was still.

A strange dawn came. The sun's path was heralded by streaks of green.

Geschwind insisted that they all had a good breakfast which he produced from thin air.

"It makes me wonder why I bothered to trudge all that way to find fish," muttered the Bear as he tore into his meal.

He looked so glum that Tom burst into laughter.

"Ssshh!" warned Geschwind, his finger pressed against his lips, but he gave Tom a huge wink.

They began to make their plans and after much discussion it was decided that Tom would attempt the rescue of his brother and Bella, whilst Geschwind and the Bear would take on Bestim.

"That's silly," protested Tom. "I'm supposed to be the Dragon Slayer. I should fight him."

"Neither the Bear nor I are nimble enough to cross that crater unseen," replied Geschwind. "I don't want to use magic force too soon. Remember, Bestim is evil, the Solanum flows through his veins. Now, should the dragon see you, then you will have to fight him first. If, on the other hand, we can keep him occupied, you will be able to rescue your brother and young Bella. Then on your return, by all means, you may fight the dragon!"

"But," persisted Tom, "you won't be able to defeat him."

Geschwind smiled, despite the pain which was surging through his mind as he guarded the Thought Barrier. "I know, you know, I imagine even the Bear knows, but Bestim doesn't."

"It's silly," said Tom again. "You could both be killed."

"I hope not," said the Bear. He looked and sounded so crestfallen that, despite the danger ahead, they all burst into laughter again.

"Tom," said Geschwind, calming the situation. "Your first duty is to your brother. Remember you both have a short time to return to your world. Pitzic will not let you down. He will be there to guide you both back to the oak tree and to safety. You must leave us here if all goes wrong."

"I understand what you're saying, Geschwind," answered Tom, "but we are not going to fail. I will follow your orders, but we won't fail."

"Come," the Bear turned to Geschwind. "Let us face this monster, Bestim."

They all solemnly rubbed noses and began to put their plan into action.

Chapter Twenty-One
Reunion

The Bear quietly worked his way around the left side of the crater. This side had a wide ledge which made it much easier for him to reach a raised platform of rock, just above Bestim's lair. There was no sign of the beast, everything was still. Geschwind made his way to the back of the Skull Rock and scrambled up until he stood on the very top. In the meantime, Tom skirted around the right side of the crater. This was a much narrower ledge but the advantage was, that as it neared the dragon's cave, it split into two. The top path carried on around the crater directly across the cave's entrance, but the second path dipped down, ran beneath the top, petering out just below the entrance. Whoever stood on that could not be seen from above. It was from here that Tom was to make the final approach. All this was achieved in total silence, not another living soul stirred on the mountainside. The only other movement came from the ever-present, ever-menacing swirling green mist which hovered and hung, as though waiting, in the depths of the crater. Tom was sure that his heart was beating so loudly it would wake up Bestim.

At an agreed signal from the Bear, Geschwind stood tall upon the top of the Skull Rock and let out a blood-curdling war cry which echoed round and round the crater. It bounced from side to side as though an army of warriors was descending upon the cave, and for a precious moment there was no answer, just an indifferent silence... Suddenly a thunderous roar shattered the air tearing it apart. From behind a rock, and directly behind the Bear lurched the menacing shape of Bestim.

Of one thing Tom was certain, this was no ordinary dragon.

Each foot thundered down like a mighty piston, and each foot had not only three giant black claws but also a fourth spur-like talon protruding from the heel. Even though his body was covered in olive-green scales, scales which flashed brown and black in the sunlight, it was still possible to see that this was a creature of remarkable muscle power, a creature of great strength. Tom felt an initial sense of awe in his presence.

'Did I really paint this?' he asked himself quietly, his thoughts in a whirl. 'Did my family help to create this monster?'

True there were gaps in the giant scales which swathed the monster's body, and there were one or two sore places on his back where he had damaged himself or perhaps had been in a fight, but there was nothing vulnerable about Bestim. His narrow yellow eyes were alert and, from his mouth full of grinning, greedy, tainted teeth, he dribbled green slime in expectant glee at the thought of battle and the sight of the Bear just in front of him. His heavily spiked tail switched from side to side, crashing against the rocks. He was oblivious to any pain.

The Bear was no fool. As soon as he heard the approaching dragon he leapt from the top of the cavern to be in amongst the surrounding rocks. It would not be so easy for Bestim to reach him there. The dragon lumbered across to stand near his cave entrance, no one would enter his cave. Tom was crouched beneath the very ledge which supported the dragon. The huge beast's tail dislodged several small stones which rained down on his unprotected head but all the time his eyes were searching for that spot, the one where both he and his great-grandfather had strangely failed to complete their work.

There, at last he saw the tell-tale sign, the broken scales just inside the left front leg. The scales ceased altogether in that small part of the leg. This could mark Bestim's death spot. It had to be.

Tom daren't move, the whole success of this operation depended on the secrecy of his presence. Once again Geschwind sent his challenge, his name, crashing around the crater whilst the huge beast's tail lashed the air above Tom's head, as it searched out its quarry.

"Ayee, Bestim!" shouted the Magician. "Come forth if you dare! Come forth and face Geschwind the Grand Master!"

A bolt of blue light burst from Geschwind's raised arm and hurtled across the crater, narrowly missing Tom.

"I can see why he's not a Dragon Slayer," muttered Tom, hoping that Geschwind's aim would improve during the day.

Suddenly another cry, a second more terrifying sound rent the air. It was the hunting call of the Bear. To Tom's ears it sounded like the roar of an angry lion. The Bear had craftily doubled back and was standing on the rocks above the dragon's cave. Bestim was confused. Now there were two enemies. There was Geschwind standing defiantly on the Skull Rock, but where was this other challenge coming from? Slowly he lifted his monstrous head, searching out every crack and crevice nearby, a great sheet of flame flew from its gaping mouth.

When the Bear called again, Bestim saw him, but turned away. Hadn't the Bear learned his lesson? They had fought before and the scorch marks on the Bear's body were the results of earlier battles which Bestim always won. No, it was Geschwind he wanted. It was as if Bestim knew that Geschwind was of the Old Magic and needed to be killed quickly. Once he was out of the way, Bestim would dispatch the Bear once and for all.

Geschwind shouted his cry of defiance again and hurtled another bolt at Bestim which merely bounced off his scales. The Dragon grunted as he very deliberately lumbered along the wide ledge on the left side of the crater away from Tom. He switched his tail viciously from side to side, landing a blow on the Bear and hurling him with a sickening thud back against the rocks. Bestim didn't even bother to finish him off, that would be something to be enjoyed later. This was the moment Tom had been waiting for, nimbly he leapt from the ledge and scrambled up the short slope into the cave.

The sudden darkness was overwhelming and startled him. He was forced to stand still to allow his eyes to become accustomed to his surroundings. That was when he was hit by something very wet and quite painful. A figure stood defiantly in front of him.

It was Charlie!

Chapter Twenty-Two
The Escape

"Tom!" shouted Charlie. "It's you!"

He flung his arms around his brother, they were both so pleased to be together again.

A girl appeared behind Charlie. "So, you are the Dragon Slayer," she said quietly. "I thought at first you were one of the Crudelis."

"Thanks very much," replied Tom, with a touch of sarcasm in his voice.

"This is my brother, Tom," said Charlie, almost crying with happiness. "We'll be okay now, we won't need the Dragon Slayer. Tom, this is Bella, she's a prisoner here too."

Bella smiled. "He IS the Dragon Slayer. Can't you see, Charlie, he's wearing Urthslean. I must say you are a bit small for a Dragon Slayer," she added. "I was expecting a great warrior, but you have Urthslean, and so it must be."

"Very funny," replied Tom. "It's enough that the Bear thinks I'm a bit small, and I don't mind telling you that if you know of anyone else who might like the job, then please be my guest. Have you seen the size of that creature?"

He knew his last question was silly, of course she had seen him. Hadn't she'd been a prisoner here for some time?

"So how are we getting home?" asked Charlie, eager to stop this banter and to start making the move home.

"We've made tons of water bombs and collected piles of small rocks. Can we use these against the Dragon?"

"At the moment," replied his brother, "Bestim is fighting the Bear."

"Oh no!" Bella exclaimed in horror. "He's no match for Bestim. The Dragon will kill him."

"Well," said Tom. "He's got some help. Geschwind is out there as well."

This seemed to please Bella even less. "They will both be killed. Neither of them is a match for that monster. You must do it because you have Urthslean."

"I know," replied Tom angrily. "I know what everyone keeps telling me."

"Who or what is this Urthslean?" asked Charlie. "I can't see anyone else with Tom."

"It's this," replied Tom, and carefully drew the sword from its scabbard. "This is the great sword that everyone says will help me kill this dragon, though I'm not looking forward to it."

Urthslean sang as Tom lifted it high above his head, but Charlie saw nothing.

"I can't see anything but you holding your arm in the air," he said frowning at Tom. "And it looks a bit silly to me. We need to be thinking about getting home and not messing about in daft games."

Tom looked stunned. "Are you really saying that you can't see or hear this sword?"

Charlie nodded. "Sorry," he said.

The noises from outside were getting louder. Great cries and crashes were echoing around the crater. The Dragon was enjoying his encounter with Geschwind.

"Look," said Bella, "we can sort that out later, but first we must make our escape, those two will not be able to keep the Dragon at bay much longer. Let's move back into the cave first. Come and see what we have made."

"You're right," replied Tom. Charlie said nothing as they trudged deeper into the cave.

Tom gazed at the pile of water bombs and the collection of small stones, and quickly realised that Charlie and Bella had made a great effort in making all these.

"These are great. Y'know we could use these, Charlie," he said, hoping his remarks would bring Charlie out of his sulk. He removed the backpack that he had carried for most of the journey. "Use this bag, which Gioco gave me, to store some of the water bombs, don't bother about the stones, there are plenty of loose ones around the crater."

Immediately Charlie brightened up. "Okay," he replied. "I'll carry it. You look after this Urthslean, or whatever you call it. It doesn't seem that heavy to me!"

Tom grinned. "You're right, of course," he said, as they all began to fill the bag with as many water bombs as Charlie could carry.

Together they made their way back to the cave entrance, only this time strange creatures began to scuttle around their feet trying to trip them. Others dropped from the cave walls and into their hair. They moved purposefully forward, brushing and kicking away anything which tried to stop them. The noise from the fighting swept into the cave so that when they reached the daylight they could only gaze in horror on the scene. The Bear was not dead but a jagged wound was running down the left side of his once golden fur, and a dark red patch of blood was staining his chest, his jaw gaped wide and his eyes rolled back and forth as he played his dangerous game of 'catch' with the Dragon.

Bestim was blundering and lurching towards the Bear but although his movements were slow he didn't seem to be harmed in any way. He was just playing with the Bear, just toying with him.

All three were able to make the journey around the inside of the crater without being seen. The Dragon was too busy tormenting the Bear, and the strange creatures, which had tried to trip them in the cave, would not venture out, so the three were able to reach the back of the Skull Rock unharmed. It was here that they found Geschwind slumped against the rock, he was in incredible pain.

Charlie looked at him in amazement.

"The Solanum is using this battle to break down the Barrier in so many places," Geschwind whispered. "I must help our people, Tom."

"I understand," replied Tom. "You take Bella and Charlie back, I will go and help the Bear. Once you are away from here you'll be able to concentrate on the Thought Barrier."

"We can't leave you," said Bella in horror. "We must help too."

"You'll help by going with Geschwind. It's important that he completes his part so that I can get on with mine," replied Tom. "I just hope you're right, Geschwind, and that I am the Dragon Slayer."

Despite his pain Geschwind managed a smile. "There is no doubt, Tom. You truly are."

Bella took hold of the Magician's arm and helped him to his feet. "We will come back for you if you do not return in time," she said. She looked at Charlie.

"I'm not coming," said Charlie.

"You must go," replied Tom. "This could be very dangerous."

"That's why I'm not coming," replied his brother defiantly. "I'm not daft, Tom. I've worked out that all of this has something to do with this new house we've decided to live in. It has something to do with Green Willow. I'm not leaving you, Tom. I can see my water bombs, I can't see your Urthslean, so let's see how we get on together against this dragon of yours. After all, you're my brother."

Tom would never be able to explain how much Charlie's words meant to him at this moment. He just answered, "Come on then, let's do it."

Chapter Twenty-Three
One has to die

Once more a great cry split the air and thundered around the crater bouncing back and forth over the rocks. It was the battle cry of a new and dreadful warrior. Even Tom was surprised by the strength of the sound; however, it had the required effect. Bestim, now standing near his cave entrance, stopped dead in his tracks and slowly turned his ugly head to glare in the direction of Tom. Even from his relatively safe position, on the opposite side of the crater, Tom could feel the heat which belched out in flames of odious breath from the Dragon. It was hard to breathe in such heat. The flames were greedily devouring the air about him.

Charlie was standing a little to his right and threw the first of the water bombs as hard as he could at the monster. It was a good aim and landed straight into the Dragon's mouth. It distracted him, and gave Tom just enough time to change his position.

"Dive!" he yelled at Charlie.

Charlie leapt behind a rock just as Bestim unleashed an enormous flame in his direction. Tom looked to his left and saw that the Bear seemed to be trapped amongst some large boulders.

"Bear, are you alright?" he called.

"It is nothing, Tom," replied the brave creature. "Go, leave me! Save yourself!"

"No!" shouted Tom defiantly. "I am the Dragon Slayer and we will kill him! Call him, Bear. Distract him, I'm coming closer!"

Tom drew Urthslean and immediately the sword began to hum. Stepping away from the protection of the Skull Rock he began to make his way across the wide ledge as, at the same time and with a supreme effort, the Bear roared his challenge.

Bestim answered by twisting around to face and attack him. One quick belch of flame would finish off this meddlesome Bear, then he could give all his attention to these stupid boys. He should never have listened to the Solanum's demands of keeping them alive, nor to the commands of Teracind. If he had followed his own instincts, the Bear would be dead by now, that interfering gnome burnt to a cinder and he would have been able to concentrate on this last irritation.

Tom ran as never before. It was not for nothing that he was the fastest runner in his school. He flew across the open terrain using the boulders as cover to reach the Dragon, but his eagerness had made him too hasty and Bestim saw the movement. Immediately the Dragon swung back and curtains of fire spattered the rocks around Tom. Charlie unleashed another round of water bombs which caused him to pause, but Bestim was no fool. Tom had been quicker than he had anticipated and, in that moment, he knew he had underestimated this boy. He had seen the flames glisten on the blade of Urthslean, this strange weapon which sang and glowed, and so it was to Tom that he now directed his fiercest attack.

Both the Bear and Charlie were alert to Tom's predicament. Whilst Charlie continued a relentless onslaught of water bombs, the Bear somehow managed to find the strength to clear himself from the boulders. He climbed back onto the platform of rocks just above Bestim's head and, with a tremendous roar and a supreme effort, he leapt from there onto the back of the Dragon's neck.

"No!" screamed Tom. The Bear mustn't die, couldn't die, it was too big a sacrifice.

Now it was Bestim's turn to screech and roar with pain. Desperately the great Dragon reared to dislodge the Bear. For the first time in this deadly struggle its great bat-like wings slowly unfurled. The effect was terrifying as they made the Dragon appear even more horrific and nightmarish. Tom could not suppress a gasp of disbelief at the size of this beast which he was supposed to kill. For a brief moment his task appeared impossible, this monstrous creature seemed invincible, but then he began to realise that the wings were beating and cracking in vain. The weight and movements of the Bear on Bestim's head were preventing him from flying, and the constant onslaught of Charlie's water bombs was proving to be, at the very least, an irritant. Flames and smoke billowed out in all directions, and Tom's nostrils took in the smell of sulphur and blood. The noise was as if a hundred trains were slamming into one another. The Bear roared in anger, and began digging his great claws into the Dragon's eyes, and in that same moment, Tom sprang forward and darted between Bestim's kicking legs.

Tom and Urthslean were as one, he could feel the excitement of the sword rushing through his hand and down into his body. He had to be quick and needed to avoid the stomping feet of the Dragon, who was able to operate his back spurs independently from his other talons. One cut from these scything blades would mean instant death. Tom began a deadly game of dodge between the monster's legs, all the time searching, searching for that one vulnerable patch just under the left leg.

Blinded by blood oozing from his eyes, Bestim moved closer to the boulders hoping that he could crush Tom against them. At that moment Tom found what he had been frantically searching for, the unfinished part of his painting, the unfinished part of his ancestor's carving, the soft scale-less part of Bestim's body.

He could hear Charlie shrieking his name as his brother realised what he was about to do. Swiftly he scrambled out from beneath the crushing legs onto a small boulder. As Bestim reared high to come crashing down, so Tom leapt, sword in hand, at the Dragon's exposed soft underbelly. With one mighty effort he swung Urthslean upwards and plunged it deep into Bestim's unprotected spot. Once there, he hung on before feeling Urthslean twist and crunch. Bestim roared and trembled as the whole of his body shook so violently that Tom fell to the ground, dragging Urthslean with him.

It seemed an eternity before anything happened, but suddenly the screams above him and the stench which filled the air became terrible. Hot green globules spattered on and around him, faster and faster, until they turned into a steady flow. It was the life blood of the Dragon. Tom frantically fought his way out from beneath Bestim's twisting writhing body but, in his eagerness to scrabble away, he missed his footing and began to slip down the crater. He grabbed at Urthslean and jammed it into the slope, digging his feet deeper into the loose surface until gradually he came to a stop.

Above him, screeching in agony, Bestim reared up high on to his back legs, all the while desperately beating his great wings.

With tortured eyes full of disbelief and terror the Dragon furiously shook its head. The Bear, who was still clinging on, was hurled through the air and landed with a sickening thud at the base of the Skull Rock. Now the whole crater was filled with the sounds of death as, Bestim the Mighty, feared by all, reared again for the last time. His claws frantically tore at the empty air, his wings, like a giant pterodactyl, cracked noisily, but they were useless. He couldn't even see his executioner, he had no wish to die, he was desperate to live, yet knew that for him there was no hope. With blood streaming from his wound he plunged down, down, down, deep, deep into the green swirling mists of the crater.

Exhausted, Tom wiped some of the sweat from his own eyes, his face was covered in a sticky mixture of Bestim's blood and his own. Slowly he turned to gaze down into the depths below him, but there was nothing, nothing at all, except an eerie, frightening silence.

Chapter Twenty-Four
Back to the Forest

It was some time before Tom could gather his thoughts together. Noises of the fight were still crashing around in his head, the smell of Bestim's blood seemed to cling to him. He imagined that he could even taste the smell of death. For a moment there was silence, then he heard a voice yelling his name. It was Charlie.

A face appeared over the edge of the crater.

"Tom! Can you climb up? I'll come down to help you."

"No," he shouted back. "Stay where you are. The sides of this crater aren't safe. I'll use Urthslean to help me get back."

To Charlie's eyes Tom was digging his hands deep into the crater's walls to slowly climb up, but in fact he was digging Urthslean deep into the treacherous scree and using the sword as a lever. Slowly he crawled and dragged his way up and gratefully took the hand of his brother as he reached the top.

"We need to move quickly, Tom," said Charlie. "Those horrible green things are climbing up behind you."

Tom looked back down the crater and saw what Charlie meant. Squat creatures were slowly making their way up towards them. He noted with satisfaction that they, too, were finding the climb difficult, with a scream one fell back down into the depths taking others with it. The sides of the crater were covered with treacherous loose rocks.

"Where's the Bear?" he asked, pausing for breath.

Charlie merely looked towards the Skull Rock and shook his head. "I think he's dead," he said.

There by the rock lay the mangled mass of fur that was once the Bear.

Together the two boys slowly made their way around the ledge towards him. Tom kept calling to the Bear but there was no reply. He had just convinced himself that the Bear was really dead when he heard a small, weary groan and, with genuine relief, he flung his arms around the crumpled figure.

"Help me sit him up, Charlie," Tom said, as he struggled to raise him. "Come on Bear, you must try to get up. You're too heavy for us to manage, and we must leave here as soon as possible."

The Bear moaned. "Leave me, Tom," he whispered. "Take your brother with you, save yourselves. Leave, before the Crudelis arrive."

"We can't, Bear," replied Tom, close to tears. "I can no more leave you than fly like Kurz. Get up! We must all leave together."

The Bear let out a deep sigh and with the boys' help slowly moved so that he was leaning against the base of the Skull. There was a great gash in his left side and the blood flowed freely.

"You may both have to leave me," muttered the Bear.

Charlie was clutching the bag which Gioco had given Tom before he had entered the Forest. "What did you bring in this?" he asked. "Did you bring any first aid?"

"Gioco said that it could be useful if I was separated from Geschwind," answered Tom. "We've already used some of it when I was attacked in the Forest. Let's see."

"Stop wasting time," implored the Bear. "Get away now whilst you've still a chance."

"Be quiet," commanded Tom. "Gioco said that there were all sorts of things in here that might help."

From the bag Tom pulled a small flagon of Hunitwede and a jar containing a strange blue liquid, on its side were written the words 'Balmbeorg... use with care'. There was also a box containing what appeared to be dried-up bits of mushroom coated in a sweet substance.

"Is there no water?" gasped the Bear.

"No," replied Tom. "But try this Bear, I'm sure it will help." He thrust the flagon onto the Bear's lips.

"It is water," the Bear sighed thankfully, as he took a large gulp. "You must both drink some."

Tom drank from the never-ending flagon but tasted only the lovely Hunitwede, and when it came to Charlie's turn he only tasted his favourite apple juice.

"It seems to taste just as you hope," said Tom.

"Let's try this stuff called Bamburger, or whatever it's called," said Charlie. "Drink your water, Bear, and I'll dab some of this blue liquid on your wounds. It might sting a bit. I did first aid at school, so I'll be very careful."

The Bear tried one of his smiles. "I trust you, Charlie," he said, and swallowed down more water.

Tom proudly watched his brother gently touch the open wounds. Immediately the first effect of the Balmbeorg was to stop the bleeding, then, to their amazement, the wounds began to slowly heal. The skin knitted together and a neat scar appeared where once a wound oozed blood.

"Amazing," sighed the Bear. "I had forgotten how clever faeries can be."

He tried to stand up but quickly realised that he was not that fit yet!

"Thank you, Gioco," said Tom to his absent friend. "Now could this be food?"

He looked at the dried-up mushrooms in the box. "I'm not too fond of mushrooms," he said, "but who cares? I'm starving. Try some, Charlie. You too, Bear."

They all took a piece.

The Bear munched happily. "It tastes like fresh salmon caught in a mountain stream."

"Mine tastes of sausages," said Charlie.

"And I've got freshly baked bread with melted cheese, just like Mum makes," said Tom, and then hesitated. He looked at Charlie. "We will get back home, Charlie, I promise."

Charlie just nodded, he didn't trust himself to speak.

"Then we must move quickly," grunted the Bear. He was getting stronger by the minute. "The sun will soon dip and the night belongs to the Crudelis. We must make our way back so that you may link up with your friends."

Tom nodded as he replaced the items in the bag. He knew all too well the formidable path which lay before them. He could remember the outward journey vividly, the stench of the rotting vegetation, the unnatural plants, the lack of air. The thought of fighting his way once more through that hostile place filled him with dread. And how would Charlie cope?

Suddenly he tensed, from behind them he heard a scrabbling noise, and swinging swiftly round he scanned the rim to see what was making the sound. Several Crudelis were slowly crawling out of the crater. Their claw-like hands scrabbled amongst the loose rocks to find a sure grip. They hesitated, unsure in the dying sunlight.

"Keep still," whispered the Bear. "They won't leave the crater until the sun drops lower in the sky. We have nothing to fear yet."

Too late. Charlie, who seemed to have an unending supply of water bombs, unleashed two large ones and hit the nearest full in the face. Startled he yelled, threw up his hands in self-defence, and promptly fell back down the crater. The others made a quick retreat.

"They'll be back," warned the Bear. "Do you never obey orders?" He looked down at Charlie who was grinning.

"Sometimes," he answered. "Best move now, I think. Looks like we may have more company."

More Crudelis had appeared on the rim of the crater. They looked as though they were sniffing the air.

"Why are they doing that?" asked Tom.

The Bear pointed to the sky. "The sun is setting. The Crudelis don't have good daytime vision. They're fixing our position by smell. When night comes they'll come straight for us and those lamp-like eyes will help pinpoint our position."

"Stop talking then," interrupted Charlie. "Let's get going."

Together they slipped and slithered their way down the treacherous path which wound its way around the mountainside. Once away from the crater, they were met again by the harsh winds, winds which had gained in strength and bitterness, winds which tossed dust, twigs and even small pebbles at them. Sometimes the path ran close to the mountain's edge and one slip would have been fatal. It was difficult to keep their balance on the loose scree, they couldn't rely on each footstep. Gradually they became aware of shapes and shadows flitting between rocks. Something was keeping pace with them. The Crudelis were on the move.

Tom's legs felt like lead. He looked at Charlie, and carefully placed a comforting hand on his shoulder.

"We can do it, Charlie," he whispered.

His younger brother nodded, a grim look on his face. "I know," he replied.

Urthslean gave a quiet hum of approval. "Thank you," said Tom, and patted the hilt.

The Bear was panting heavily. "Let's stop for a while," he gasped. "I think your friend's medicine is wearing off. I feel so weak. We must stop."

"No," replied Tom, leaning against a rock. "It's not wearing off, it's the air. We're quite low down now and we're very close to that dreadful Forest. Oh Bear, if you knew how much I hate it."

It was true. Despite the treacherous surface, they had made good headway and now, as the sun was sinking in the green heavens, they found themselves on the lower slopes of Mount Ondraedan. The air had lost the sharp bite of the upper slopes, instead it was replaced by a heavier and more humid atmosphere, and it was beginning to sap their strength. Tom looked about him, the shadows had crawled away and everywhere was filled with a strange uncanny silence. It became so intense Charlie thought his ears would burst, but then a sudden wild wailing split the air, a screeching so terrible that in agony he clasped his hands over his ears.

The Bear leapt to his feet, his eyes wide in terror.

"What is it?" shouted Tom above the noise.

The Bear groaned. "It's the Banshee, Tom. The foreteller of death, my death."

"I don't believe it." Tom tugged angrily at the Bear's arm. "It's a trick. The Crudelis can make you believe anything. Come on, Charlie! It just means we must move faster. We can't give up now, Bear, not after all we've been through. Come on, both of you!"

Urthslean hummed so loudly that even Charlie looked about for the source of the sound.

The Bear faltered as the wailing Banshee came closer, but the dark shape swept on and twisted through the skies as though driven by some invisible force. Great brush strokes of black moved, first one way and then another, it was like watching a flock of starlings, a murmuration, surging through the skies just before roosting time. The boys watched mesmerised. She, the Banshee, had come for someone or something, that was certain.

As they neared the start of the Forest, Tom felt panic welling up inside him, his heart began to beat faster, he hated everything about this place but go into it they must if they were going to get home. Urthslean began to hum again. They paused.

The Bear looked down at both boys. He too was worried, but even so, he gathered them both up in his giant arms, and gave them a hug. "Don't worry," he said. "You're right. We can do it. Let's go!"

Despite his fear Tom managed a grin. "If we get many more hugs like that, Bear, we won't have to worry about anything!"

Charlie just said, "Wow!"

Without another word they plunged into Ferlian Forest.

Chapter Twenty-Five
Beweglic

"I don't like this place, Tom," said Charlie, clutching the few small rocks he'd collected earlier.

"Neither do I," replied Tom, "but we have to go through here to get home. I don't know any other way."

"Did you come this way to rescue me?" asked Charlie. Tom nodded.

"You're very brave," said his brother. "Thanks."

"That's okay," replied Tom, trying to sound as if it was no problem. "Keep your wits about you, Charlie. There are some nasty things in this Forest."

The Bear was pushing his way along the path, Tom was at the back and Charlie was grateful that he was in the middle.

The only good thing was that the ground was a little firmer and so they were able to make better progress. Tom began to feel more positive, but this was short-lived; he stumbled and tripped on a tree root that had slithered unseen across his path. Immediately a sharp pain shot through his right leg as claws sank deep into his calf muscle. He tried to grab hold of something, anything, but it was no use, he was slowly being dragged away.

"Urthslean!" he screamed, and felt the solid hilt of the sword leap into his hand. One enormous thrust into the darkness beyond his leg was answered by a squeal and a grunt from a Crudelis. Another grunt came from a second as Charlie hurled a rock in the same direction. It was all over as quickly as it had begun.

The Bear spun around. "Are you all right?" he asked. His voice sounded dry and hoarse.

Tom nodded as Charlie quickly rubbed some Balmbeorg into his leg.

"Where is all this light coming from?" asked the Bear looking around. Everything had become bathed in an eerie green light.

Tom looked at Urthslean, the blade was covered in green slime. "I don't know," he answered. "It was a bit like this when Geschwind and I came through, but it didn't seem so bright."

If Tom had but known it, the green light was coming from the Crudelis themselves, they were massing in the glade where Tom and Geschwind had rested earlier.

The wail of the Banshee tore through the air once more. It began to whip up a great wind which caused the twisted trees to crack and moan as they swayed and danced their unnatural rhythms to her tune. The Forest was jerked into life as dead branches were snapped off like dry matchsticks in the violent wind, dry matchsticks which, in their turn, became lethal spears driven towards them. So fearful was the noise that it felt as if a giant airliner was bearing down on them. They became aware of many eyes watching them as they fought, punched and kicked their way through the tangle of roots, branches and limbs of the plants. Their senses were being battered and bullied by the howling wind. The Crudelis patiently waited, waited until they reached the glade.

It was here that they met him. Standing at the far end of the glade was a lone dark figure, Beweglic.

Everything within the glade became still as if frozen.

Charlie drew in a quick gasp of air. At first he thought it was Teracind, but he quickly realised that this was a smaller being, but nonetheless one to be feared.

Tom gripped Urthslean once more.

"It is Beweglic," muttered the Bear. "The leader of the Crudelis. Teracind and Slaf do not intend us to leave this glade alive. They have sent their General to stop us."

Beweglic was about the same height as Tom, but his head was dominated by huge upward slanting eyes. His skin was made of green scales, and his yellow teeth were more like fangs. He was dressed completely in black, and clutched between the four talons of one hand, he held a cruel-looking dagger. There were unmistakeable signs of blood on it. Geschwind's? Bella's? Tom cast a quick look around the glade. There were no bodies visible, but slowly emerging from behind every distorted tree and ugly stump stood the silent figures of Beweglic's followers. The Bear snorted and grunted nervously.

"We've got to cross this glade," whispered Tom. "Don't take your eyes off any of them. We'll go forwards very slowly."

Beweglic lifted his head. It was such a slight movement but it was enough. It was a signal.

Two Crudelis rushed screaming and screeching towards them, their talons extended, and once again Urthslean sang as Tom wielded his sword to the right and to the left. Great scything actions. Down. Across. Across again. And up. The head of one Crudelis rolled away, the other lay writhing on the ground, mortally wounded. Tom felt sick. Beweglic laughed. Another movement and four rushed forwards. Charlie hurled rocks at them and Tom swung Urthslean. The Bear tried to tackle one but was wounded before Urthslean could dispatch these suicide fighters.

"What's he doing?" asked Charlie. "Doesn't he care about his troops?"

"He's playing with us," replied Tom, looking at the baying mob of Crudelis encircling them. "He's like a cat playing with a mouse, only we're the mice."

The Crudelis were shouting at their leader, begging to be given the chance to attack. Suddenly Beweglic raised his hand… and all was silent.

"I think this is it," whispered Tom. "Good luck, Bear. Charlie…" he hesitated.

"Don't say anything, Tom," Charlie's voice sounded a bit croaky as he fought back the tears. "Just don't say a thing."

"Let's do it," said Tom. "Urthslean, this is it." He gripped the sword and amazingly the sword sang and suddenly bathed all three of them in a beautiful blue-green light. It was so spectacular that it caused a small murmur to ripple through the ranks of the Crudelis. No one moved. Leering at his followers, Beweglic stepped forward.

When or how the attack started, Tom was never really sure. Beweglic must have given a signal, for suddenly they were fighting for their lives. Screaming, shrieking Crudelis were leaping on them from all sides. The Bear hit out in every direction but in the end the sheer weight of numbers was enough to gradually force him to his knees. Charlie was holding a rock in each hand and hit out savagely. The boys stood together fighting with a grim determination to survive, and all the time Urthslean sang just as it had in those early distant days when it was first forged.

The stench of the Crudelis' blood was like rotten eggs and decaying flesh. Tom could just make out the figure of Beweglic standing on the fringe of his army, baying and encouraging them forward. If only Tom could reach him, he felt sure that the others would give up if their leader was dead.

"Stay close, Charlie," he ordered, as he slowly fought his way across the glade towards Beweglic.

He began to feel as if he and Urthslean were invincible, but it couldn't last.

Suddenly he felt a great pain in the back of his neck as several Crudelis hurled themselves on top of him. He heard Charlie shout and then… a scream. The poisonous talons sank deep into his body. With a groan he sank to his knees, his grip on Urthslean faltered and the sword hung limp in his hand. As he looked up he saw the evil, sneering face of Beweglic gazing down at him. The dagger came down… and all was blackness.

Chapter Twenty-Six
The Banshee's Reward

Pitzic waited silently for the Banshee to claim him. He had done his best. Was this to be his end? He'd never given death much thought until this moment.

'How would it be?' he wondered as he gazed about him. 'Would it be the Banshee or the Crudelis?'

He looked to the Forest, there was movement again, he gripped his sword tightly, he knew he wasn't going to give up without a fight. Suddenly he dropped his weapon and shouted with joy at the top of his voice, for there out of the Forest and running towards him came Geschwind and Bella. They flung their arms around each other, laughing and crying with relief and happiness. At least they were safe.

"Where's Tom, and his brother?" Pitzic had to shout above the increasing wind. The noise of the cracking branches was like a rifle shot.

"Back there!" Geschwind pointed back into the Forest. None of the Magician's previous hardships were apparent, he had regained all his old strength. It had surged through him once Bestim had been killed. The Solanum had been thrown into complete disarray, they had not believed that their Dragon of evil could be destroyed, not even by Tom, and their confusion had allowed Geschwind to repair the Thought Barrier which protected his people from the Dark Forces. Once this had been achieved, Geschwind was ready to give his formidable attention to Tom and Charlie's well-being. No one was more aware of their impending danger than

Geschwind. He was determined to save the boys or die in the attempt.

"What has happened to Kurz?" he asked, looking down at the crumpled figure lying on the ground.

"We were attacked by the Crudelis," began Pitzic. He didn't finish as at that moment they heard voices shouting and the noise of ponies. Looking back across the plain they could see Gioco returning with a small band of friends.

In minutes they were all together again, delighted at the safe return of Bella.

"What made you return?" asked Geschwind.

"We could see all the strange lights around Mount Ondraedan, and we quickly realised that a Death Battle had begun," explained Gioco. "Then we heard the Banshee… so we came," he added simply.

Geschwind shook his hand warmly.

"Now listen all of you, we must hurry," said Geschwind. They all huddled together to listen carefully to his plan. "Some of you must return with Bella and Kurz, who is badly wounded because—"

"No, I don't think so," interrupted Bella quietly." You're going to need everyone to go back to save Tom, Charlie and the Bear."

If anyone was surprised at the mention of a Bear they didn't say so.

"I can manage Kurz on my own, and then I can return with more help if needed," she sounded very confident, but inside she was trembling.

"The plain is a very dangerous place, Bella," murmured Pitzic.

"I know," she replied smiling. "So many of you have risked your lives trying to save me, now let me do this. Let me do something for myself. I'm sure I'll get through, I won't let you down. Get back to the others as quickly as you can. Just leave me two ponies."

"Then take this sword, Bella," said Pitzic. "I just hope you won't have to use it."

"Thank you," replied Bella, and gently rubbed noses with him. He looked suitably embarrassed but secretly he was delighted.

Geschwind quickly explained the situation to them. He felt certain that the Banshee had not come for Tom, but she was a law unto herself, and it was clear she was here for one of them, though they would do all in their power to stop her. As if in reply, the Banshee let out another high-pitched cackle, which brought icy fear into the hearts of everyone. They drew lots for one of them to stay to care for the ponies, the rest followed Geschwind into the Forest of Ferlian.

* * *

The Forest was in its own death throes. As the force of the wind increased, so branches snapped off with ever growing rapidity. Once Bestim had been killed, Teracind had abandoned his followers, they must cope as best they could. Trees were being stripped of their leaves, and poisonous plants were crushed underfoot as the small band bravely fought its way into the depths of this mangled mess. Geschwind strode ahead leading the way, his eyes glinting with determination as he thrust aside the branches with ever increasing strength. The others gained confidence from him, their progress was swift and certain. They were not prepared, however, for the scene which greeted them when they broke through to the glade.

The Bear had fallen and a group of Crudelis were hunched around him, as vultures do around a corpse. From their reluctance to make the final attack it seemed that the Bear might not be quite dead. Pitzic rushed swiftly to his aid and several followed him.

Geschwind frantically searched the scene. A group of Crudelis was beginning to encircle Charlie, and quickly Geschwind directed his forces to help him. But where was Tom? He was just in time to see the black figure of Beweglic, with arm raised, standing over Tom's body. It was then that Geschwind became the Mighty, a true descendant of the Great Sorcerers, and all his ancestral powers came into being.

With a great cry and sheer willpower, he froze the arm as it came down for the final kill. A blaze of light snaked from his finger tips and across the glade. With a snarl of rage the black figure spun around and Geschwind found himself, at last, face to face with Beweglic. For a brief moment they stared at one another, as though unable to believe what each of them saw in the other. The moment of recognition lasted barely a second. Then all magic was cast aside and, uttering cries of anger and rage, they hurled themselves at one another, both with the single purpose in mind, death.

The others, following the example of the new war-like Pitzic, charged at the remaining Crudelis. Overhead, ever wailing, ever patient, hovered the dark shape of the Banshee. It was as if she knew that this would be the time, the moment of reckoning for someone below.

Geschwind and Beweglic were locked in deadly combat. Beweglic constantly tried to use his fangs and talons to attack the Magician's throat, but Geschwind was quick and fearless and his grip was one of iron. They rolled back and forth, then Geschwind fell and immediately Beweglic was upon him, but Geschwind gripped his scaly wrists and held him fast. The yellow eyes leered down at him, and a hideous mouth opened wide to reveal long discoloured fangs. Deliberately Geschwind bent his knees and firmly planted his feet in Beweglic's stomach. With a mighty heave, he pushed him away.

The Banshee swooped and a black shadow, like a giant hand, scooped up the writhing body of Beweglic. She dragged him high into the storm-filled skies, and his cries and screams of terror brought fear into the hearts of even the bravest amongst them.

All became still.

The Crudelis fled, and the little band of warriors wearily lowered their swords.

Charlie rushed across to his brother who was lying motionless on the ground.

Of the Bear, there was nothing. In his place lay the body of their King, Bella's father.

Chapter Twenty-Seven
Bella's Journey

Bella finished tying together the last of the ropes and stood back to survey her handiwork.

"That will make a good litter, Tuzzy. Help me to place Kurz on it."

Despite her protests, Geschwind had insisted that one of the elves should go with her and so Tuzzy, the smallest of the group, had been selected.

Together they half carried, half dragged the unconscious Kurz onto the sledge.

"He won't like being tied onto that," said Tuzzy, frowning.

"Well, he'll just have to put up with it," replied Bella, curtly. "We can't risk him falling off."

She wasn't too pleased at having Tuzzy with her.

"Now listen," she continued. "You ride Calan, he's the smallest, Barus can pull the litter, and I'll ride Thencan. Treo can walk beside us."

Geschwind and his men had already left, and the guard left to care for the ponies wanted them to wait until dawn, but Bella insisted that they leave as soon as possible, as it was obvious that Kurz needed some very strong magic if he was to survive. Treo was very weak, and no one really knew when Geschwind and the others would return, or even if they would.

"We'll be alright," said Tuzzy, though he didn't feel it.

They travelled along dried-up river gullies, and all the time they could hear the distant sounds of the battle. In contrast their journey seemed to be remarkably quiet.

Bella began to think that the whole journey would be easy, when suddenly Tuzzy gave a shout.

"Over there!" He pointed to the left. "Moving shadows!"

They stopped and Treo gave a nervous snort. It was difficult to see in this eerie light. Heavy clouds blotted out much of the moonlight.

"Whatever it is," whispered Bella, "we won't be able to outrun it. Barus can't pull the litter any faster. We'll just have to keep moving but watching."

"Psst! Psst!" Tuzzy was trying to attract her attention.

"For goodness sake, Tuzzy," said Bella angrily. "Stop whispering. What are you trying to say?"

Tuzzy took a big breath. "I just want to say," he said. "THEY'RE COMING!"

As he spoke there was a terrible howl and out of the gloom rushed four grey-green shapes. The Crudelis had decided to attack.

"Keep close!" shouted Bella. "Don't let them pull you off of your pony!"

Tuzzy was riding Calan who had decided to become a bucking bronco, rearing up and crashing down, he immediately killed one of the Crudelis. Bella dispatched another one by using Pitzic's sword to strike off its head. The remaining two Crudelis hesitated but then, without warning, seized Kurz from the litter.

No!" shouted Tuzzy, and leapt from Calan to defend Kurz. Bella followed.

The two last Crudelis grinned maliciously. This had been their intention all along, now they stood a better chance of defeating Bella and her friend.

They decided to attack her first, but they had not bargained on the ponies. Gentle, small Calan hated the Crudelis with a fierceness that could not be underestimated. With a soft whinny he nudged Tuzzy to one side; Thencan trotted forward and Treo stood in front of Bella. The three ponies raised their heads, snorted and pawed the ground. It was five versus two.

The Crudelis launched themselves at the ponies, they might be short and squat but they were very powerful and strong. Bella and Tuzzy joined in the attack but in the frenzy, the ropes securing Kurz became loose and he rolled from the litter into a thorn bush. Barus could do nothing to stop this, so he turned his attention to helping the others.

Suddenly, from the Forest, there came an horrendous scream. Bella turned just in time to see a nightmarish, black form rising from the trees and moving away across the sky.

The Crudelis hesitated, Calan lashed out with his hooves and the Crudelis ran whimpering away into the gloom.

The two friends looked at one another, relief on their faces.

"Where's, Kurz?" said Bella in horror.

"Kurz!" shouted Tuzzy, as neither of them had seen him leave.

A small groan came from the thorn bush. Quickly they rushed to him and tried to pull him out.

"No, no." Kurz staggered up and started to push them away. "Get off! Go away! You're Crudelis! I'll fight you. Go away!"

No matter how they tried, he fought them, desperately hitting out in all directions.

"What shall we do?" asked Tuzzy. "How can we help him? He's delirious."

Bella approached Kurz, a look of determination on her face. "I'm sorry, Kurz but we have to get you back on that litter." She hit him so hard that he was knocked out. "Come on Tuzzy, help me get him back, we've still got quite a journey to make."

Tuzzy gave a little chuckle and did as asked.

Looking behind they could hear great shrieks and groans coming from the Forest. They didn't know if it was good or bad. All they did know was that there was a great fire which might be coming their way. The sky looked as though it was burning, and even from where they were, they could feel the heat from the flames as tongues of orange and red began to eagerly eat up all the air. Some of the trees exploded in the heat and sparks of fire burst into the sky like giant fireworks. They needed to travel faster.

For some time they travelled in silence until they stood at the edge of the swamp.

"Oh, Tuzzy," said Bella, sighing. "I think we should rest here for a while. The swamp will be dangerous, we need to keep our wits about us."

Tuzzy was about to agree when they suddenly heard voices. Quickly they drew their swords. The little elf stood up on Calan's back to peer into the distance.

"It's alright, Bella," he cried. "It's alright. They're coming from Campandella, from home. They're coming to help us. I can see Poco."

Sure enough, picking their way through the marsh came several of the little people, some were carrying lanterns to light their way.

"We've found them," shouted someone.

"Stay where you are," shouted another. "We'll come to you."

Two faeries swooped down in front of Bella and Tuzzy.

"We are so pleased to have you home," they said. "We were so worried."

Soon they were surrounded by many friends, and there was much hugging, kissing and laughter. Poco took charge of Kurz and the ponies, and it was during this hubhub that there was a sudden splash of a rainbow and there before Bella stood Lusinga.

"Oh," cried Bella and rushed into her arms. It was only then that she allowed herself to cry.

Chapter Twenty-Eight
A King's Story

When Tom opened his eyes, he was surprised to find himself lying on a bed surrounded by many happy smiling faces, only Charlie looked worried.

"Charlie?" he whispered hoarsely. "Did we do it?"

As soon as he heard Tom say his name, Charlie punched the air and gave out a great cry.

"Yes!" he shouted happily. "You're alive! We can go home!"

Tom struggled to sit up. Many of the little people were gathered around his bed. The small room was crowded with his friends and a few unfamiliar faces. Everything began to come flooding back.

"Welcome back, Tom," said Geschwind softly, his craggy face breaking into a great smile. "You've had a long sleep. How are you feeling now?"

"I'm fine, I think," he replied, a little bewildered. "Are we back in the castle?"

Everyone nodded.

"Are you okay, Charlie?"

His brother nodded. "Just a few bruises, that's all," he answered. "How about you?"

Tom nodded. "The last thing I remember…" He looked around the room. "Where's the Bear? What happened to him?"

"I'm here, Tom." A fair-haired man stepped forward. He was slightly taller than those standing around him, his features were similar to his cousin, Kurz, they had the same green eyes, the same pale skin but, unlike Kurz, his golden hair flowed past his shoulders. He too had the ability to fly.

Geschwind gave a slight cough. "This is Bella's father, Tom, and the King of the Faeries."

"Wow!" said Charlie.

"I don't understand," said Tom. "How could you be the Bear?"

Everyone began talking at once, all eager to explain it to Tom, so that in the end Geschwind had to raise his arm and called, "Silence!"

"Perhaps," said the King. "You would all be good enough to leave us, so that I can explain it to Tom."

"I'm not leaving Tom," replied Charlie defiantly.

"I didn't expect you to," said the King kindly. "But everyone else please leave, except Geschwind and Charlie."

So, they did, and the King began his story.

* * *

It was late at night when most sensible folk were in bed. The messenger hammered hard on the castle door, desperate to get a message to the King and to Geschwind.

"Take your time," said Geschwind, gently calming the distraught young elf. "Tell us slowly what has happened."

"It's our village," he gasped. "A marauding bear of great strength has attacked our homes. Several have been killed, we need your help."

A look of disbelief crossed Geschwind's face. "If this is true," he said, rising from his seat, "then this is no ordinary bear but one possessing evil powers." Suddenly he grunted in obvious pain and held his head. He looked at the King. "I must leave, Your Majesty, there is urgent business to attend to in the north. Please, no matter how bad this appears, please do not attempt to capture this bear on your own. The magic being used must be very powerful for him to come so close to our kingdom. I will return as soon as possible."

Geschwind left. He had only been gone a few minutes when a second elf appeared stating that the bear had broken into the home of one of the Fringe elves, elves who chose to live outside the castle at the edge of the village, and carried away their young son.

The King looked at his friends. "We can't stand by and just wait until Geschwind returns," he said. "They need our help, and they need it now."

So, with a few trusted followers, he left for the Fringes. There they found the elves huddled together by the roots of a giant tree.

One minute they had been happy in their homes and the next this ferocious bear had broken in and Tint, their little one, had been snatched. They pleaded with their King to find him and to return him to them.

The King looked at their terrified faces. He knew he had to attempt the rescue.

To his followers he said, "If any of you want to turn back now I will not judge you, but I intend to rescue this child."

No one turned back.

The Plain was dark, and soon each one of them was engulfed in a total blackness never before encountered. Each time they sent out a light, the darkness swallowed it. This was powerful magic.

Suddenly one of his followers, Gar, said, "Listen, I can hear a child crying."

They all stopped as they heard the crying turn to screams of terror. As they followed, so the sounds seemed to come from a different direction. They began changing course, only to find that they were no closer. They had been swallowed up in a clever Crudelis trap. As the darkness lifted slightly, they began to make out even darker shapes flitting in and around them.

Suddenly Gar let out a scream as he was dragged from his pony and killed, and then Dan… it became a bloodbath. Only Kurz and the King remained.

"Go back, Kurz," ordered the King. "Go back and warn our people that the Crudelis have become much stronger, I think that they are planning an attack on the castle."

"I can't leave you," answered Kurz. "You will be much weaker on your own. I should stay."

"I am ordering you to leave," replied the King firmly. "Go now to warn the others, I am relying on you."

So, a reluctant Kurz left the King on his own. Immediately the Crudelis moved in. First, they killed the King's pony, secondly, several leapt upon him and tore the wings from his body. The pain was indescribable. He was taken to Mount Ondraedan.

* * *

"What about the bear?" asked Tom, who had been listening intently to the account.

"There was no bear," replied the King bitterly. "It had been invented to tempt us out of the castle."

"But the little boy," asked Charlie. "What about Tint?"

"He had been placed in a trance and was found later, warm and well in a cupboard in his own home," replied the King. "I should have waited until Geschwind returned before riding off into the unknown."

"You were very brave," said Charlie kindly. "I've seen lots of these Crudelis. They're really horrible and cruel."

The King smiled. "I was bound to one of the boulders. The smell and stench of rotting flesh was something I will never forget. Flames kept spattering the rocks around me. The Crudelis were dancing and jumping about as though taking part in some unnatural dance. I began to realise that they were playing a game of 'dodge and dare' with their monstrous Dragon. Then I saw the reason for the stench. These demented creatures were actually cheering as members of their group were being melted alive by the Dragon's fire. When they saw that I was awake, they suddenly stopped dancing and sat down and stared at me."

"They did that when I was put in front of Teracind, the Claw," said Charlie quietly.

The King nodded and continued his story.

"I had a great wound in my back, where my wings had been torn from my body. The searing pain would not let me forget that, but I was not prepared for what followed. Bestim thundered before me and lowered his head so that his great yellow eyes blotted out all else. His foul breath blew into my face and soaked into my skin. Then he suddenly reared up on his back legs and roared. I closed my eyes expecting to be crushed but nothing happened. The Crudelis began to cheer..." The King paused, the pain of that moment was still raw. "As I watched they fed my wings, my own living wings, Tom, to Bestim... and all they could do was laugh."

The room became full of silence.

It was only broken when Charlie went forward and gave the King a great hug. The King smiled and patted the boy's head.

"What happened next?" asked Tom.

"The Crudelis just sat and waited again."

"For Beweglic?"

"No, it was for Spithra, their own sorceress. They knew that in time my wings would grow again and with them my magical powers. When Spithra crawled out of that crater she was one of the most grotesque sights I have ever seen. A giant black spider-like creature with the distorted face of a half-human – blank, white, staring eyes, a short snout and fangs for teeth. Her movements are a mixture of half crouching and half running. Even the Crudelis backed away from her. She spun her fine web about me and soon I was encased in one of her shrouds, hardly able to breathe. For one horrible moment I thought she would be my end, but they hadn't finished. I was kept on a ledge, high above Bestim's cave, where I was able to see all that went on. My worst nightmare was realised when I saw them drag my beloved daughter, Bella, into the crater."

The King stopped, he was fighting back the tears.

Bella, who hadn't left with the others put her arm around her father's shoulder.

"It's all right, Father," she whispered. "I'm safe now, I'm here."

Bella continued. "I didn't know that my father was there. I couldn't see who or what was wrapped up in that cocoon. They told me that if I didn't agree to marry Beweglic then I would be killed, and that they would attack the castle. They said my father had died looking for Tint and that they had made certain that everyone at the castle believed this. The Solanum has such great mind control. In fact, at that time, it was only Geschwind who stood between them and the complete surrender of Campandella."

The King coughed. "Then, Nhiamar, the Bringer of Nightmares arrived."

"He's one of the Solanum, isn't he?" said Tom, shifting his position in the bed. He was getting a bit uncomfortable. "What does he look like?"

"He is your nightmare," replied the King simply. "Whatever is your worst dream, he will take that fear and twist it into a shape of nightmare proportions. As soon as he arrived, the Crudelis threw themselves to the ground and hid their faces. I decided to concentrate on the so-called bear that we had come to kill. Nhiamar picked up on that thought and believed it to be one of my greatest fears. Within seconds I began to take on the shape of a bear. He made me golden because he believed hunters would want to kill me for my coat. Then they called upon Bestim to drive me away, knowing that I would return again and again to see Bella."

"Why didn't you tell us all this when we first met?" asked Tom.

"I couldn't," replied the King. "Nhiamar is not stupid. I was unable to reveal my identity to anyone."

"So, when Beweglic was killed, the spell was broken."

"That and the fact that, thanks to you Tom, Geschwind was able to restore his own considerable powers. For if Bestim had not been destroyed, who knows what might have happened?"

Chapter Twenty-Nine
I want to go home

Charlie looked at Tom. The others had left the room and the two brothers were on their own.

"I want to go home, Tom," he said. "You do too, don't you?"

Tom nodded. "Let's go as soon as possible," he replied. "Though to be honest, Charlie, I don't know how we do it."

Geschwind came into the room. "I am thinking," he said kindly. "That you must be ready to leave."

"Yes," said Tom. "We would like to leave as soon as possible."

He was now dressed in his normal clothes and somehow once in these he didn't feel much like the Dragon Slayer any more. He picked up Urthslean and handed it carefully to Geschwind.

"I suppose you should keep this now," he said.

"No," replied Geschwind, shaking his head. "You must keep it, Tom. Have I not said that your home of Green Willow is built over a time fault, and that Skadmeer is intent on breaking through into your world? You are the Master of Urthslean."

"But how do I explain to my parents that I've got to wander about wearing a sword?" asked Tom. "They'll think I've gone nuts!"

Charlie began to giggle.

"They won't be able to see it," said Geschwind. He turned to Charlie. "You can now see it. Can't you, Charlie?"

Charlie nodded. "It started to appear this morning," he answered. "I thought I was imagining it at first, but then I realised it was real. I don't know why I took so long to see it."

"I believe it was because you first met Teracind. His thoughts made it hard for you to accept the existence of Urthslean. You are a very strong boy, Charlie, to be able to overcome such evil. Well done."

Charlie grinned. Such praise from Geschwind made him feel nine feet tall!

Geschwind continued. "As a reward for such bravery, Charlie, I would like you to accept my little friend as a gift." From his robe he produced a small metal elephant, and handed it to Charlie.

Tom laughed. "It's one of your messengers. Can it change shape?"

"If necessary," replied Geschwind. "If you ever need me, just tell it to find me and I'll come straight away." He looked hard at Charlie who was staring at this little creature in amazement. It just fitted on the palm of his hand.

Suddenly the little elephant lifted its trunk and trumpeted. Charlie nearly dropped it.

"Has he a name?" asked Charlie.

"Thank you for asking," said the elephant politely. "Indeed, I do have a name, but I have to say, Charlie, that I am not a 'he' but 'she'. My name is Arula, and I will protect you should any evil come your way. You may keep me in your pocket, it will not bother me, unless you have sticky sweets in there."

Charlie assured her that it was quite clean and turned to Geschwind. "Thank you, Geschwind," he said. "I promise I'll look after her."

"You must," replied Geschwind sternly. "Your lives may depend on her later."

The boys looked at each other.

Geschwind clapped his hands. "Now come, both of you. We must leave at once if you are to get home safely."

'At last,' thought Charlie. 'Home.'

Chapter Thirty
The return of the Master

They made their way through the castle and out into the courtyard. Many had come to shake their hands or rub noses. Everyone was so happy. They all knew about Tom and Charlie's bravery, of how Tom had killed Bestim and their battle with Beweglic, and had come in their hundreds to thank the two boys.

In the courtyard they met Gioco, Pitzic and Kurz. They had brought Treo along to say farewell.

"He is a very brave little pony," said Pitzic. "He saved my life and I thought he was going to die. I will care for him until you return, Dragon Slayer."

"Thank you, Pitzic. Take care, Treo," he murmured, as he buried his face in the pony's neck. Treo gently nuzzled him back.

Charlie stood before Bella. "Are you really five hundred years old?" he asked in disbelief.

She giggled. It was that same sound that he had first heard when he met her in the cave. It still filled him with happiness.

"Yes," she said. "I'm quite young, you see."

This time they both burst into laughter.

"You will return, Charlie?" she asked hopefully.

"I hope so," he replied. To his embarrassment she rubbed noses with him.

Together Tom, Charlie and Geschwind made their way out of the castle back to the track where, only a few days previously, Tom had made his way through the blizzard to the castle. This time it was a leisurely stroll.

There was no snow, no sharp bitter winds. A few spring-like flowers were appearing on the grassy mounds.

Geschwind explained that after they had left Ferlian Forest, it had burst into flames. It had screamed in defiance like a wounded beast, but it was no use, it was destined to die along with the Crudelis and Beweglic. Since its passing, several changes had been noted on the plain. Lush meadow grass was returning, small wild animals and insects had been seen, and the elves were particularly pleased that the flowers were beginning to yield a good crop of Hunitwede again. Even the marshes and bog lands were disappearing.

They stopped by the mighty oak.

"Do we really have a murderer in our family?" asked Tom.

Geschwind shook his head. "No, Tom," he replied. "It will be hard for you and Charlie to prove this, but I believe you will do it. There are many secrets hidden in Green Willow. First there are the paintings, some of which are portals to other places and times, to different dimensions, and together they form a powerful key to controlling time. You must never sell them, they must never leave the house."

"Dad says nothing must be sold or moved from the house," replied Tom.

"Mum's not too pleased about it," added Charlie. "She says much of it is rubbish!"

Geschwind laughed. "I expect she's right," he answered. "Remember this, both of you, there are many who know about the secrets within Green Willow. They know it has been built on a time fault and are searching for the keys to unlock it. You must protect the paintings."

"What all of them?" asked Tom, thinking of his mother's reaction to this.

"No," replied the magician. "Seek the ones that have been painted by Jonathan Ferriston. It is because I failed in my duty that Jonathan painted these many years ago, and now a bridge exists where no bridge should ever have existed. A bridge across time and other worlds."

"I don't really understand," said Tom.

"Neither do I," added Charlie.

"Magic may work in many strange ways," continued Geschwind. "Your family has been caught up in the battles for the control of Glencyndal, and the land on which Green Willow stands. If you need me," he looked at Charlie, "send Arula, she will find me and I will come. Remember it is not only in the paintings that the evil ones are present."

"What do you mean?" asked Tom. He could sense some sort of movement in the oak tree. "What are evil ones? I mean, how are we supposed to recognise them in our world? We've never met an evil one."

"But you have, Tom, you both have," replied Geschwind kindly. "In your own world it can take many forms and shapes, and as the Master of Urthslean you will be able to recognise it and defeat it."

A deep rumbling was coming from the heart of the oak tree.

Geschwind's next words caused them even more confusion. "You will find Jonathan Ferriston in one of the paintings. Seek him and much more will be explained."

"I thought you said he painted these years ago. Surely he must be dead?" said Tom.

The noise from the tree began to increase. The grumbling began to grind and whine.

"You must go!" shouted Geschwind, above the noise. "Leave now! Keep Urthslean by you, Tom, and take care of Arula, Charlie!"

With that he pushed them both forward and immediately they were engulfed in a sea of paint. Charlie grabbed hold of Tom's shirt just as they were swallowed by an enormous vortex of colour. Tom turned to look back at Geschwind but already the magician was a distant figure. A wave of nausea swept over him as he reached out to get hold of Charlie. They couldn't speak. The noise was deafening. They were trapped. It became difficult to breathe and just as Charlie was beginning to panic, it all stopped and they were tossed out onto the bedroom floor.

"Wow!" whispered Charlie. "Where have we just been?"

"I don't know, Charlie," answered his big brother. He was staring at the sword still clutched in his hand. It began to sing. "But I think it must have been true. Have you still got Arula?"

Charlie smiled and opened his hand. There stood the little elephant.

They both looked back at the painting. It had changed. The green sky, the snow, all had disappeared. Instead of a winter's scene it was now springtime and the old oak tree was beginning to sprout leaves. There was no sign of Geschwind, just a castle nestling on a hillside deep within the painting.

"Are we going to tell Mum and Dad?" asked Charlie.

"They'll never believe us," replied Tom with a grin.

"Do you think there really are some horrible people trying to steal these paintings, and trying to get into this house?" asked Charlie, fearfully.

"Yes," replied Tom. "Geschwind seems right about most things. There are lots of secrets in this house, we need to ask Dad about it. We need to find out about the blacksmiths and the smugglers that Dad was talking about the other day."

"What about that girl?" asked Charlie. "I know I saw her, Tom. Do you think we can find her?"

Tom nodded. He looked around their bedroom. "The most dangerous thing we will have to do," he said quietly, "will be to explain to Mum why we haven't sorted out all these paintings yet!"

Charlie groaned.

Chapter Thirty-One
Sorting

"At least we know that this one is a special painting," said Tom. He lifted up the painting of the castle, and put it on top of his bed.

"The paint looks bright," said Charlie. "And look, it's got a name on the bottom – Jonathan Ferriston – but I bet they all say that."

"No, they don't," replied Tom. "This one just says JF, so perhaps that's not special."

"I've found another one!" Charlie sounded excited. It was a ship in full sail ploughing through a deep-blue ocean. There amongst the waves was the artist's name again, Jonathan Ferriston.

Eventually the boys found four paintings with his name; the castle on the hill, the ship in full sail, a painting of Green Willow (undated) and the garden by the terrace, and finally, the most upsetting one, the house in ruins, completely shattered and open to the sky. None of the others sported the full name of the artist.

"What shall we do with the rest?" asked Charlie.

"We'll take them back to that end bedroom," said Tom. "That girl can sort them out."

"That's not funny, Tom," said Charlie. "Supposing she's a Crudelis or a ghost, or…"

"You've got Arula and I've got Urthslean," replied Tom. "So, she's not going to bother us even if she tries. C'mon, let's get these other paintings back. At least we can tell Mum we've done something."

"They don't seem to have missed us," said Charlie, a little disappointed in his parents.

"Geschwind said that time is very different in his dimension, in fact according to the clock we've not been away more than a few minutes," replied Tom.

It was true, the hands on the clock had barely moved.

They spent the next half hour taking the remaining paintings back to the little end room. There was no sign of the girl. It was hard work as the paintings were heavy and very dusty. Tom looked at Charlie and laughed.

"You've got dirt all over your face, Charlie," he said.

"So, have you," retorted his little brother.

Their mother called up the stairs. "Lunch ready, boys!"

They raced each other to the bottom of the stairs and into the kitchen.

"It sounds as though we've got a couple of elephants thundering down the stairs," said their father.

"Three," replied Charlie, before he could stop himself.

"Pardon?" said Mr Ferriston.

"Have you washed your hands?" asked their mother. They thankfully rushed to the sink before their father could ask any more questions.

"Be careful," whispered Tom, as they dried their hands.

"Sorry," replied his brother. "I couldn't help it."

"So, how far have you got with all those paintings?" asked Mrs Ferriston whilst they were enjoying their meal.

"Well," answered Tom. "We've put most of them back in that end room, but we'd like to keep a few back in our own bedroom, if that's okay."

"Whatever for?" asked their mother.

"Well, we like them," replied Tom.

"You like them!" repeated their father. "They're probably covered in dust, looking at the state of your faces, and they'll take up far too much room. What on earth do you want with them?"

"We like them," said Charlie, feeling it was his duty to support his big brother.

"Have you sorted out your toys and books yet?" asked Mrs Ferriston.

"We've been really busy," replied Charlie. He was beginning to feel quietly confident about everything.

"Busy, doing what exactly?" said his father, smiling at him.

"Well," burst out Charlie. "Tom has fought the most humungous dragon and I helped to rescue a fairy princess who's five hundred years old!"

Tom looked at him in horror. What else was he going to say? But he needn't have worried, both his parents began to laugh.

"One day," said their father. "I hope you two get together and write down all these adventures. They'll make good stories for other children. Not the Grimm Brothers but the Ferriston Brothers. We'll earn a fortune!"

"Perhaps this afternoon you can find time, between fighting dragons and rescuing princesses, to find homes for all your toys," said their mother. "And we need to talk about this kitchen," she added, looking at her husband.

The boys nodded, pleased that the conversation had now turned to boring things.

After lunch they both went to look at the dragon carving on the front door. It had changed. The carving was definitely beginning to disintegrate, they could detect a growing split from its head to its tail and from this there seemed to grow several small sprays of delicately carved flowers.

"Hunitwede," said Tom firmly, as they both went upstairs to sort out their toys.

Part Two

More Frames

Shadows and Graves

Chapter Thirty-Two
Caught!

"What do you think you are doing?" the man shouted.

Mandy was so startled that she almost fell from the fire-escape. She looked down and saw that he had grabbed Andrew by the arm.

"Get down here at once, I say, at once!"

She began to hurry down but the fire-escape was so old and rusty that she slipped.

"Don't shout at her like that," said Andrew, trying to free himself from the man's grip. "You'll make her fall. Take your time, Mandy. Go carefully."

"It's her own fault if she falls," retorted the man. "She shouldn't have gone up there in the first place. Come here!"

Mandy did as he asked.

"This is private property," said the man. "You shouldn't be here."

"Neither should you," answered Andrew bravely.

For a brief moment, Mandy thought that the man was going to hit him. Instead he shook him before putting his face very close to Andrew's.

"Listen very carefully, little boy," he hissed. "I repeat, you shouldn't be here. What were you looking at up there through the window?" He directed this question at Mandy.

"We're just looking, that's all," answered Andrew. He could see that Mandy was close to tears.

"If you hadn't noticed," sneered the man, "I was talking to the young lady, not you."

"Nothing sir," said Mandy. "Just looking."

"Come, come," a jovial voice broke through the tension. It belonged to a large, plump woman. A great contrast to the tall, thin man menacing them.

"Where…?"

"Where did I come from, dear?" said the woman, as though she had just read Andrew's thoughts. "Why I was at the front of the house all the time. I heard Mr S shouting and so I thought I'd better come and investigate. He does take his duties very seriously. Don't you, dear? Now leave go of the boy's arm, there's a good man. Leave go." She said these last words very firmly, and there was a certain anger in her face. "He won't run away. So, leave go."

Mr S reluctantly did as she asked.

"Now what are you doing trespassing here?" she asked. In her own way she seemed just as menacing as Mr S.

Andrew stood close to Mandy. "We often come here," he answered. "Lots of our friends come too. The house has been empty for so long, we just play in the grounds. Who are you? Are you the agents? Has someone bought 'Green Willow'?"

"My," the woman laughed, "you do ask a lot of questions for a young lad, don't you?"

"It's none of your business who we are," burst out Mr S, glowering at them.

"Now, now dear," replied the woman, obviously angry at his interruption.

She took a long hard look at them both, especially at Mandy. "So, you saw nothing when you were up on the fire-escape, my dear?"

Mandy shook her head. "The windows are full of cobwebs and are very dirty," she replied.

The woman sighed. "Well, in answer to all of Andrew's questions. Yes, we are the estate agents. We've been asked to keep an eye on things in readiness for the new owners. They will be here soon, so it would be sensible to let your friends know that no one must come and play here again. Do you understand? NO ONE."

She almost growled the last two words and her whole body seemed to fill the air around them. Mr S grinned.

"Just one more time, dear," she said and made to approach Mandy. "What did you see?"

"She's told you," retorted Andrew, standing between the woman and Mandy. "She didn't see anything. We're going now," he added, and pushed Mandy away from the other two. "We won't be coming back here again, you can be sure."

With that, the two of them raced from the garden. They could hear the laughter of Mr S following them as they ran.

They didn't stop until they were out of the grounds and in the village. Mandy burst into tears.

"C'mon," said Andrew. "We'll go and tell my dad. He'll sort them out. Don't cry, Mandy. They can't hurt us."

Mandy wiped her eyes. "They were horrible. How did they know your name, Andrew?"

"I don't know," he replied. "Perhaps they heard you say it."

She shook her head. "And did you see their eyes? They were a strange sort of yellow. Do you…?"

"No more now," replied Andrew. "Look we're here. Let's go and see my dad."

They both ran up the path to the vicarage.

Chapter Thirty-Three
Friends or Foes?

A few days had passed when Mrs Ferriston announced that she was going to the village to 'have a proper look around' and did the boys want to come with her. They both agreed. Tom wanted to have another look at the village school which he knew they would be attending after Easter, and Charlie wanted to buy some sweets. Their mother said she would take the car, and that they could explore the village whilst she did a little shopping.

As they came out of their driveway, a large black car sped by and blared its horn.

"Really!" exclaimed Mrs Ferriston. "There was no need for that!"

It tore off in the direction of the main road and they could hear the squeal of its brakes as it shot round the bend. Mrs Ferriston carried on sedately to the first car park in the village right next to the village hall, still muttering about 'mad drivers'.

"I'll meet you back here in about half an hour," she said. "Now, Tom, you will keep an eye on your brother, won't you? And don't forget to buy a granary loaf for us at the baker's."

Tom nodded. Charlie protested that he didn't need anyone to 'keep an eye on him' and their mother left.

There seemed to be a lot of activity around the Church Hall. People were going in and out of the building carrying boxes, and all sorts of bric-a-brac. When they looked inside, Charlie saw the skinny, mousy-haired girl again, the one who'd stared at him when he had visited the school.

"Look, Tom," he whispered. "It's that girl again."

"Is she the one you saw on our first day in the corridor?" asked Tom quietly.

Charlie shook his head. "No," he said. "She's much bigger. Is she playing with those ducks?"

"No," replied Tom. "It looks like she, and that dark-haired boy, are sticking labels on them."

The boy saw Tom and said something to the girl so that they both turned to stare at the brothers. Tom and Charlie decided it was time to leave when a woman, who was sorting clothes, saw them.

"Hello!" she called out. "You must be the new boys up at 'Green Willow'. How are you settling in? Well I hope? If you're lost for something to do, or want to help, then you'll be most welcome here. We're quite a friendly bunch."

Tom decided that she had definitely not seen the inside of 'Green Willow' or she would never have said that! There was enough work there to last a lifetime. Still he knew that she meant well and was only trying to be friendly, so he smiled, said, "Thank you" and ushered Charlie outside.

They passed the church and there was the school. It looked very different from their school in Oakbridge. There was a small playground in the front, and the great high windows were more like church windows than school ones; under each one there was a lovely window box full of primroses and daffodils. It looked so old. They knew there was another small playground at the back, but there didn't seem to be a school field. They'd lived in West Lee and attended a town school at Oakbridge with a fabulous playing field, and now here they were in a country school with no field, very strange. In fact, the whole village had a strange air about it, as if it had never moved into the 1970s but belonged in a past era. Then they saw the baker's shop and so crossed the road.

They'd never been in a bakery like it! The little bell tinkled as Tom opened the door and the smell of freshly baked bread was fantastic. There was only one customer in the shop, an elderly lady, so Tom didn't think they'd be too long but he hadn't bargained on the shopkeeper's curiosity. Several generations of Smithsons had owned the bakery but it would be true to say that the present Mrs Smithson held the record for gossiping!

Tom was becoming so used to wearing Urthslean that he had almost forgotten it was there. As he approached the counter his hand brushed against the hilt of the sword, and he heard a quiet hum. Charlie looked up at him. "Is it…?" he began.

Everything happened so quickly. Mrs Smithson froze in mid-sentence. The whole shop became silent as the customer slowly turned to face them. As they stared, horrified, her features melted to reveal the unpleasant face of a Crudelis. She stretched out her talons and moved forwards to attack Charlie, but Urthslean was already in Tom's hand and he swung it down to cut off her head. When she saw Urthslean she let out a hideous scream and crumbled into dust.

"Wow!" said Charlie. "What happened to her?"

"I don't know," replied Tom visibly shaken. "I never really expected to find a Crudelis here even though Geschwind warned us. Urthslean just seemed to leap into my hand. I don't remember drawing it." He carefully placed the sword back into its sheath.

Mrs Smithson gave a cough and a splutter. "And so, you're enjoying your move to Green Willow, are you boys?"

Tom grinned at Charlie. Mrs Smithson was obviously unaware of what had just happened in her shop. She hadn't even noticed the disappearance of her customer.

"Yes, thank you," they answered.

Tom bought the loaf for his mother and Mrs Smithson gave Charlie a free gingerbread man to welcome him into the village.

"She's nice," he said as they left the shop, and immediately bumped into the mousy-haired girl.

Chapter Thirty-Four
What do you want?

"Hello!" said the girl. "You've just moved into 'Green Willow', haven't you?"

They both stared at her. Tom thought that the boy with her looked a bit uncomfortable, almost embarrassed, but the girl carried on.

"My name's Mandy. My mum runs the local Post Office and General Store, you came to our school didn't you, just after Christmas to look around? I remember," she said, hardly pausing for breath. "What's your names?"

She gave them both a big grin as she waited for their answers. Tom could see that she wasn't going to move out of their way. The boy smiled and said, "My name's Andrew."

They both answered almost together. "Tom, Charlie."

Tom then said, "I suppose you both live around here?"

"Yup!" Mandy pointed across the road. "I live over there above the Post Office and Andrew's dad's the Vicar." She waved her arm in the direction of the church.

"The vicarage is behind the church and the school," explained Andrew.

"Well, you both know where we live," replied Tom. "It seems that everyone knows where we live," he added with a touch of sarcasm.

"Well, it's quite exciting," explained Mandy. "I mean, no one's lived in that house for years and years and years, and now you've moved in and well… we're just being nosey, that's all!"

"Cheek," muttered Charlie quietly.

"Oh really," replied Tom with mock severity. "So, what are you being nosey about?"

"Everything," she laughed, ignoring his tone. "What's it really like inside your house? It's big, old and musty, isn't it? We know your garden well, don't we, Andrew, 'cos we used to play in there lots, but we've never been inside. I mean, is it true that there are ghosts in your house and…" She caught sight of Andrew's face and stopped.

"Oh dear," Mandy took a deep breath. "I think I'd better stop talking."

"Mmmmm," Andrew looked at Charlie. "It's just local gossip, that's all. The old house has been empty for so long that people make up stories about it. It's a very nice house, even though it's so big."

"Did you play in our garden then?" asked Charlie.

Tom didn't like the thought of others in the garden. He was already feeling quite possessive about it even though they'd only been there a few days.

"Everyone did! Old Mr Ferriston didn't mind," laughed Mandy, but seeing their faces added quickly, "Well, perhaps not everyone, but lots of us did. We didn't do anything wrong, just played there. It's a lovely garden, isn't it?"

Tom nodded. He couldn't help thinking of Geschwind's words, *'Others know about the paintings'*. Supposing Mandy and Andrew knew about them. Was she lying? Had they been in the house? Was she the girl Charlie had seen on their first day? He thought of the creature in the bakery and turned back to look. Mrs Smithson was in deep conversation with a new customer, she looked up and waved. Slowly the woman turned to fix Tom with a penetrating gaze. It was as though she was trying to probe the very depths of his soul, an icy shudder passed through him as he saw the look on her face. Urthslean hummed and the spell was broken.

Charlie tugged at his sleeve.

"Are you all right?" asked Andrew. "You've gone very white."

"I'm fine," muttered Tom. "Just a bit tired, it's probably the move." He began to edge Charlie away from the shop front.

"I know what it's like," replied Mandy, in a motherly sort of way. "It can be exhausting."

"You've never moved house," laughed Andrew. "How do you know what it's like?"

"I've heard customers talking to Mum about it," she retorted defensively. "I can imagine what it's like."

The boys laughed and Mandy began to giggle.

"We've got to go back and meet Mum in the car park," said Tom. "She'll be wondering where we are."

"We'll come back some of the way with you," Mandy began, balancing on the edge of the kerb. "We can show you a short cut if you like?"

They both nodded.

Mrs Ferriston didn't mind that they were going to walk back with Mandy and Andrew. It was good she felt that they were making friends with children they would meet at their new school. After all, she thought, she had already met Andrew's mother in the village hall, and Mandy's in the Post Office. No, they would be fine, what on earth could go wrong in such a beautiful and friendly village? Such silly rumours from so long ago, it was just nonsense. She took her loaf and drove home.

Chapter Thirty-Five
Through Caddy Copse

They walked towards Carter's, the newsagent's, which was opposite the school. There was a narrow pathway, a twitten, between that and the garage and gradually, as they made their way back, they began to realise that they had a lot of things in common, such as sport and football teams. Tom and Charlie were pleased to learn that St. John's had a great football team, the best in the area, according to Andrew! Mandy told Tom that he would probably be in Miss Durmast's class with Andrew.

"How do you know that?" he asked.

Andrew laughed. "We've only got two classes in the Juniors, you'll be in Miss Durmast's class with me, and Charlie will be with Mandy with Mr Crindle."

"Only two classes," said Charlie in surprise.

"I expect your other school was much bigger," said Mandy.

The boys nodded.

They had reached the copse behind the newsagent's. Andrew pointed out the track which led to the boundary wall of Green Willow.

"This is called Caddy Copse," he said. "There's a lake up there," he pointed to the right. "We'll show you the way to your house if you like," he added.

"Okay," replied Tom. He looked at Charlie who nodded. To tell the truth they had both been shaken by what had happened in the bakery. The sight of that woman's face had been unnerving, neither of them had expected to meet any time-travellers like the Crudelis in

Chepham village. She had looked as though she really hated them. Even though the Magician had warned them, they had not been prepared to meet such creatures so soon and in Chepham.

Suddenly Charlie stopped. "Look, Tom," he exclaimed. "It's the oak tree, and someone has tried to cut it down!" He ran towards it. The oak tree from the painting was in a sorry state. Some branches had broken away and lay scattered around it, and it was obvious that someone in the past had used an axe on it.

Mandy and Andrew looked puzzled.

"It's been like that for ages," said Andrew. "Have you got a thing about trees, Charlie?"

Tom could see that the next few minutes could prove awkward to explain, so he laughed and said, "No, it's just that it looks very much like an oak tree in one of the paintings we've got indoors. Of course, it's not the same one, is it Charlie?"

Charlie had his back to them but Tom knew he was upset. Suddenly he shrugged his shoulders and turned back to face them. "No 'cors it's not," he said. "Silly me." But Mandy was sure that he had been crying.

They carried on walking and for a while no one spoke.

"There's a small lake in Caddy Copse," said Andrew. "A lot of your early family were iron masters."

"How do you know that?" asked Tom. In a strange way he still didn't like so many people knowing so much about their new house or their family before they'd found out about these things for themselves.

"My mum told me," he answered simply. "She's an historian, when she's not organising jumble sales!"

They had reached a stone wall, some of which had fallen away and so left a natural stile.

"This is the way we used to get in," said Andrew, looking a bit uncomfortable.

"Sorry," added Mandy.

"There's no need to be sorry," replied Tom as he climbed over the wall. "We'd have probably done the same if we'd been in your shoes." He paused as Charlie clambered over and jumped down beside him. "How about you both come round tomorrow afternoon? You are on holiday, aren't you?"

"Yes," replied Andrew. "We finished last Friday. That would be great. We've got to help at the village hall in the morning, but the afternoon would be fine."

"I'll ask Mum, but I'm sure it will be okay," added Mandy. "We'll show you where we put our camps, if you like? You can get rid of them if you want."

"Don't sound so worried," said Tom. "I'll tell you what, you show us the camps, and then we…" he paused and lowered his voice, "we'll show you the ghosts."

Mandy giggled nervously. "I told you there were ghosts in there, Andrew," she looked hard at him but then realised that he was laughing. "There's no such thing as ghosts. There aren't, are there, Andrew?"

He didn't answer but just raised his eyebrows in an exaggerated sort of way.

"That's not what you said earlier, Mandy Hurst," he said, trying to sound like his father.

"It depends," added Charlie, clutching hold of Arula, his elephant, which he had in his jacket pocket.

"You're quite right, Mandy," said Tom kindly. "There's no such thing as real ghosts, so don't worry. We won't show you the two-headed ghost under the stairs." They began to make their way across the grass back to their house.

"Only the one in the cupboard!" shouted back Charlie.

"See you tomorrow," they both called as they ran home.

Chapter Thirty-Six
Equal Shares

Mandy and Andrew pulled nervously on the old weathered bell rope. It felt hard, cold, and reluctant to be used again after all this time. The entrance to Tom and Charlie's home was protected by massive oak doors which had been magnificently carved many years ago by their ancestors.

"It feels funny coming here like this," whispered Mandy. "We've never been up to the front door before. It all looks so different."

"I know what you mean." Andrew gazed at all the carvings on the door. There were lion faces, deer, some really ugly characters, and a badly-cracked winged dragon winding its way down the full length of the door, and all held together with some elaborate ironwork. It really was a magnificent piece of work.

Mrs Ferriston opened the doors, she gave them both a big smile. "Come in, come in!" she said. "The boys have been waiting for you... They're here!" she called up the staircase.

She had the same blue-green eyes as Tom and a mop of mousy-coloured hair which seemed to have a will of its own, she also had a dark smudge on her nose, the result of cleaning out more cupboards.

A great noise from above signalled the arrival of Tom and Charlie via the bannister. It was their turn to feel confident, after all this was their home, but both Mr and Mrs Ferriston were so welcoming that the others soon lost their nervousness. They all went into the Long Room.

This was a magnificent room, it literally took up the whole of one side of the house. This one room was, as Mr Ferriston kept saying, "Bigger than the whole of our previous terraced house!"

To which his wife replied each time, "Don't exaggerate, dear!"

Shelves and display cabinets lined most of the walls, and there were quite a few gaps caused by missing items. The remaining books, it must be said, looked a bit dull and musty. The room itself was overwhelming with its high ceiling and long casement windows, light was obviously important for reading in such a room. One wall was dominated by a large decorated stone fireplace.

"Would you like to have a look around the house?" asked Tom. They both nodded.

Mrs Ferriston brought in some biscuits and orange squash and then left to 'clean out yet more cupboards'. She sounded tired.

"Have you really not been in here before?" asked Charlie. They both shook their heads.

"Do you see that date at the back of the fireplace?" They both bent down to have a look.

"1702," mumbled Andrew, through a mouthful of biscuit crumbs.

"Well," said Tom. "Our dad says that that's when our family gave up their iron works. We didn't know that we'd lived here for so long, in fact we hardly know anything about our ancestors."

"That's right," added Charlie.

"There's a horrible looking dragon carved on the back of this fireplace," muttered Mandy, who was still bent down trying to look up the chimney.

"Bestim," murmured Charlie.

"Pardon?" Andrew frowned. "What did you say?"

"Nothing," replied Tom. "Come on, if you've finished, we'll show you around, and then if it stays sunny you can give us a tour outside!"

They went from the library through the hall and into the short passageway which led into the kitchen.

"Why does it say, 'Do not enter'?" asked Mandy, as they passed a dark green door just before the kitchen.

Tom grinned. "Do you remember what I said about the ghost? Well..."

"Tom Ferriston!" It was their mother's voice coming from the depths of one of the kitchen cupboards. "Don't you go scaring your new friends." She came into the room, and looking at Mandy she said, "Mr Ferriston has sealed it up, dear, because it leads down to the cellar, and the bottom steps have all rotted away."

Tom and Charlie gave them a good tour of the other rooms, including the smaller library. Each room in this enormous house had a large fireplace with ornate decoration on it.

"Let's go upstairs," said Charlie, and tore up the stairs two at a time. "Come and see our bedroom!"

"Wow!" said Andrew when they entered. "It's big!"

"Everything about this house is big," answered Tom. "Mum and Dad have really got their work cut out to make this into a guest house." He paused. "But I don't ever remember seeing them so happy. They really seem to enjoy it."

"Come and see this," said Charlie suddenly, and led them down the corridor towards the end room but before they reached it he took them into a small room opposite.

Mandy looked bewildered. "There's nothing in here," she said. "So...?"

"Da-da!" answered Charlie dramatically, and opened the cupboard to reveal the spiral staircase.

"We said we weren't going to bother about this until later," said Tom, a bit annoyed by his young brother's enthusiasm.

Charlie wasn't put off. "I thought it would be good for Mandy and Andrew to see it. We don't have to go up there."

Mandy went in and stood on the bottom step. Urthslean had been silent all day, but now suddenly began to hum loudly.

"No!" shouted Tom. "Don't go up there, Mandy."

Mandy looked frightened as she turned to come back.

"I'm sorry, Tom," said a shaken Charlie. "I didn't know, I didn't think…"

"It's not your fault, Charlie," whispered Tom. Loudly he said to Mandy, "Sorry, Mandy. I didn't mean to frighten you, it's just that Dad says the steps up there are not safe."

"I wouldn't have gone up there anyway," replied a white-faced Mandy. "I don't mean to be rude, but have you ever smelt it in there?"

Tom shook his head and ventured into the cupboard, he started to go up, but Urthslean increased in volume, so he quickly came down.

"I see what you mean," he said. "I'll tell my dad. It's horrible. Sorry about that."

Andrew had said nothing. He approached the cupboard and made a face. "Perhaps," he said, "you might need my father. It smells as if something has died up there."

"Let's get out of this room," said Tom. "I'll lock the door and tell Dad. Come on back to our room."

Charlie kept apologising to everyone, Mandy kept telling him it didn't matter, and Andrew kept very quiet.

They sat on the floor and for a moment there was an awkward silence.

Suddenly Andrew said, "Let's share all that we know about this house and its history. 'Cos it seems to me that you are hiding something and I know we are!"

Charlie looked at him in amazement. "What?"

"We'll begin," said Andrew. "That's only fair. Then you can tell us what you know if you like. Or you can keep it secret. What do you think?"

"Yup!" replied Tom. "I think that sounds good. Don't you, Charlie?"

Charlie nodded. "Yes. It sounds good, like when Mum shares a cake between us. Equal shares in everything," he said.

They all agreed.

Chapter Thirty-Seven
What do you know?

There was a sudden flash of lightning followed by a distant rumble of thunder. Charlie looked anxiously at Tom.

"It's alright," his brother said quietly. "It's just the weather, nothing else." He patted his side. "Urthslean isn't bothered."

Mandy and Andrew exchanged puzzled looks.

"Who's going to start?" asked Andrew, eager to move on.

"I will," announced Mandy. "I don't know that much about your house. Andrew knows much more 'cos his mum and dad have told him extra things."

The boys nodded.

"I never met old Mr Ferriston. Mum used to deliver the post and things but even she never saw him. He used to have people to look after him. Then when it became empty, we used to come round here from school to play in the garden. No one minded. We used to dare each other to go round the bit by Jay's wood 'cos that's where we pretended the ghosts lived. Of course, there aren't any ghosts, we knew that, but it was spooky just pretending, so that's what we did! Then one day, it was last year, I came here with Andrew and we were peering in at one of the windows. We'd climbed the fire-escape, you see…" She paused seeing the look of disapproval on Tom's face.

"I know, I know we shouldn't have done it, the staircase is rusty and might collapse and…"

"Get on with it," muttered Andrew.

Mandy glared at him and continued, "Anyway I saw, I mean, we both saw, lots and lots of paintings in one of the upstairs rooms." She pointed to the corner of the boys' room where they still had the four paintings. "Probably those," she said. Tom just nodded.

"Andrew can tell you more. Except that one day the paintings were there and the next they'd gone. We met a horrible Agent man here and a strange woman. Well, we thought that they were Estate Agents. The man was very angry with us. I thought he was going to hit Andrew. We told Andrew's dad and my mum and they were cross and banned us from coming here again. The police came and wanted to know what the man and the woman with him, well, what they both looked like. They said that there'd been several burglaries from big houses in the area. Terry Liner, in my class, said that it just went to prove that there were ghosts here, which made it even worse when we weren't allowed to come back to find them!" She looked at Tom and Charlie. "There I've finished!"

"Wow!" said Tom in mock horror. "Did you take any breath?"

"Don't be rude," answered Mandy with a smile.

Andrew stood up and sat on the edge of Tom's bed. "Since we all last met I've been doing a bit of thinking."

"Careful," said Mandy. Charlie grinned.

"Shush!" replied Andrew. "You both seemed a bit cagey last time we talked about your house. I began to wonder if something had already happened here."

Tom looked at Charlie, who was already sitting on his bed. They said nothing.

"Y'see, Mandy and I have played in your garden on and off for ages, and so have lots of our friends. I began to wonder if the two strangers we met here were linked to the other two."

"What other two?" asked Mandy, jumping up to join Charlie.

"Get on with it," said Tom, who was standing by the window. The storm seemed to have blown over, leaving the garden looking very bedraggled.

"It was last August, I think, and we were having our usual crop of visitors coming to look at the church windows, and some of the old paintings on the walls. Dad sent me to the church to give Mum a message. She was on the flower rota. There were these two tourists standing by the South Porch. One was a man, tall with greasy hair, and the other a large woman with ginger hair."

"Why didn't you say so earlier?" asked Mandy.

"Sorry," replied Andrew. "I was more worried about the man you and I met. He was pretty angry, wasn't he? I'd forgotten about the others."

Mandy nodded.

"Anyway, they were asking Mum about 'Green Willow'. I thought they were going to buy it, but of course they didn't, because you did."

"I expect lots of people have been interested in 'Green Willow', so what was so special about them?" asked Tom.

"Well, Mum said they wouldn't come into the church, they just stayed by the porch. She said they were very odd and kept asking about any artwork that might be in the house."

Charlie asked, "What happened after you saw the paintings?"

"It was strange," replied Andrew. "They were definitely there. We saw them, even though the windows were so dirty and dusty, but when we took our parents back the next day, well, they'd all gone. Then the police said that all the stolen property, including some paintings, had been found in Munty's barn, he's a local farmer, but Mr Munty said he had no idea where they had all come from. Any way they can't have been stolen, 'cos you've got them here, haven't you?"

"I don't think my mum believed that we'd seen anything," murmured Mandy. "I was too frightened to tell anyone else about what I'd seen."

Andrew agreed. "My dad said if they were valuable, then they wouldn't have just been left in an empty house."

"He's right, y'know," Mandy nodded wisely. She looked so solemn it made Charlie laugh.

"So, what else do you know about this house?" asked Tom.

"Not much really," answered Andrew. "It's always had a bit of a reputation."

"Reputation?" repeated Charlie.

"Yes," whispered Mandy. "Magic."

"Magic?" Tom and Charlie looked at one another.

"Well, not fairy-tale magic," replied Andrew grinning. "I mean we all know that's not true."

The brothers just stared at him as a quiet ripple of laughter ran through the house.

"What was that?" asked Mandy, she looked frightened.

"Just the wind down the chimney," said Tom.

"It happens a lot," added Charlie.

"It's not real magic, just folklore, superstition," continued Andrew. He was trying to sound very adult-like, but he too had felt the ripple run through the house, and he didn't like it.

"I believe in magic," said Mandy quietly.

Andrew just shrugged his shoulders.

"You said equal shares," said Mandy. "But you haven't told us anything yet. We've told you lots but you've said nothing."

Tom and Charlie looked at one another.

"What do you think?" said Tom to Charlie.

"We did promise we'd share," said Charlie quietly.

"I'm not sure that they'll believe us," said Tom. How could he explain to this older boy that they had met with pixies, elves and fought a dragon. Now, in the real world, it all seemed impossible, and yet…

"If we tell you, then you must promise not to tell anyone else," he said.

"As long as it's not something very bad," said Mandy. Andrew agreed.

"Okay," said Tom. "Here goes."

And so, he began his telling of the land of Glencyndal, and the killing of the mighty dragon known as Bestim.

Chapter Thirty-Eight
Urthslean Speaks

When Tom and Charlie had finished their story, the other two just sat on the beds in silence.

"Oh my," whispered Mandy. "Do you really mean that you've been inside one of these paintings, and lived and walked in another world?"

Tom nodded. He was looking hard at Andrew. If this boy didn't believe them, then he knew it would be hopeless. Andrew's face gave nothing away.

Eventually he spoke. "I've heard about things like this in story books but not in real life. Are you really telling the truth? Do you honestly believe that that's what happened to both of you?"

Both boys nodded.

"Think of this house, perhaps even the whole village, as sitting on a time fault. Not a fault in the rocks but a fault in time. Sometimes the fault shifts and you fall into another dimension. The keys to this seem to be linked to the paintings. Something odd happened when 'Green Willow' was built," said Tom. "Who's to say that back then there weren't other beings living around here. After all you haven't seen real dinosaurs but you believe in them, don't you?"

"That's different," replied Andrew. "It's been proven that they existed, and besides they left their bones behind, fossils and things."

Charlie said, "But so have the faeries. They gave me this elephant, and Tom has Urthslean!" He put his hand in his pocket and pulled out Arula. Only Tom could see the little elephant.

"Sorry," she whispered. "I must remain invisible."

Without thinking Tom drew Urthslean from its scabbard.

"This is Urthslean," he announced grandly, and almost at once wished he had never said it.

The look on Andrew's face was one of complete disbelief, only to be rivalled by Mandy's expression of utter bewilderment.

"What on earth are you talking about?" said Andrew. "There's nothing there."

"What is it you are trying to show us, Tom?" she asked frowning.

Tom bit his bottom lip. This was going to be hard. They had to understand.

"When I was in Glencyndal, Geschwind, the Master Magician, gave me this sword. He told me that it was a very special one, forged many years ago by the first settlers here. He said that they were probably our early ancestors and had decided to set up home on this Dunnlin…"

"Dunnlin?" Mandy asked,

"It's what Geschwind's people call the hills and the downs in this area," explained Charlie.

"They made this sword for the Dragon Slayer and buried it on the side of the hill. In those days people believed that there were dragons in Sussex. If anything bad happened, the slayer would know to come to this Dunnlin. Geschwind found it many years later, rusted and neglected. He took it back to Glencyndal and restored it, but not before he had added a few magical improvements of his own."

"And you think that you were holding this sword just then?" asked Andrew quietly.

"I didn't THINK I was holding it," retorted Tom. "I WAS holding it!"

There was a long silence.

"Geschwind told us that no one would be able to see our gifts in this world," muttered Tom. "Only those from Glencyndal, like that woman in the baker's."

"What Mrs Smithson?" gasped Mandy.

"No," replied Tom. "Her customer. She looked really weird."

"What customer?" asked Andrew.

Tom closed his eyes and took a deep breath. Had he seen her? He looked at Charlie who nodded.

"I saw her, Tom, she definitely was there," he said.

"What's the point of having a sword, if no one can see it?" asked Mandy.

"Can you prove you've got one?" asked Andrew. He stood up as though preparing to leave. "'Cos if not, then I think…" He raised his eyebrows, and didn't bother to finish the sentence.

Charlie looked from Andrew to Tom.

"Show them, Tom," he said firmly. With that he rummaged around in one of the cupboards and found an old T-shirt. "You can use this." He handed it to Tom.

"Okay," said his brother. He gave it to Andrew and Mandy.

"Hold this out between you. Tightly so that it's stretched right out."

They both began to look a little worried.

Tom grinned. "What are you so worried about? If you don't think I've got a sword then there's nothing to be afraid of, is there?"

"We're not afraid," growled Andrew. The house gave a little chuckle.

"It's just the wind down the chimney," said Charlie. He was beginning to enjoy this.

Tom drew Urthslean. "Hold the T-shirt tightly, and don't move," he commanded.

Slowly he raised the sword high above his head, and taking careful aim he cleanly sliced through the shirt causing Andrew to fall with a grunt against a cupboard. Mandy let out a loud squeal and fell onto Charlie's bed.

"How did you do that?" gasped Andrew.

Urthslean hummed and Tom grinned.

"What will your mum say about Charlie's T-shirt?" giggled Mandy holding up her half.

Charlie hadn't thought of that.

"Well?" Tom looked at Andrew.

"You're saying that you've got an invisible sword in your hand?"

Tom nodded.

"Can I hold it?" asked Andrew.

"I don't know," replied Tom. "You can try." He held Urthslean out across both palms and offered the sword to Andrew.

Andrew shivered as the sword passed right through his hands and clattered silently to the floor.

"Something felt very cold, and my hands feel like ice," he whispered.

"Can I try?" asked Mandy.

"Okay." Tom nodded.

Once more the sword passed right through her and she shivered.

"It's like a ghost moving through your body." She looked a little afraid.

Tom picked up Urthslean. "This is the sword of the Dragon Slayer," he said. "This is Urthslean, and I am the Dragon Slayer."

Charlie was holding Arula and she gave him a little nudge. He held her close to his ear.

"Arula has a message," he said to Tom. "Geschwind says that you must be careful as others can pick up the sound of Urthslean, and that they are already nearby searching for it."

Tom nodded and replaced the sword into its scabbard.

"That was fantastic," said Mandy, clapping her hands together.

"It was…" Andrew paused, "very strange, very strange indeed."

"Look," said Charlie. He pointed to the painting of the castle which they had hung on the wall. "This is the painting which we went into. Show them your painting, Tom. See it's just the same."

Tom rummaged amongst his old school paintings and found it.

"It's very much like it," murmured Mandy, gazing at both pictures.

"It's not like it, it is it," retorted Tom.

Andrew said nothing.

"Then there's this," carried on Charlie. It was the painting of 'Green Willow'. And this…" He began pulling out more paintings.

"Stop, Charlie," said his brother kindly. He could sense that it was all a bit overwhelming for their two new friends. He looked at both of them.

"You're right," he said. "It must sound really strange to you but it's true, we did go into another dimension. And you're right, this house is weird, sometimes it seems to have a mind of its own. Charlie has already seen a girl in the house who shouldn't be here." He looked at Mandy. "We don't know who she is or how she gets in. We thought you might have some ideas." She shook her head.

"I'm hungry," announced Charlie. "Can we go downstairs and see if Mum's got something to eat?"

Tom nodded, but before they moved, they made plans to meet up again soon to see if they could persuade Andrew's mother to let them know a bit more of the history of 'Green Willow'. Apparently, a great deal of information was contained in documents which were housed in the church vestry.

Chapter Thirty-Nine
White Elephants and Bric-a-Brac

The next few days went by very quickly. Charlie and Tom searched the house from top to bottom but there was no sign of the little girl whom Charlie had seen in the passageway. They kept well away from the spiral staircase having told their father about the strange smell there.

Mr Ferriston gave it a good check, but could not detect much of a smell but he did, however, forbid them to go up.

"It's an absolute death trap," he told his wife. "The spiral goes up to a door and you open it, and you're immediately out on the roof, only there's nothing between you and a complete fall to the ground, except a small ledge no wider than a metre! You're not to go up there, boys. I'll get it sealed off and later have a proper rail placed up there to prevent any accidents. It's a nightmare of a design!"

In between times of helping their parents sort out the rooms, they also helped with the jumble sale which was rapidly turning into a full-blown fete. They were even given a stall to run between them. It was the 'Tin Can Shy'. Charlie couldn't stop having a go himself, he had quite a good aim and a great throw.

"Are you and Dad coming to the fete?" he asked his mother.

"I'll try to pop round in the afternoon but your father won't be able to come. Uncle Arthur is coming over to talk about family business and planning applications. I expect it will take some time."

"Don't forget we've both been invited to Andrew's for tea," said Tom.

Their mother nodded.

"See you later!" they both called as they rushed out of the door.

Mrs Ferriston closed the side door and returned to the hallway. She was pleased that the two boys had begun to settle in. The move had been a great struggle and a complete change of lifestyle for all of them. There was that scurrying sound again, she gazed up the staircase and around the landing, the house must be riddled with mice. She just hoped that Jack and Uncle Arthur would be able to find out where these creatures were getting in, and then stop up the holes. The sounds were beginning to get on her nerves.

* * *

The fete was proving to be a great success. People from the village and the surrounding areas turned out in force to support the Youth Club's efforts. The boys were pleased when they saw their mother coming towards them, it was close to three o'clock.

"Come and have a go, Mum," called Charlie. "You can do it!"

"There are a lot of people here, aren't there," she said glancing about. "I didn't expect it to be so crowded. Uncle Arthur didn't stop talking from the moment he arrived. Alright then, I'll have a go."

She threw the wet sponges at the tins and somehow one of them managed to hit Charlie.

"Sorry," she grinned.

"You did that on purpose," he said laughing.

It must have been about a quarter to four when things were beginning to die down. Tom had taken to wearing Urthslean all the time, and now in these quieter moments he could hear the sword gently humming.

Andrew came rushing over to their stall. "Don't look now," he said breathlessly, "but your mum is being followed by those two people. I'm sure they're the same ones that came to the church, and the ones that were in your garden."

It was only then that Tom realised that the sword had been trying to warn them.

Mandy came over to join them. "What's up?" she mumbled through her ice cream.

"It's those two," indicated Andrew. "It's them."

"They're following our mum," added Tom.

Charlie looked at Mandy. "C'mon!" he shouted, and they both ran across the field towards his mother.

Charlie held on to one side of his mother, whilst Mandy pulled her towards the village hall.

"What on earth are you two up to!" laughed Mrs Ferriston.

"Please can I have an ice cream like Mandy, Mum?" asked Charlie.

"And you haven't been to my stall yet, Mrs Ferriston," added Mandy. "I'm sharing it with Sophie Hibson. We've got a doll which her mum's made and you've got to guess its name." All the time they were both steering her away from the strangers.

"Wow!" whistled Tom, looking at the small group moving out of harm's way.

"That was some quick thinking by your brother and Mandy," agreed Andrew.

Urthslean began to hum loudly as the man and woman suddenly turned to stare at them.

Tom gripped the hilt of his sword and the two just laughed. The man raised his arm and pointed at Tom, then they walked away.

"Why are they laughing?" To Andrew their behaviour seemed very odd.

"I'll explain later," replied Tom through gritted teeth. He took a step forward but the two just waved to him before turning to leave.

"What was that all about?" asked Andrew. "I feel really peculiar. I'm icy cold."

"They saw Urthslean," muttered Tom. "I'm sure of it. It can only mean one thing. They came from Glencyndal, from another dimension. But how did they get here? I must let Geschwind know about them. Look, they're leaving."

The unwelcome visitors made their way to the car park next to the church hall. A few moments later a large black Rolls-Royce slid silently past the hall and purred its way towards the main road. Its very silence made it seem sinister.

Chapter Forty
Tea

In less than a quarter of an hour peace reigned once more in the village hall and on its tiny field. Everyone had pitched in to help clear away the rubbish. The small marquee, which had earlier been the home of the much-needed tea-urn, was dismantled. The tables were stacked away, the hall floor swept and helpers were just waiting around to find out how much the Treasurer thought they had raised.

"So, what do you think we've made, Mike?" asked Mrs Smithson.

"I can't say for sure, Jean," replied the Youth Leader, who was also acting as Treasurer. "But I think it must be in the region of £1200, give or take a little for expenses and unknowns."

"That's brilliant," beamed Mrs Thomas, the Vicar's wife. "Thank you everyone for all your hard work. I'm sure we'll be able to get some really good camping equipment for all the youngsters with the money raised."

There was a round of applause, everyone was pleased. It made all their work over the past few days and weeks seem worthwhile. People began to drift home.

"You children may go home to the vicarage," said Mrs Thomas kindly. "I expect you're feeling quite hungry. Letty will be there, tell her I'll be along later, Andrew."

"Okay, Mum, he replied.

They made their way through the churchyard, behind the church to the wide pathway which ran at the back of the school, and then up the gravel drive to the vicarage. Neither Tom nor Charlie had been in a vicarage before.

"Who's Letty?" asked Tom.

"Well it's a bit difficult to explain," replied Andrew. "She lived here in the vicarage before we came, she was the housekeeper for the previous vicar. Apparently, his wife took Letty in after the war when she was about our age. All Letty's family had been killed."

"That's awful," said Charlie.

Andrew continued. "When Mum and Dad came here, she had already packed her bags because she thought they wouldn't want her but, of course, they did, and so she's stayed doing more or less what she's always done. She can live here for ever, if she wants to. Mum made the Bishop agree to that!"

"Your mum scares me a bit," admitted Charlie.

Andrew laughed. "She scares a lot of people. I think she even scares Dad sometimes! She works very hard, y'know, helping Dad and organising things. She also does research on old manuscripts – she went to Oxford," he added proudly. "That's where she met Dad."

They walked around the side of the house.

"Letty!" called Andrew. "Letty, we're back."

A small plump woman came out of the kitchen door to greet them. She was wearing a brown flecked woollen dress, her snowy-white cropped hair seemed to highlight her rosy red cheeks. Her face broke into a beaming smile when she saw them.

"Hello, my dears," she said opening her arms wide. "You must be Tom, and you must be Charlie."

Charlie smiled, he liked her already.

They had a great tea and afterwards helped Letty to clear everything away.

"Mum said she wouldn't be long," said Andrew as he dried a saucer.

"You know your mother, Andrew," answered Letty. "If someone's caught her, and wants to talk over a problem, she'll listen to them as long as needs be. Now off you go, into the garden all of you."

Mandy gave her a big hug before joining the boys on the old rickety seat by the edge of the lawn. They were talking about the two strangers at the fete.

"Move up," she said wriggling onto the seat. "You'll just have to ask this magician friend of yours, y'know, the one who's been telling you that some of the paintings are portals into new dimensions, if he knows anything about the strangers. If they know about the paintings, then of course they're going to want them. Wouldn't you, if you thought you could time-travel through them?"

"I don't think they're ordinary burglars," murmured Tom.

"And," added Andrew, not wanting to be outdone, "they may be after more than just those paintings. Didn't you say, Tom, that Geschwind gave you the sword for your protection?"

"And for my family," added Tom quietly.

"Well, there you are then," said Mandy, grandly.

Tom just looked at Charlie who made a face.

"But how did they get here?" asked Charlie.

"Could they have come the other way, through your paintings?" asked Andrew.

"Oh no," Charlie shuddered. "I don't want to think of them sliding out of the paintings and into our bedroom."

Tom agreed.

"They must have come much earlier," said Mandy kindly. "If they're the 'agents' that Andy and I saw, then they were here before you moved in to your house."

"We'll ask Geschwind about them," said Tom firmly.

Mandy, Tom and Charlie didn't stay much longer. Mrs Thomas hurtled back, obviously tired but she couldn't stop. She had popped in to see one of the parishioners only to find that she'd fallen downstairs. The doctor had been called and Mrs Thomas was going back to see if she could be of help to the family.

She said she hoped Tom and Charlie would join the Youth Club which she said included virtually all the children in the village regardless of age.

As they turned to go down the twitten which led to Green Willow, they heard a car come up behind them. Fearfully they looked around expecting to see the black Rolls-Royce, but it was only a small family car, they breathed a sigh of relief.

It was a bit useless being a Dragon Slayer, thought Tom, if he was going to jump at every strange sound and not use his common sense.

"What do you think, Charlie?" asked Tom, as they climbed the stile. "Do you think Geschwind will come if I call him?"

"I'll send him a message," replied his brother grinning as he gently whispered to Arula.

Chapter Forty-One
Shadows in Time

"It's good to see you, Tom, and you too Charlie," Geschwind smiled. "So much has happened since you were both last here."

For a moment the boys had forgotten that a minute at home was as many months in Glencyndal.

"You don't look any different," replied Tom. "How much time has gone by?"

"A number of times," replied Geschwind vaguely. "Time means very little in eternity."

They were sitting on a small boulder inside the painting. Arula had returned very quickly from delivering her message to Geschwind, and he had responded almost immediately.

Charlie gazed at the scene before him. The rich green valley stretching away into the distance, the little cluster of houses around the foot of the castle, and far away on the horizon, the mountains.

'One of those peaks must be Mount Ondraedan,' he thought.

This was where Tom had fought Bestim. Of Ferlian Forest there was nothing, it had been consumed by fire.

"Are these people linked to the Crudelis?" asked Tom impatiently. "How do you think they got into our world?"

Geschwind smiled. "You haven't changed much either, Tom. You still ask too many questions! I believe, however, that you are partly correct. These 'people' are in fact from another dimension."

"From Glencyndal?"

"No." Geschwind stroked his beard. "Much further afield. I think they have been sent by the Solanum."

"But how did they get here?" Charlie sounded worried. "I thought you were the only one who could cross into our world."

"I'm not certain as to how," replied Geschwind. "When, however, is different. My guess is that they, and probably others like them, entered many years ago. They may even be trapped in your time, but I do know why. They are here to steal the paintings of Jonathan Ferriston, and, also the paints. If you, or your family, die in the process it will be of no concern to them."

Charlie gave a shiver.

"Then they must be stopped." Tom stood up and looked down at Geschwind.

"Calm down," Geschwind answered gently. "Sit down whilst we think about this carefully."

Reluctantly Tom did as he asked.

Geschwind continued. "I believe they are Margar and Stincan. As I said once before to you both, the Solanum is controlled by Skadmeer, the Destroyer. He is prepared to go to any lengths to gain control of all dimensions and time. His battle commanders are Teracind the Claw, Nhiamar, the Tormentor and Bringer of Nightmares, and Slaf the False One. Margar works for Teracind, she is really malevolent and spiteful. Stincan's master is Slaf, he's an odious and revolting creature."

"I've met, Teracind," said Charlie quietly.

"And you showed great courage, Charlie," said Geschwind.

Arula gave a little trumpet of agreement.

Tom sighed. "And we're supposed to stop this lot from getting into our home, into Green Willow?"

Geschwind laughed. "Now where's the conqueror of Ferlian Forest, the mighty Dragon Slayer? You must remember that you are not alone. You have Urthslean, and without sounding too pompous, you have me! Not forgetting all your friends in Glencyndal."

"And me," interrupted Charlie.

"And you," chuckled Geschwind. "Most definitely you, Charlie."

"Now," he continued. "Your advantage is that I doubt if they realise yet that you know exactly who they are. They're not very bright, but you must never trust them. Never let yourself be alone with them. Make certain that you are with your new friends, Mandy or Andrew, or even someone like the Vicar or Mrs Thomas."

"Or Mum and Dad," said Charlie.

Geschwind's answer sent a chill down his back.

"No, Charlie," replied Magician. "They are even more at risk than you. You see they aren't aware of any of the danger. These creatures are enemies of your whole family, of your very existence at 'Green Willow'. Sadly, your ancestors didn't realise this until it was too late."

"So, what do we do now?" asked Tom.

"You must find Jonathan Ferriston," replied Geschwind.

"But he's dead!" answered Tom in frustration. "How do we find someone who is dead?"

Geschwind smiled. "He will be very much alive in one of his paintings. Of that I am sure."

"Which one?" asked Charlie.

"I don't know," answered the Magician.

"Then how are we supposed to find out?" asked Tom angrily.

"I can't help you in this," replied the Magician. "I can say that his body is buried somewhere in the local churchyard but he cannot rest in peace until he is reunited with his reflection, his shadow, which you will find in one of the paintings. He is a shadow of a different time but, when you find him, he will be able to tell you how all this began. He will be able to help you to solve the riddle of 'Green Willow'.

"Those other two…" began Tom.

"Well, I think their appearance means that the Solanum is worried. Stincan is a Warlock and Margar a Witch. We will be much better prepared this time." He gave a chuckle as though looking forward to a battle.

The pale ice-blue canvas of the sky was dotted with pink feathery clouds. "I think you must both return home," he said. "The sun is beginning to sink."

"You know," said Tom ruefully. "All we ever wanted to do was to prove our great-grandad's innocence, to prove that he wasn't a murderer."

"And you shall, O Master of Urthslean," answered Geschwind. He placed a hand on Charlie's shoulder. "And remember you are not alone, Charlie. Arula will always find me." He paused. "Now off you go, both of you!"

Chapter Forty-Two
Even the best laid Plans

It was not going to prove easy.

They had all been to the Palm Sunday service given by Andrew's father. Mandy listened carefully to Tom's news, especially the bit about Stincan and Margar. She sat on the broken south wall which separated the churchyard from the school playground.

"Well," she said, as she plucked a daisy from one of the stones. "I really don't see how you can be sure of finding this Jonathan Ferriston even if you can go popping in and out of those magic pictures."

"But we have to try, don't you see," answered Tom earnestly. "The alternative, as far as we can see, is disaster for our family—"

"And the whole village," interrupted Charlie.

Andrew and Mandy looked at the brothers in disbelief. There was a moment's silence.

"It's crazy!" said Mandy.

All this time Andrew had been quiet, just listening to them and pushing little piles of stones together with his shoes, but now he said, "I've been thinking. If you can wait until next week, I'll ask Mum and Dad about the history of your home. If, as your friend Geschwind says, that early painter was an ancestor of yours, then there may be evidence of him in the parish records. Anyway, I can find out if you like."

"Thanks, Andy," said Tom. "Are you sure your parents won't mind?"

"They'll be pleased, especially my mum. She loves doing that sort of thing. Oops!" he added as he realised he had just buried his Palm Sunday cross in one of his gravel towers. He dusted it off and crammed it into his pocket.

"Yes," added Mandy. "I'll ask my mum too. She knows ever such a lot about the village, she's lived here all her life."

"Thanks," said both boys.

They made plans to meet up the next day, but, when they reached home, Tom suddenly said he didn't feel very well.

"You've caught a chill," replied his mother in a matter-of-fact voice. "I expect you caught it standing out on that field yesterday in that cold wind, and trailing around all week collecting jumble."

"I haven't got a chill," said Charlie. "And I did the same."

"That's because you're a tough old man," replied his father, giving him a firm slap on the back.

"I'm not that tough!" replied Charlie making a face.

"But I enjoyed doing all that for the fete," protested Tom feebly.

"Enjoyment has nothing to do with it," she smiled. "A few hours in bed is what you need, you'll soon feel better. Make sure you're quiet when you go upstairs, Charlie," she added.

In fact it was more than a few hours, as Tom developed a bad case of tonsillitis confirmed by Dr Manders the next day.

"If you or your husband can pop into Chepham, to Hibson's the chemist, you can start the medicine straight away, and I'm sure Tom will show real improvement very quickly," he said as he left.

Charlie was worried that his parents might want him to move to another room, but luckily his mother said he could stay if he promised to be quiet and to come for her if Tom needed anything, so of course he agreed.

As he explained to Tom later, so much happened in that last week of the Easter Holiday that it was obvious that they were getting closer to solving the problems about Green Willow. The first was on the night after Tom had started to take his medicine.

* * *

Tom was woken up by someone crying. At first he thought it was Charlie, but then he realised someone was sitting on the end of his bed. Framed in the silver moonlight was the grey shadow of a boy. He wasn't much older than Tom, but was dressed in clothes of an earlier time. Gradually Tom realised that it wasn't the effect of the moonlight which made this boy seem grey, he really was grey. His face, his clothes, his hair, his skin, everything about him was as a grey shadow. His shoulders were hunched and his face was buried in his hands. He was quietly sobbing his heart out, completely unaware that Tom was watching him.

At this point Charlie woke up and let out a yelp when he saw the boy.

"Who is he?" he whispered.

Tom shook his head. "Ssshh! I don't know," he replied with difficulty. His throat was still sore. "You ask him."

"Who are you?" he asked. "Why are you crying?"

The boy sprang off the bed and turned to stare at them.

"Come and sit on my bed," said Charlie, feeling more confident by the minute. "My brother can't talk very well, he's got a sore throat. So please, who are you?"

The boy's eyes were sad and mournful, his clothes were in a bad state. Tom thought he was the saddest person he had ever seen.

"My name is Joshua," he murmured quietly. "Joshua Ferriston, and I know you. We've been watching you both. You're Tom and Charlie."

"Why do you say 'we'. Who's 'we'?" asked Charlie.

"We used to live here. We used to play in that garden." He pointed to the window and beyond.

"You said 'we' again," persisted Charlie.

"The man used to visit us—"

"Who is 'we'?" asked Charlie in frustration. He began to worry that they might wake up their parents.

There was a rustle from behind the curtains and out stepped a small girl. She was probably a bit younger than Charlie but again it was difficult to tell. Not only was she grey but she had faint holes in her body. They could see right through her.

"It's her," whispered Charlie in amazement. "The girl I saw on our first day!"

"This is Elli, my sister," explained Joshua. "She's very ill."

Elli climbed up on Tom's bed and sat on his legs. She was so light, if Tom had not seen her sit down he wouldn't have known she was there.

"How can she be ill?" asked Tom. "You're ghosts. You're already dead!"

Joshua sprang off Charlie's bed and Elli looked suddenly frightened.

"We are not ghosts!" he shouted in his hollow voice. "Not ghosts! Not yet!"

"Calm down. I'm sorry," said Tom. "I didn't mean to upset you, but you have to admit, you are getting a bit grey and thin."

"So how did you get here?" asked Charlie.

"I'm not sure that you'll believe me," said Joshua.

"Since we moved here," said Tom, "some very strange things have happened in this house. It'll take quite a bit to surprise us, honest."

Charlie nodded.

Joshua sat down again.

"One day we were playing in our garden when a man appeared. He said his name was Jonathan Ferriston. He seemed very worried and told us a sad story about the death of his younger brother. Then he said that our garden was only a painting, it wasn't real at all."

Elli gave a little sob.

"He then said that we were not real people but just people he had painted in his picture and that our world and the other worlds of which he had spoken were in great danger. He had foolishly allowed himself to come under the influence of some very bad people. They had strange names. Stincan and Margar."

"We know those names, don't we Charlie?" said Tom. Charlie nodded.

"We asked him to stay with us, but he said he had put us in enough danger. He said he would go away but asked us to keep a careful watch over all the paintings."

"How could you do that?" asked Charlie. "Could you see out of your painting?"

"Jonathan taught us. He even taught us how to concentrate so hard that we could leave our painting."

"Wow!" said Charlie.

"We were quite good at it," replied Joshua proudly. "Nothing much happened for many years. People came and went. We were hung in various rooms. We learnt of World Wars and such dreadful things. Then your great-grandfather and his beautiful bride, Mary, came to live here. It was such a happy place. She transformed the real garden into a little piece of paradise. Then came the tragedy and he would spend days wandering the house moaning and sobbing and calling her name."

"Do you think he killed her?" asked Charlie.

"No!" Elli's strangled whisper sent a chill down their backs. Even the house shivered.

"Rest, Elli, rest. You mustn't speak, you'll wear yourself out." Her brother patted her hand.

"I think the troubles were something to do with us, the paintings. I remember clearly when your great-grandfather had us bundled up into a room and called us 'accursed'. And there we stayed until children came and stared at us through the window. By now we had learnt to leave our painting and wander the house. We were used to children playing in your garden but not staring at us through the window."

"Mandy and Andrew," whispered Tom. Charlie nodded.

"You know them?"

Both boys nodded.

"It was you," said Charlie. "It wasn't mice at all. It was you I heard when we moved in."

Elli giggled.

"And you're the girl I saw in the corridor," he added. She nodded.

"It was about then that we realised we couldn't return to our painting. The magic will not obey us."

They both began to weep.

"Don't cry," whispered Tom. "You'll do more harm to yourselves," Tom's throat was beginning to ache again.

It was true, Elli was almost fading away before their eyes.

"We'll try to help you, but first you must help us. Do you know where we can find Jonathan Ferriston? It's vital for us, for all of us, that we find him soon."

Joshua shook his head.

"Try," urged Charlie.

"I think," replied Joshua, frowning, "he might be in a land where he can easily reach the sea. He was very fond of ships and told us many stories about them."

"You've hit it!" Tom sounded excited. "He must be in the painting of the sailing ship. That's it! Thank you,

Joshua, thank you. Now we have a friend who might just be able to help you both."

Charlie held up Arula and sent her on a message.

Chapter Forty-Three
Jigsaw Pieces

Andrew and Mandy were disappointed when they learnt of Tom's illness. They'd cycled round to his house hoping to meet up.

"How about Charlie?" asked Mandy. "Would he like to come out with us?"

"I wish he would," replied Mrs Ferriston. She looked worried. "But since Tom's illness he won't leave him. It's almost as though he thinks he's protecting him."

Andrew said, "Don't worry, Mrs Ferriston. Tell Charlie that we'll carry on as arranged. He'll understand."

Mrs Ferriston smiled. "Alright, Andrew, I will." She had no idea what he meant and neither did Mandy.

They turned their bikes around and began to cycle back to the village.

"Tell Charlie we'll carry on as arranged?" Mandy said. "What did that mean? You made it sound very important."

Andrew grinned. "We'll go back to my home, and we'll see if Mum can start finding out things about the Green Willow for us. Come on!"

"I thought you didn't believe them," she said. "Y'know, all that stuff about the house and the paintings."

Andrew just smiled and pushed down hard on his pedals.

When they arrived back at the vicarage, Letty and Mrs Thomas were having a cup of coffee in the kitchen. The Reverend Thomas was busy in his study preparing one of his many sermons to be delivered in the week. They could hear him practising as they passed the door. Everyone was sorry to learn of Tom's illness.

"I'll pop in and see him later in the week," said Mrs Thomas. She looked quizzically at the two of them. "So, what are you two up to today?" she asked.

Andrew took a deep breath. "If I tell you something, Mum," he said, "do you promise to keep it a secret?"

His mother just raised her eyebrows over her mug of coffee.

Letty smiled. "It depends what it is, young man," she said.

Mandy looked worried. They'd promised Tom not to tell of his secrets, surely Andrew wasn't going to break that promise, but she needn't have worried, Andrew had no intention of breaking his word.

"Tom wants to trace his ancestors," he blurted out. "He knows that his family has lived in Green Willow for hundreds of years but he can't find out anything about it in the house. I wondered if we might have anything about his family in the Parish Records. I've heard you tell Dad that our records go back years and years. I thought that as Tom is unwell, it might be a nice surprise for him when he gets better."

"Yes," added Mandy, trying to make it sound official. "Help him in his enquiries."

Andrew's mother was not so easily fooled.

"Surely the family solicitors have all the records. Then there must be lots of information on the Deeds. His parents must know all this. Why doesn't he just ask them?"

"He wants to surprise them," said Mandy hastily. "I think he's very keen on history, got that funny sort of mind." She blushed as she remembered that Mrs Thomas was an historian.

"Stay here," commanded Andrew's mother, and left the room.

The two friends looked at each other. What next they wondered?

"Listen," whispered Letty, putting a finger to her lips.

Mrs Thomas had gone across the hall to her husband's study. They heard low mutterings, a soft chuckle and the clink of keys. A few moments later she appeared in the doorway in her old brown coat.

"Come on then," she smiled. "Let's go and find out."

Mandy and Andrew ran after her.

* * *

The heavy church door groaned and protested as it swung open and the musty, cold smell of the church wafted towards them. Since the recent thefts and vandalism in nearby churches it had been felt sadly sensible to keep the church locked.

Mandy hated going into the church when it was empty, the cold air rose from the flagstones and hung around them. She could hear their echoing footsteps bounce from pillar to pillar as though someone or something was shadowing their path. She kept close to Mrs Thomas. They went straight to the vestry door, unlocked it and quietly closed it behind them. After jiggling about with her keys, Mrs Thomas opened a small cupboard set back in the corner of the room. With Andrew's help she lifted a heavy metal box from a shelf, and together they placed it on the table. The box was well padlocked, in fact there were three to open. They seemed to suggest that the contents must be of great value. As soon as it was opened Mandy peered in, the smell was old and stale and immediately made her sneeze. Mrs Thomas laughed.

"Help me to lift this book out," she said. "We must place it very carefully over there on that small table."

It was an enormous, heavy tome and they laid it gently down on the green cloth. When it was opened it covered the whole of the table top.

"Now let's see," she muttered as she solemnly put on her glasses.

"Mum's in her element," whispered Andrew to Mandy.

"I heard that." Mrs Thomas laughed. She turned to Mandy. "You never know, we might discover something. There are some very interesting records in here, and what is more…" She turned back to the box and began searching it again.

"Aha! Here it is!" She held aloft an old tatty exercise book. Mandy wasn't sure what it all meant but, if it meant helping Tom and Charlie, then perhaps another 'Aha!' was needed.

"Aha!" she exclaimed, in such a way that the other two burst out laughing.

"Look," said Mrs Thomas. There in ink on the inside cover and in large spidery handwriting was written the following…

'An unauthorised history of certain members of the family known as Ferriston.' by The Reverend Matthew Woods. 1920.

On the first page was written, 'Born in the Parish of Chepham at Green Willow 1867 William Thomas Joshua Ferriston.'

"Now he died…" Mrs Thomas paused searching her memory, "in 1970, I think. He was very old. The house was empty for some time before your new friends arrived."

"Is this book important, Mum?" asked Andrew, looking at the tattered papers which his mother was holding so gently.

"I think so," she answered. "I've never looked at it properly. I'd forgotten it was here until a moment ago. This old exercise book belonged to the vicar who was here during the First World War. That was around the time of Mary Ferriston's death. The Ferristons are a long living family and have lived at Green Willow for centuries. Apparently, they were very secretive, and here was one of them in the national news when the country was involved in a world war! I've never bothered to read this properly but I'll do my best to find out all I can. I was told that the Reverend Woods fancied himself as a bit of a detective, and became really involved in the case."

"Mum," said Andrew. "You won't tell…"

"Look," replied his mother. "I volunteered to do this, so stop worrying. Just promise me that no one is going to be upset."

"No one will mind," answered Andrew. "Tom and Charlie will be really pleased."

"And their parents?" queried Mrs Thomas.

"They won't mind," said Mandy. "In fact, I think it will make them very happy." She had no idea why she added that last bit but it felt right.

Mrs Thomas laughed. "Off you go," she said. "How can I get on with my sleuthing with you two hanging about!"

"'Bye," they called as they ran out of the church and thankfully into the fresh air.

Chapter Forty-Four
Life at Sea

"No!" Charlie said very firmly. "You're not well enough yet. Mum said you were to stay in your room and rest. Anyway, it's nearly midnight, and I'm tired even if you're not."

"Oh, c'mon, Charlie. All I'm asking is for you to put the painting at the bottom of my bed. That's all," whispered his brother.

Charlie hesitated.

"Okay," he said, "but just to look at."

Tom nodded.

"Just looking," said Charlie again, as he propped up the painting of the ship at sea. They both stared at it.

"Can you see what I can see?" asked Tom, a little too eagerly.

"Oh no," groaned Charlie. "We're not, are we? I mean, I can't swim very well. Tom! Aah!"

This time the painting didn't invade their room, as the castle one had done, this time it literally pulled both of them towards the ship, and they landed with a thud on the deck.

"Ow!" shouted Charlie. "That hurt!"

A tall man grinned and looked down at him. "Up you get little one!" he said and gave a deep laugh. "It looks like your friend has found a softer landing."

Charlie looked up and saw his brother entangled amongst some ropes attached to a sail.

"Help!" yelled Tom, as two sailors rushed forward to cut him down from the rigging.

Several sailors now gathered around them and began laughing, especially as both boys were still in their pyjamas.

"Where on earth did you come from?" asked the tall man, as he helped Charlie to his feet.

"We're looking for Jonathan Ferriston," replied Tom angrily. He didn't like being laughed at.

"We live in 'Green Willow'," said Charlie.

"Ah yes, I thought you might," replied the man. He signalled the others to leave and then told Tom and Charlie to follow him to his cabin. He was obviously the captain.

He bent low in order to go under the doorway and down to his cabin which was at the stern. This allowed him a full window across the width of the ship. He was taller than their father, well over six feet. His hair was long and curly and just turning slightly grey, but his eyes were the deep blue of the sea and, when he smiled, so did they.

"Sit down," he said, pointing to two chairs in front of his large desk. "I am Captain Jonathan Ferriston of the *Merry Willow*. Who might you two be?"

"I'm Tom Ferriston and this is my brother Charlie," replied Tom. "We've just moved into Green Willow, your old house I think. We've found all your paintings and we needed to find you."

Jonathan smiled. "I hoped someone would come one day. Tell me all that has happened since my departure."

So, Tom and Charlie told him about their move to Green Willow and their adventure with Geschwind. They told him all that they could think of, though it took some time, as Jonathan wanted to know more and more about the world. Cars, planes, trains, all these things were unknown to him. He couldn't believe it was 1975. Charlie thought they'd never get to the point.

Eventually Charlie broke in and said, "And someone has cut down the oak tree, and I'm sure it's the one you painted in the castle picture."

"It is," replied Jonathan quietly. "I cut it down." He looked intently at Charlie. "You look so like my little brother, Joshua. It's uncanny."

"Why? Why did you cut it down?" asked Charlie horrified. "It was a beautiful tree."

"You're right," replied Jonathan. He stood up and walked to the large window. For what seemed a long time he just stared out at the ship's wake. Suddenly he turned and sat back in his chair. He lit his pipe and began.

"Joshua and I used to climb it regularly. Almost every day. We even built a small cabin amongst the branches, but one day we found the tree covered with large black birds. They were attacking our cabin and causing great damage. Joshua was ten years old and I was fourteen. I told him to stay down whilst I climbed up to clear them away, but he didn't, he followed me."

"Typical," murmured Tom. "Charlie never does what I say either, it must be something to do with being little brothers."

Charlie grinned and nodded.

Jonathan smiled sadly. "As I reached these birds I realised that they were not normal but were more like grotesque goblins, with large eyes and talons."

"Like Crudelis," said Charlie.

"Yes, so I discovered much later," replied Jonathan. "It was impossible to stop them destroying our cabin, and then they turned their attention to Joshua. They were so quick and nimble around the branches, before I could stop them they gripped hold of him and threw him into the air. I tried to help him but failed. I will never forget his screams." Jonathan broke off and took some deep breaths. "He crashed down through the branches on to the ground below. Amidst a babble of hideous laughter, these creatures leapt on him but I scrambled down as quickly as I could and fought with them. I thought all would be lost, they were biting and kicking and trying to cut us with their talons, but then at a signal, a long penetrating siren, they all stopped and disappeared into the ground."

Tom asked quietly. "Did they have large lamp-like eyes. Yellow and dull?"

Jonathan nodded. "I carried Joshua back to the house but he was already dead." He paused again. "So, I found an axe and went straight back and began chopping down this dreadful tree so that these creatures would never be able to use it again."

"But then you painted it, and put it in the picture with the castle," said Tom. "Why?"

"Yes, but that was much later, after I had nearly ruined the family by gambling our money away at the gaming tables in Tunbridge Wells. It painted itself into the landscape."

"So, then what happened?" asked Charlie. He was beginning to shiver from the cold and damp.

Jonathan smiled and poured a dark liquid into two small goblets. "Drink this," he said. "It will help to keep you warm." He handed them to the boys and then poured a large drink for himself.

"My father was very good to me," he continued. "He realised that my stupid behaviour was because I blamed myself for Joshua's death, for not being able to save him. I don't think anyone believed in my story of the strange creatures, even though several such sightings had been reported in the village over many years. Eventually I came to my senses. I had been a promising artist, and so I took up painting again and sold a few landscapes in London. I did quite well with a couple of portraits too." He paused.

"We've found some," said Charlie.

"I was in the cellar when I found the paints. Tiny stone jars full of wonderful colours. I tested them out and was alarmed, but then excited to find that they seemed to take over. They guided my brush, even mixed themselves on my palette, they didn't seem to run out or dry out, but I couldn't predict the final result."

"Wow!" said Tom. "I wouldn't mind paints like that."

Jonathan shook his head. "My first painting was of the oak tree and the castle beyond, and that's when I first met Geschwind. I should have given him the paints there and then."

"Why didn't you?" asked Charlie.

"I wasn't sure," replied Jonathan. "You see I'd met those evil creatures. Some even came in disguise to the village. I couldn't be certain that Geschwind wasn't just some clever trick. I wasn't sure whether or not he was part of some evil plan, so I kept them. Created my own Joshua and poor Elli. They will be all right, won't they?" he looked hard at the boys.

They nodded.

"The paints began to take on a life of their own, even completing a painting of 'Green Willow' which I hadn't intended. I began to realise that others were after them, so I hid them. My so-called gambling friends were not all they seemed. They were from another dimension. The rest you probably know."

"Well not really…" began Tom.

The cabin door burst open.

"You best come up top. Cap'n," said a breathless seaman. "There's a storm brewin' and we're sailing right into it."

All three of them went on deck. There stretching across the horizon was a long dark menacing cloud. Distant rumbles of thunder could be heard and the odd streak of lightning shot down only to bury itself in the sea, a sea which had taken on the colour of distressed seaweed with waves that shuddered from side to side.

"It's comin' this way, Captain," shouted the bo'sun, holding hard on the wheel.

"You must go," said Jonathan. "They know you are here. You must leave for your own safety. Tell Geschwind I am tired of all this."

"Who are they?" asked Charlie, trying hard not to show he was frightened.

"It will be Skadmeer and his followers," shouted back Jonathan. The wind was beginning to screech as it tore through the ship's sails. The sailors were frantically trying to lower them but by now the lightning was striking all around, and a huge sea was rising up before them threatening to swamp the ship and all on board.

"Where did you hide the paints?" persisted Tom, but his voice was drowned by the howling of the wind. "And how are we supposed to leave?"

For once he didn't feel like the Master of Urthslean. The sight of the mountainous waves was terrifying.

"I know," said Charlie, suddenly taking charge, and immediately sent Arula away.

Within seconds they tumbled out of the painting and onto Tom's bed. The painting was now a battleground between the sea and the little ship. It was as if they were watching a film or a TV programme. For a few minutes neither of them spoke. The knowledge that a few minutes ago they had been part of it was impossible to understand, and then suddenly it ended. The churning sea became calm and the sun returned.

"Wow!" said Charlie, as Arula landed gently on his hand.

Chapter Forty-Five
Unwelcome Visitors

Tom started to shiver. The visit to Jonathan Ferriston had not been without its consequences.

"I told you we shouldn't have gone," complained Charlie. He was worried by the change in his brother. "I'm going to fetch Mum and Dad."

"Not now," whispered Tom. "Wait until the morning. I could be better by then. Just wait."

Charlie wasn't so sure but he did as his brother asked.

It was obvious by early morning that Tom was no better and so he rushed into his parents' bedroom to tell them.

"Good gracious, Charlie," said his father. "You're very early. It's only just six o'clock. Whatever's the matter?"

"It's Tom," said Charlie. "He's worse."

Mrs Ferriston was already in their bedroom.

She immediately phoned Dr Manders who came at once.

He was puzzled as to why Tom hadn't responded to the medicine, so changed the dose. He asked Mr Ferriston to collect a different prescription as soon as the chemist was open and left, muttering something about the hospital. Charlie didn't like the sound of it. As soon as he could, their father went off to Chepham, he used Tom's bike to ride there. Mrs Ferriston sat on the edge of Tom's bed.

"You should be getting better by now," she said to her eldest son. "You were so looking forward to starting at your new school and…"

There was a ring at the doorbell.

"Who can that be?" she said looking at Charlie. "Oh, I know, it's probably Mrs Thomas. She said she might pop round."

Charlie felt the hairs on the back of his neck prickle. He could hear Urthslean humming from beneath Tom's bedclothes. Arula gave a quiet trumpet. Something was wrong.

"I'll come down with you, Mum," he said looking at Tom. His brother appeared to be asleep, the medicine was working fast.

His mother opened the great door and was confronted by two of the strangest people she had ever seen.

Mr Sebastian Caven-Smythe and Miss Marguerite Watson stood on the doorstep.

He was a tall, thin man, with a sallow complexion and sunken, dark eyes that were never still but shifted around searching everywhere. His nose was too long for his face, and from his nostrils, and his large ungainly ears, sprouted thick black and grey hairs. When he smiled, his thin lips parted to reveal uneven tombstones of stained yellow teeth.

Mrs Watson was not a pretty sight either, she looked as though she had fallen into her clothes whilst still asleep. She wore a dark brown suit which had seen better days. The jacket was open as she was too large to button it up, and revealed a crumpled and stained, yellow blouse. Her stockings were a thick brown, matching her heavy brown shoes and she carried a large battered, brown shoulder bag. They were a very strange couple and yet there was something familiar about the both of them.

Mrs Ferriston looked down at the card which had been thrust into her hand.

Caven-Smythe and Watson
Qualified Electricians
High-Class Interior Decorating

"May we come in?" asked Mr Caven-Smythe politely. "We heard of your husband's predicament…" he paused, "so we thought the personal touch would be best. So here we are!"

"No!" shouted Charlie, who was standing by his mother's side. "No! Go away!"

Mr Caven-Smythe just stared at him.

Charlie shot off upstairs and Mrs Ferriston heard him close his bedroom door and lock it. Later she recalled how she felt both angry and frightened at the same time and, she said, she must have said 'come in' for the next minute they were all standing in the hallway. Mrs Watson was running her oily fingers over the wallpaper, and writing something down on a pad which she had produced from her shoulder bag.

"I do all the power jobs, whilst my colleague here adds the high-class interior touch," Mr Caven-Smythe gave a smirk as though he had made a funny remark. It wasn't a pleasant sight.

Mrs Ferriston's mind was in a total whirl. Had her husband really asked these dreadful people to provide an estimate? She couldn't remember. He had certainly not mentioned that anyone would be calling this morning, and the name of the firm did not seem at all familiar. She turned unsteadily to close the front door. A large black shining Rolls-Royce stood in their driveway. Where had she seen it before? Turning back, she was just in time to catch Mr Caven-Smythe preparing to leap upstairs. A flicker of annoyance registered in his eyes, but he quickly regained his composure, spun round and came across the hall to her.

"My husband is out," she said, hastily trying to hide her fear. "But he'll be back soon. In fact, I'm expecting him home any minute."

"Of course, you are, dear lady." The tall figure of Mr Caven-Smythe swayed above her like a giant cobra about to strike. "We'll begin on the ground floor." He paused at the entrance to the long room. "All our estimates are free... but... you will all have to settle your account eventually." He gave a long drawn-out breath of hopeful satisfaction.

Mrs Ferriston followed them from room to room as though in a trance. She was vaguely aware that Marguerite Watson was opening cupboards and drawers, which seemed very odd. How it happened she wasn't too sure, but suddenly they were standing outside the boys' bedroom.

Charlie came out of the room and deliberately closed the door behind him. He had already sent Arula with a message to Geschwind, and he had alerted Urthslean to the appearance of the strangers. He stood by his mother.

"Go away!" he shouted at Mr Caven-Smythe. "You're not wanted here. Go away!"

"What a rude little boy you are," exclaimed Mrs Watson. "I was never allowed to speak so to adults." She gave a disapproving look at Mrs Ferriston.

Before his mother could speak, Charlie said, "My dad didn't ask you to come here. I know he wouldn't have asked you. I've sent for Geschwind, he's coming here to help us."

Mr Caven-Smythe let out a loud hiss, and looked at Mrs Watson. "I told you we should have killed her as soon as she opened the door, but no, you said it had to be a soft, gentle approach." With that he turned to Mrs Ferriston again.

Charlie's mother was frightened, her face was pale and she was trembling, but she held on tightly to Charlie's hand and stood her ground.

"You may not enter my son's bedroom," she said. "I'm sorry if Charlie seems rude but he is quite right, you may not disturb my other son, who is unwell."

Mr Caven-Smythe began to grow, he towered over Mrs Ferriston, a writhing monstrous shape. His face contorted savagely and his top lip curled up to reveal his yellow fangs. His odious breath engulfed her as his true self, Stincan, prepared for the kill.

"Anyone at home?" Mr Ferriston had returned, his voice filtered through the cobwebs which were beginning to tie up his wife's mind.

"Jack! Jack!" she screamed. "Quickly! We're up here."

Mr Caven-Smythe clenched his teeth, his menacing manner changed abruptly, he made a benign, futile gesture with his hand as he and Marguerite Watson moved away.

"Come, Marguerite, come, we mustn't disturb the little lad. Let us leave quickly."

They didn't stop to talk to Mr Ferriston but swept past him on the stairs almost knocking him over in their eagerness to leave. They appeared to be arguing.

"If only you'd let me—"

"Our orders were to be careful and not to—"

"Orders! THEY'RE not here. THEY don't know what it's like to be—"

"Shh!"

"Don't shh me! And where did you get that stupid name of Marguerite from?"

"Hark who's talking… Sebastian… Huh!"

Within seconds the Rolls-Royce slid silently out of the driveway.

It wasn't until she'd had a good cup of tea that Mrs Ferriston was able to tell her husband of all that had happened.

"Charlie was so good," she sobbed. "He tried to warn me but I didn't listen. I don't know how he knew that they were imposters but somehow he did."

"Just knew, that's all," replied Charlie. "I just felt it."

"Good lad," said his father. "Well done." Charlie felt nine feet tall.

"Why did you come back so soon, Dad?" he asked.

"It was the strangest thing," replied his father. "When I collected Tom's medicine they handed me this note. I thought it must be from you," he said, looking at his wife. "It just said... COME HOME QUICKLY. I've never cycled so fast in all my life!"

"I didn't send it," said Mrs Ferriston. "But I'm so glad you did." She hadn't heard Charlie mention Geschwind, so had no idea of his part in saving them.

"What's all the fuss about?" It was Tom. He had come downstairs in his pyjamas and was leaning against the kitchen door. "I'm really hungry, Mum."

"Come and sit down at once," said his mother giving him a big hug. "We've been so worried about you. The doctor even came and ordered you more medicine. You shouldn't be out of bed. Go back and I'll bring you up some food."

"No, I want to stay up now. I want to know what I've missed," he answered looking at Charlie.

Charlie grinned. Arula had just landed quietly in his pocket.

So, whilst Tom tucked into bacon and eggs, they all told him about their unwelcome visitors.

Chapter Forty-Six
Tea with Geschwind

Later that day Charlie asked Tom how he had made such a 'miraculous' recovery. Well, that's how Dr Manders had described it.

"When you sent Arula back to Glencyndal, she told Geschwind all that was happening. He sent me some medicine and she delivered that note to the chemist. Remember time is different there. I'm glad you did send for him. Thanks, Charlie."

"But," persisted Charlie, "what was really wrong with you? Why were you so ill?"

"Geschwind thinks that Stincan and Margar put some sort of spell on me. Y'know when they pointed at me at the fete, well, I've been feeling groggy ever since," replied his brother. "It's all gone now, thank goodness."

"Everyone was worried about you," said his brother. "Even me!"

Tom grinned.

"I'm going to ask Mum to let us go into Chepham so that we can have a talk with Mandy and Andrew. We'll see if they've any news about the so-called burglars."

"Good idea," replied his brother.

It took a bit of persuasion, but the next day their mother agreed, providing that she drove them in. She was still unsure about Tom's sudden recovery. After all, only the day before, the doctor had been talking of a hospital visit. It seemed too good to be true, but by the time they had reached the village the boys had persuaded her to allow them to walk back on their own via the twitten and

Caddy Copse, on the condition that they phoned her if Tom felt at all unwell.

Their mother decided to do a small shop in the village and the two boys wandered off. It was then that they saw Mrs Robertson who ran the village tea shop. She waved to them.

She was a small person with a very homely smile. Her white hair was tied up in a neat bun, and her rosy cheeks always made her appear very happy. People said that her cream teas were the best in the area and that secretly she probably sampled too many of them!

"Come in, boys," she called. "Come in. I hear you've not been too well, Tom. Come in both of you and I'll find a cream cake for you! There's someone here I'd like you to meet."

They really wanted to visit Andrew and Mandy but they knew they couldn't be rude.

"How does she know your name?" whispered Charlie.

"It's a small village," muttered Tom. "Remember Dad said that everyone knows everyone else's business, and we must be careful what we say. We'd best go, but be careful we don't know who she wants us to meet." He patted Urthslean.

There were two steps up into the tea shop. It was a very old building which had once been a private house. The floor was on two levels. In the lower level two ladies were deep in conversation about their grandchildren; the upper section was empty, save for someone sitting in the corner next to an alcove which had once been a large fireplace. He or she was reading a newspaper so they couldn't see who it was.

"Now boys," said Mrs Robertson. "What would you like? Choose any cake that you fancy. After all, Tom, we need to make you strong, and Charlie needs a special treat, as I hear he was very brave in helping your mum deal with those horrible people."

"Do you mean—" began Charlie.

"The burglars," interrupted Tom. "Yes, he was brave."

Charlie had never seen such beautiful cakes all sitting under the glass cover begging to be eaten! In the end he chose a chocolate éclair and Tom a vanilla slice. Mrs Robertson brought out two glasses of her 'special', as she called it. A lovely fruit juice. They sat at the small table next to the stranger.

Mrs Robertson gave a small cough. "I'd like you to meet my cousin, Archie Rushforth," she said proudly. "He's a great traveller. He's been all over the world. Archie, put your paper away and say hello to these two brave boys."

Mr Rushforth slowly lowered his newspaper and smiled. "Hello, boys," he said quietly. "It's good to meet you."

Tom choked on his drink, and Charlie missed the cream from his éclair so it dropped back onto his plate.

It was Geschwind.

His hair had been cut and his beard trimmed. He looked very distinguished in his tweed suit. It was very much like the old-fashioned suits worn by golfers, only he wasn't wearing shoes but large tartan slippers. He had on a green checked shirt and a large red bow tie with matching red braces.

"Hello, boys," he said again, smiling at their amazed expressions. "It's very good to meet you here."

"Are you, are you…" stammered Tom.

"Mr Rushforth," he answered, and extended his hand, a hand which Tom knew so well. Immediately Arula rose from Charlie's pocket flew round the table and settled on Charlie's éclair.

"Naughty," said Mr Rushforth laughing. At once the little elephant returned to Charlie. "Eat your cakes up, boys. I haven't much time. Things are changing fast but I wanted you to know that you are not alone in Chepham. There are many folk here, like my 'cousin', who can, and will, help you, for the time is fast approaching when we shall all be tested—"

"Why haven't you come before?" interrupted Tom, puzzled and a little angry.

"The negative forces have been too strong to allow it," he explained. "But I believe, thanks to the two of you, we are winning. They didn't like being sent from the house. We will soon be able to prove once and for all, the innocence of your great-grandfather, and rid Green Willow of the unwanted visitors who still lurk in its shadows."

Charlie felt sick, and it wasn't the chocolate éclair. He didn't like the idea of visitors 'lurking'.

"Did Jonathan tell you where he hid the paints?" asked Mr Rushforth.

"No," replied Tom. "He said he found them in the cellar but didn't say any more, but I'm sure that they're in the house."

"That is certain," replied Mr Rushforth. "I must leave quickly, but we will meet again soon. Go and see Andrew and find out what his mother has unearthed about your family. Take care brave boys." He stood up and Tom noticed with horror that his hands were beginning to fade.

Before they could say anything more Mr Rushforth left the room and disappeared into the back of the café.

"More cakes boys?" It was Mrs Robertson. "I'm sorry my cousin dashed off like that. He doesn't mean to be rude but time's pressing and he's such a busy man."

The boys declined her kind offer and left.

"Let's go and see Andrew," said Tom when they were outside in the cool air.

Charlie nodded. He'd always hated shadows. What could be lurking in the shadows of Green Willow? He dreaded to think.

Chapter Forty-Seven
The Reverend Wood's Diary

"Come in, come in!" said Mrs Thomas, when Tom and Charlie knocked on the back door. "It's lovely to see you, Tom. We were told you were so ill. How did you get here? Surely you haven't walked all the way?"

"Mum brought us round in the car," replied Tom grinning. "I've made a 'miraculous recovery' according to Dr Manders."

Charlie smiled as he heard Arula chuckle. Andrew came into the kitchen and looked surprised to see the two brothers.

"It's good to see you," he said, "but we all thought you were very ill, we didn't even think you'd make it back to school next week."

"Dr Manders has some good medicine," replied Tom.

Suddenly the back door burst open and in rushed Mandy. "I saw you crossing the road," she said breathlessly. "I thought you were very ill so…"

Everyone laughed. "That's what we've all been saying," said Mrs Thomas.

Letty brought two more glasses of her special fruit juice, the Reverend Thomas just ruffled Tom's hair before going back to his study, and Mrs Thomas sat down at the table with her cup of tea. Andrew looked at her. "Shall we?" he whispered.

"I thought you wanted to keep it a secret?" said his mother.

"Only whilst Tom was getting better," answered Andrew. "Can we tell them now?"

His mother nodded and left the room.

"Now you've done it," said Letty, sitting down at the table with them.

Mrs Thomas returned carrying the battered looking exercise book.

"Well," she said with a triumphant sigh. "Andrew told me that you were interested in your family history and so I thought I'd look up one or two things in our Parish records that might help you. I hope you don't mind."

"That's really kind, Mrs Thomas," replied Tom. Charlie nodded.

"Did you know," continued Mrs Thomas, "that your ancestors have owned Green Willow since 1699 when Charles Ferriston had the house and some land given to him in payment of a debt? The house was known as 'Buckshill Farm' but later it was changed to Green Willow, and your ancestors bought up much more land."

"No, we didn't know all that," replied Charlie so emphatically that the others laughed.

"I won't bore you with all the bits and pieces," said Mrs Thomas smiling at Charlie. "There are, however, one or two quite interesting moments in your family history. Would you like to hear them?"

"Yes please," replied Tom. Despite already having had a vanilla slice, he was enjoying Letty's home-made biscuits. He felt as though he hadn't eaten for years.

"It would appear that in 1716 there was a dreadful accident and Joshua Ferriston died from a fall from a large oak tree."

"Yes, we know," muttered Tom. The others looked at him in surprise. To cover up his embarrassment he added, "Uncle Arthur mentioned something about it when he visited the other day." It seemed to satisfy everyone.

"I believe his brother, Jonathan, took it really badly because that is about the time when your family had to sell away much land to pay for his gambling debts. The reason the Reverend Wood found all this out is because Jonathan became a famous painter of his time, and then suddenly disappeared!"

She placed a number of faded letters on the table. "These are copies of letters sent between Jonathan and his solicitors in Tunbridge Wells. I don't know why the Reverend kept all of them but they have proved very useful. You see there are lots of letters from 'Coaster, Coaster, Coaster and Sons'."

"So many Coasters," said Mandy.

"There's a firm called 'Coaster and Coombs' today in Tunbridge Wells," said Mrs Thomas. "I wonder if they're related."

They are," replied Tom. "Dad told me, they're our solicitors now."

Charlie gave a sigh. He hoped they weren't going to talk about boring things.

Mrs Thomas smiled. "It appears that Jonathan wanted to be buried with his relations in the churchyard here, but the Reverend of the time, a Mr Collins, wouldn't agree. You see Jonathan had left a letter and a great deal of money, two hundred pounds, I believe, for a memorial stone to be placed near his brother Joshua's grave in the event of his death."

"Wow," said Andrew.

His mother nodded. "Mr Collins was a cautious man and kept all these letters between himself and the solicitors. There was some doubt about Jonathan's death. When did he die? How did he die? Was he murdered? Did he commit suicide? Where was his body? Mr Collins was not a happy man."

"But if Jonathan Ferriston had paid so much money, why didn't he just get on with it?" asked Tom.

"Well eventually he did," replied Mrs Thomas. "There's a marker stone somewhere in our churchyard, though I can't say I've ever seen it."

"So why did the Reverend Wood later keep an exercise book full of all these things about our family?" asked Tom. He was a bit annoyed at the thought of a stranger going through all his family's history.

Mrs Thomas paused. "I think the Reverend Wood fancied himself as a bit of a detective. He appears to have been fascinated by the trial of your great-grandfather accused of the murder of your great-grandmother. Then he came across these other papers and the story of Jonathan, so he put it all together and created quite a history of your family. I will give you this book to take home to your father. You should have it." She pushed it across the table to Tom.

There was a hush in the room. "Thank you," said both boys.

"Let's go and have a look now," said Andrew eagerly. "Let's have a quick look for the marker stone."

"Well," began Tom. "We promised not to be too late getting back."

"I'll drive you back," said Mrs Thomas. "I'll phone your parents now to let them know… that is, if you think you are well enough. I don't want you to overdo things."

"I'll be okay," replied Tom. "We had a tea over at Mrs Robertson's this afternoon and we met her cousin, Mr Rushforth, so we're fine."

Letty laughed.

"I didn't realise she had a cousin," said Mrs Thomas.

"He does a lot of travelling," said Letty. "I'm glad he was able to pop in. I haven't seen him for such a long time. Did he seem well?"

Tom looked puzzled. "He looked great," said Charlie and grinned.

Chapter Forty-Eight
Graves

They all went to the churchyard. Mr Philpott was there busy at work, cutting down weeds and generally tidying up. He had worked as an accountant in London for many years but three years ago had retired because of ill health. Now he busied himself caring for the church grounds. He said that working outside in the peace and quiet had given him a new lease of life. He looked up when he heard their footsteps.

"Hello, Mrs Thomas," he said, pausing in his work. "What brings you here this afternoon?"

"Well, Geoffrey, we need your help. Am I right in thinking that the oldest graves are on the south side?"

"Yes, I believe they are, in fact I have a rubbish dump over there as the weeds are particularly bad in that area. It's where I have my bonfire. Why do you ask? Does the smoke bother you? I'm really sorry if it does, I'll move it if you like."

"No, no, it's nothing like that," she replied. "Tom's looking for his ancestors' graves. Are there any Ferristons buried along there?"

Mr Philpott smiled at Tom. "I believe there are," he answered and turned in that direction. They all followed.

They crunched along the gravel path as though their lives depended on it. Mr Philpott had no idea why they were hurrying so much and neither did the children, but Mrs Thomas was eager to see the stones. She had never realised there were so many Ferristons buried in the yard. Why, she thought, weren't there any plaques in the church? Such an old family should be recognised in some way. What had happened in their history, in their past, she wondered?

The weather had worn away so much of what had been written on these old and pitted tombstones. Some were almost black, but nevertheless they stood tall and straight.

Tom looked dejected. Where was the marker for Jonathan Ferriston?

Mrs Thomas saw his look and mistook it for the after-effects of his illness.

"I'm going back to the vicarage," she said gently. "I'll phone your parents and let them know that we're on our way. We can leave all this to another day; after all, the graves are not going anywhere. They'll be here tomorrow."

Tom made a weak protest, but to be honest he was beginning to feel tired.

"Thank you, Mrs Thomas," he said. "That would be good. We'll come back tomorrow."

Charlie looked relieved. He was feeling hungry.

Mrs Thomas drove them home and explained everything to their parents. Then she presented Mr Ferriston with a large brown envelope containing the Reverend Wood's exercise book.

"There," she said. "You should have it. It's just a few notes about your family. I expect you know most of it. Tom and Charlie can explain it all to you if necessary."

After a short chat with Mrs Ferriston she drove off. She didn't notice the large black Rolls-Royce which glided silently along the road behind her.

Chapter Forty-Nine
It's here!

It was about half-past ten the next morning when Mandy shouted, "Look! It's here!"

Underneath a bushy, thick, green-leaved plant some two feet high, was the ashen-grey shape of a small marker stone. The friends had been searching the churchyard since nine o'clock that morning. Mr Philpott had arrived around ten to finish off a few jobs and had been surprised to find the four of them examining each stone as if on an archaeological dig.

"Ugh!" she said holding her nose. "What a stink! What is it?"

"Ah," answered Mr Philpott. "It's that weed. It's a terrible plant and quite unnatural."

"Why?" asked Andrew. "It's only ivy, isn't it?"

"No, it isn't." Tom's voice was sharp. He knew he had seen this plant before.

Mr Philpott looked at him with approval. "You're quite right, Tom," he said. "It's henbane and it's poisonous. It ought to flower in the summertime, you know from June onwards or thereabouts, but this plant seems to flower all the year round, whenever it feels like it." He leaned heavily on his spade. "By rights it ought never to be in flower at the moment, but no matter what I do, back it comes and dare I say it, just lately it appears to have a new lease of life. I hate it!"

Mandy bent down as if to smell the yellow flower with its dark purple centre but Tom pulled her back. Even so she wrinkled her nose, the smell was like bad meat. "Ugh, it's really horrid!"

"I know," muttered Tom. "They were in Ferlian Forest, only much larger. They hung from everywhere, from branches and rocks, just everywhere." He looked very white as though he was going to be sick.

"I remember," whispered Charlie.

"I don't know about that," replied Mr Philpott, not understanding Tom's meaning. "But I'll tell you one thing about this particular plant…"

The children looked at him as he dug his spade deeper in the ground.

"Well," he continued. "Not only does it grow but it also does so in a specific direction." He pointed to the graves of the Ferriston family. "I've cleared it away from them time and time again, but back it comes with its horrible, hairy, sticky stems and leaves." He grunted in disgust. "Sorry, Tom, sorry Charlie, but it seems to like your ancestors best of all."

The friends prepared to attack the plant.

"Be careful," warned Mr Philpott. "I'm not sure you should be doing this." It was too late they had all begun swinging their spades. Mr Philpott went quickly to his shed and produced some masks and gloves, insisting that they should wear them. No one spoke, they hardly dared breathe in case they took in some of the deadly fumes, and the masks made them feel claustrophobic. Tom felt really sick, the smell soaked up the atmosphere, and once again he was reminded of that dreadful journey with Geschwind through Ferlian Forest. Mandy and Andrew began to cough but still no one uttered a word.

Ten minutes later the site looked like a battleground, the plant lay in pieces, cut to shreds. They stood back to survey their work. Mr Philpott was the first to break the silence.

"Well," he said. "If I had you four working with me for a few days we'd soon have this churchyard looking wonderful in no time!"

The others didn't answer, they were staring at the small, grey marker stone now completely free of the henbane.

"Jonathan Ferriston b. 1702. In Remembrance," read out Charlie.

"That's funny," muttered Mr Philpott. "It doesn't say when he died. Most unusual."

"I'll get Mum," said Andrew, propping his spade up against the wall. He dashed off before Tom or Charlie could say anything. He was back with his mother and a very breathless Vicar whilst the others were still leaning on their spades.

"There, James," she said, linking her arm through her husband's. "Now what do you think of that?" Before he could answer she continued, "I don't think he's there."

Charlie and Tom looked at her. What did she know? Did she know about Jonathan's ship or the paintings?

"This is what the Reverend Wood was writing about, what his predecessor was worried about. I don't think they ever had a body to bury. He's not there."

Her husband looked at her in horror. Mr Philpott gave a nervous cough and shuffled his feet in the gravel. The four friends remained silent.

"Really, Mary, I hardly think you need to be quite so melodramatic!" responded the Vicar, misjudging the look of alarm on the children's faces. "You don't have to frighten us all. I'm sure that there's some perfectly simple explanation. He probably died abroad, just as those letters suggested. It wasn't easy in those days to bring back a body from far-off places. Not everyone could afford to be pickled in brandy like Nelson. He could even have died of plague so his body wouldn't have been returned. This was just his way of ensuring that he should be remembered with the rest of his family. Perhaps the engravers of the time forgot to put the date of his death on the stone. Oh, there are hundreds of possible reasons why the marker is in this spot. All of them better than your assumption that it's not a proper grave."

"Then why isn't he over there with the rest of his family?" persisted his determined wife. "Why was his grave hidden here in this dark corner, under this disgusting plant?" She pointed to the henbane which lay like a wounded animal all over the site.

"I don't know," replied the Vicar in frustration. "The plant probably wasn't there when the marker was laid down." He turned to go back to the vicarage, his wife went with him. The friends could hear them discussing the grave as they made their way along the path.

"She'll be wanting the grave exhumed next," muttered Mr Philpott, leaning on his spade. "It'll mean the Coroner and probably the Bishop all getting involved." He smiled kindly at Tom and Charlie. "Not forgetting your dad, of course. He might not look too kindly on all of this."

Mandy sighed. Why did adults always want to take over?

Mr Philpott said he'd rather tidy up everything himself. He didn't want the children to be near the henbane any more than was necessary.

They made their way along the path to the vicarage.

"I'm sorry my mum got so carried away," said Andrew.

"Don't worry," replied Tom. "I've been thinking. We'll let the adults check the grave if they want to, we know the real reason why Jonathan's body won't be there. It could be part of what Geschwind meant when he said things were about to happen. Anyway, I don't think we should interfere at this stage."

The others agreed.

A great kerfuffle was going on when they walked into the Vicarage kitchen. Letty was making some very noisy coffee, and the Vicar was talking animatedly to his wife who had just put the phone down.

"How could you ask Tom's father such a question? What on earth must he think?"

"He didn't mind a bit," she answered defensively. "He's a very nice person and was quite amused by the whole thing."

"Amused!" The Vicar's eyebrows almost took off into space.

"He couldn't understand what all the fuss is about."

"Neither can I," interrupted her husband.

"He gave his permission, said to keep him informed and not to touch the grave unless he or a member of his family is present. If I speak to the Coroner will you contact the Bishop, please James?"

They left the room.

"Now what mischief have you children started?" gently scolded Letty.

"You know what Mum's like," explained Andrew.

"Oh, I do, I do!" laughed Letty. "It'll be alright, Charlie," she whispered in his ear. "We'll be ready this time, don't you worry."

Charlie nearly dropped his glass of orange squash when she said this.

"Don't spill it!" she smiled seeing his bewildered expression.

Chapter Fifty
The Storm

The air was lifeless. Tom and Charlie lay on their beds, the bedroom window was wide open but it made no difference. Tom found it especially hot and sticky. Every time he turned over, his pyjamas refused to come with him. Even Urthslean, lying beside him, seemed to moan rather than hum. Something unpleasant was coming, he felt sure.

They talked in low tones about the meeting with Mr Rushforth, the finding of the marker stone, until there was nothing more to say.

Charlie was puzzled by Letty's remarks about 'being ready this time'. What did she mean?

Their mother decided that the weather was unnatural for this time of the year. It was too hot. Weather like this came in the summer.

"There's a storm brewing," she had announced at tea time.

"The weather men haven't forecast one," replied their father, though secretly he agreed with her.

"It's coming," she replied firmly. "A piece of seaweed on the back door would agree with me!" Then she burst into giggles. "I sound just like my mother!" she added.

She was right. As the boys lay on their beds they heard a quiet rumble of thunder in the distance. They both decided to look out of the window to see if there was any lightning.

Night had swallowed the tail end of the day. Jay's Wood was a sea of dark uneven patches. Very few trees had grown their spring canopies which made this warm weather seem even more strange. Hot weather came when trees were heavy with summer coats of leaves, not when their spindly arms were still bare from winter gales. In the distance Fox's Gulley looked dark and menacing.

"It looks as if there are strange shapes moving in the trees," whispered Charlie.

"Don't be silly," replied his brother. "It's just your imagination. Urthslean isn't bothered so why should you be?"

Charlie nodded, though he wasn't too sure.

The sky in the west still clung to the last remnants of light, its navy-blue canvas was haphazardly streaked with lines of dark yellow and orange. Occasionally a reckless bird chirped from the hidden depths of a bush as though reassuring himself, and anyone else who might be listening, that he wasn't afraid or bothered by this unnatural weather, only to be rewarded by an ominous rumble in the distance. In between these sounds came the odd glimpse of sheet lightning, nothing dramatic just a nervous twitch on the horizon. Nothing moved, everywhere was stillness. It was as though the garden had turned itself into a painting, a very dark painting. Eventually even the brave lone singer folded his wings in resignation and settled down for the storm to break. Somewhere in the distance a lone dog gave a couple of futile barks.

Charlie flopped back down on his bed and Tom soon followed. They were still awake when their parents came upstairs to go to bed.

"Try to get to sleep soon," said their mother, as she came in to close the bedroom window.

"Please don't," groaned Tom. "It's so hot."

"I know," she answered softly. "But it will rain hard tonight, I'm sure, and I don't want it coming in through your window. I'll leave the bedroom door open, that will bring in some fresh air. Now try to get some sleep, both of you." She left.

Urthslean began to hum but both boys were so tired that despite the heat they soon fell asleep.

Tom wasn't sure why he woke when he did, but something had disturbed him. He could hear the steady hiss of the rain even through his closed window, and the thunder seemed to be boiling away quietly in the distance, creeping ever closer. He lay there in the darkness, waiting for the lightning so that he could count the gaps to see how far the storm had come. A disappointing blink of blue light swept around the room and in a few moments was answered by a stronger roll. The storm was coming closer. A sudden deluge of rain pounded on the window and the broken gutter let a constant flow of water drum on the butt below.

Urthslean was quietly humming a warning.

"Did you wake me?" Tom looked at the sword. He really wanted to go back to sleep.

"Tom." The whisper sounded right by his ear.

He swung round in his bed to face the door, half expecting to see someone standing there, but it was only inky blackness.

"Who's that?" He gripped the sword, his voice sounded hoarse and dry with fear. "Who's there? Is it you, Geschwind?"

There was no reply. Another brief sweep of blue light lit the room only to be answered by an enormous clap of thunder. The rain pounded like icy hailstones against the window. His heart beat so fast that it felt as if it had leapt into his throat. It hurt and the pain reached into his ears. He was frightened, scared. The gutter was overflowing so much that the rain was pouring down the side of the house. A great streak of lightning lit up the whole room followed almost immediately by a harsh clap of thunder, then, as suddenly as it had started, the rain ceased, it was all over. Only the sound of a gentle wind could be heard. It had not woken his parents, he could hear his father's snoring, and Charlie had slept through it all.

The whisper came again. "Tom, get up. Come."

Urthslean's humming was becoming more urgent.

"It's no good, Urthslean," murmured Tom. "I must go. This must be the time. The moment we have all been working for. Geschwind said that we would be tested."

Silently, and as quickly as his trembling fingers would allow, he dressed. The storm was returning, and a sense of purpose was growing in the wind as it moaned its way about the house and rattled the windows. He moved to the top of the stairs, there had been no need to open the squeaky bedroom door, and he knew his way well enough not to switch on any lights.

"Tom," the whisper twisted and writhed its way up the staircase and drew him down.

"Where are you? What are you?" he asked. He was beginning to wish he had woken up Charlie. His head began to throb as he moved into the waiting well of darkness hovering at the bottom of the stairs. As if in a dream he dragged open the great doors and collected his bike from the shed. He didn't even flinch when a clap of thunder broke directly overhead.

The voice was all around him, in the trees, in the air, and yet at times it seemed as if it came from within his own head. If he had looked down, he would have seen a pale blue glow surrounding Urthslean, just as it did when they had battled with the dragon, Bestim.

"Tom."

Obediently he rode his cycle along the driveway and out onto the deserted road. The wheels hissed quietly on the tarred surface and, as the lightning increased, so he became vaguely aware of the trees on either side standing tall and still like silent sentinels, watching his every movement. It came as no surprise to him when he stopped outside the church gate. The storm was turning ominous, as if something or someone was waiting for the next move to be made. Suddenly it was as if the sky had turned to paper, and the thunder was shredding it apart. A single bolt of lightning smacked hard into the old yew tree, splitting it from top to bottom.

Tom hesitated.

The rain had stopped but the wind now returned to torment him, and with great difficulty he pushed back the gate dropping his bike in the entrance. Instinctively he knew where to go and so his footsteps scrunched their way along the path, past the silent tombstones and down through the churchyard towards the grave of Jonathan Ferriston. He stopped as he rounded the corner and automatically rested one hand on the hilt of his sword. Urthslean was desperate to wake him from this trance-like state. It began to glow but this time it was no blue flame but a vicious white heat which made Tom yell and come to his senses.

The sudden fury of the storm woke many people that night. With a frantic crack, jagged streaks of forked lightning scuttled down from the heavens and dug deep into the soil. At last! The wind seemed to shout as it tore into the bushes and wrapped itself shrieking around the trees. Paper on the deserted village street began to dance eerily as it was tossed into the air. Foolhardy cats rushed for shelter, wise ones were already in bed, and dogs whined and barked just to show that they were not afraid. As the first drops of heavy rain spat angrily on the ground, windows were hastily closed, and Tom's mother smiled in her sleep, remembering that she had closed the boys' bedroom window because she knew the storm would break. People snuggled down deeper in their beds, just grateful that they were in the warmth and safety of their own homes.

Tom stood alone in the churchyard, a solitary figure, facing the unknown darkness.

Chapter Fifty-One
Charlie

Charlie woke with a start. The last clap of thunder felt as if it was in their bedroom. He turned over to look across to Tom's bed.

"Where are you, Tom?" he whispered as loudly as he dared. He had no wish to wake his parents. There was no reply. The bed was empty.

He went to the top of the stairs and saw that the great front doors were wide open. Instinctively he knew that Tom must have gone back to the churchyard. He rushed back to their bedroom and changed out of his pyjamas. Tom was in danger, of that he was certain, he said as much to Arula.

"Then I must go to Geschwind," she said simply. "You too must take care, Charlie. There's a great deal of harmful energy in the air tonight. Wish me luck!" And with that she flew straight through the castle painting.

"Be careful!" called Charlie, forgetting his parents were in the next bedroom.

"What's going on?" called his father. Charlie could hear him getting out of bed.

He decided that the only thing to do was to tell his parents where he thought Tom had gone. By this time both his parents were out of bed.

"What on earth are you doing dressed like that?" said his mother, in amazement. "And where's Tom?"

"Why's the front door wide open?" asked his father.

"It's Tom," replied Charlie. He was becoming agitated. "Tom's gone to the churchyard, I know it. He's gone to that grave. He's in danger. Please Dad, we've got to go, he needs help." All this came out in one breath.

"But..." began his mother.

"Please believe me, Dad," implored Charlie. "Please..."

But he needn't have worried. Both his parents were throwing on their outdoor clothes on top of their pyjamas, and together they rushed down the stairs. No one spoke as they jumped into their car.

In a matter of minutes they had screeched to a halt outside the church gate. Tom's bicycle was lying by the lychgate, the back wheel was still spinning.

"Oh, Tom," Mrs Ferriston sounded fearful.

"Stop!" shouted Mr Ferriston, as Charlie leapt out of the car and ran to the back of the churchyard.

As he and Mrs Ferriston tried to follow, so the car doors slammed shut and all the locks clicked into action. They were trapped inside. Desperately they tried to escape, to wind down the windows, but nothing would work. Mr Ferriston searched in vain to find something inside the car to break the windows.

Charlie rushed round to Tom as a bolt of lightning revealed two very dark shapes standing by the grave of their ancestor. The thunder raged in fury around him, and unleashed a new deluge of torrential rain which stung his face, and a sudden frenzied wind pushed and battered him, it was hard to reach Tom. He flung himself at his brother.

"You shouldn't have come," said Tom. "But I'm glad you have."

Together they turned to face the dark figures.

The tall one was Stincan whilst the smaller squat one was Margar. There was no pretence now, the boys could see them for what they were. Their ghastly faces glowed unnaturally in the light of the storm. Stincan's presence was almost overwhelming. He was tall, very tall. A thin skeletal figure, hollow-cheeked and death-like. His eyes were set back and ringed in thick black circles, which contrasted strangely with his yellowing parchment-like skin. From his sleeves protruded his wizened hands, almost fleshless in their appearance. He wore his cloak like a monk, with the cowl well over his head. Margar, on the other hand, wore hers down. Tom thought how much she resembled Prince Beweglic with her slanting yellow eyes and her pointed ears. Her hair was now dark, unkempt and straggled over her shoulders, it moved and wriggled. At first the boys thought it was the wind moving it, but then to their horror, they realised that it was alive with worms. They wanted to run, but it was too late.

Tom drew Urthslean and prepared to fight.

"So," sneered Margar, in a voice which screeched like a tormented cat. "You have brought dear Urthslean for your protection as well as your little brother. You'll find us much harder to dispatch than that overgrown lizard Bestim."

"Tom," Stincan's voice caressed the night air and slithered towards them. An ominous rumble of thunder punctuated the moment. "Come here, Tom, the time is right."

Charlie grabbed hold of Tom's sleeve. There was no way he was going to let his brother go anywhere. Smaller dark shapes began scurrying through the churchyard and moving in and out of the tombstones. Margar leered at Tom and it took all Charlie's strength to stop him lurching forwards. Urthslean growled and began to glow.

The grave lay open.

"There's no body in here, Tom." Stincan's voice was mocking as he pointed to Jonathan Ferriston's empty grave. "No body. Dear me. Let us give them one, Tom. Let us give them a body." He paused. "Yours."

Margar went into peals of laughter. "Yours, Tom," she chortled. "Your little body."

Tom felt as though a million ants were crawling over his brain as the two slowly began to pull him forwards. He stumbled towards the yawning hole dragging Charlie with him.

"I'm sorry, Tom," said his brother, and kicked him really hard on the shins. "Wake up!" he screamed. "Wake up, Tom! Call for Geschwind!"

Tom grunted but the kick had worked. Together he and Charlie fought their way to the South Porch of the church.

* * *

The noise of the lightning splitting the yew tree caused Andrew to wake up. He sat up. Something was wrong, but what was it? He jumped out of bed and went to the window, from here he had a clear view of the back of the churchyard. Another burst of lightning lit everything up as though it were day, and in that fleeting moment he saw Tom and Charlie below. His quick eye also took in the two dark figures standing amidst the battered henbane.

"Tom!" he shouted, forgetting his parents were asleep in the room next door, and Letty was only across the hallway, but no one heard him above the storm.

He grabbed his clothes and feverishly pulled them over his pyjamas. Another clash of lightning caused him to glance out and he could see Charlie holding on to Tom, trying to drag him away from the two strangers. He rushed downstairs and began to tug at the backdoor forgetting that it was bolted at the top and bottom.

"I must hurry!" he gasped, as he placed a chair by the door in order to reach the top bolt. He abandoned all attempts to be quiet, he didn't have time. He threw the chair to one side, opened the door and rushed out into the storm.

"Tom! Charlie!" he yelled into the wind, but his voice was swallowed up as the violence of the storm increased. The old gate, which connected their garden to the churchyard swung crazily aside as the wind seemed to take pleasure in banging it back and forth after he had gone.

"Tom! Charlie!" he shouted again, as he saw Charlie kick his brother in an attempt to stop him moving forwards.

The boys turned to look at him. "Go back!" shouted Charlie. "It's dangerous."

"No." Andrew stood firmly by the side of his two friends. When Stincan saw this, he let out a hiss of anger. Andrew helped Charlie to pull Tom away from the grave, away from the henbane and towards the South Porch of the church. They had to get out of this unnatural storm. Stincan and Margar followed stealthily. Never before had Urthslean glowed so fiercely, and despite their earlier taunting they had no wish to confront the sword's spirit nor the Master of Urthslean in a physical contest.

Margar snorted pig-like. "Well, well, well. We can now have three bodies and not just one! You will not get away from us so easily!"

The storm, too, had not given up, not a household in the village was allowed to sleep peacefully that night.

Suddenly Tom saw smaller, darker figures emerging from behind every tombstone.

"Crudelis!" he shouted.

Andrew looked to where Tom had pointed. All he could see were masses of dark shadows moving through the graveyard. A trick of the light? Somehow these shapes filled him with dread. The hair on the back of his neck began to prickle, he felt sick. Tom and Charlie saw Crudelis climbing over the tombstones delighting in scraping their claws over the headstones, and relishing the discomfort this hideous sound was causing the boys.

"Throw these," commanded Charlie. He picked up one of the many stones lying around the porch entrance.

"Where?" asked a bewildered Andrew.

"At the shadows," answered Charlie, hurling one straight at an advancing Crudelis. It gave a screech and hastily retreated.

Andrew did as he was told but then turned his attention to the two strangers. Was it his imagination or did they seem like two giant bats waving their arms about? What was happening? The night air was full of the noises of the storm. Strange sounds of shrieking and groaning. It was a storm like no other. Tom was scything down Crudelis as Urthslean sang. It was all too much for Margar.

"Go on, you miserable creatures," she screamed. "They're only boys. Go on or I'll make short work of you myself." With that she sent a searing bolt of light into a Crudelis who burst into flames.

"They're playing with us," panted Tom. "Go home, Andrew. Quickly save yourself before it's too late."

"No, I'm not leaving," replied Andrew. "I'm not sure what I'm fighting but I know it's evil. I'm not leaving you two." He hurled another stone into the dark.

Charlie felt something land in his pocket, it was Arula. "He's coming," she whispered.

"Enough!" commanded Stincan. "I see that I will have to complete this task myself."

Margar sniffled and snorted with glee.

A green bolt of light smashed into the wall close to Tom's head, followed quickly by another at his feet. The church bell began to toll.

Margar could not conceal her delight. "Again! Again, Stincan. Quickly, kill him this time! Kill all of them!" she screamed.

Charlie hurled a large stone at her. "Geschwind is coming!" he yelled. "Leave us now!"

Now it was the turn of Stincan to falter. He looked around, an expression of fear and hatred on his face as, with a rush of wind and a crack of lightning that fairly flew from the skies, Geschwind stood before boys. Oh, but this was no ordinary Geschwind. This was Geschwind of the Old Magic, the Master Magician. A second much taller figure appeared by his side. It was Jonathan Ferriston come to protect his young descendants.

With a snarl, Stincan rushed at his old enemy, but Geschwind was ready for him and quickly turned the attack to his own advantage. Stincan was hurled high into the sky and crashed against a headstone, but as quickly as he fell, the Warlock was up on his feet again. A bolt of green light shot from his fingers only to be parried away by Geschwind. Jonathan threw himself onto Margar but was soon engulfed by the many Crudelis who came to her aid.

Above the storm the boys could hear a weird singing sound, and there on a small mound stood the figure of Pitzic who had come with a band of warriors to aid his leader. From all sides, winged creatures appeared moving so quickly that at first Tom could not make out their shapes. Amongst them was Kurz and his followers.

"Take care, Kurz," whispered Tom, as Crudelis began to unleash their cruel talons upon the gossamer wings of the faeries.

The shadows and shapes lurched back and forth as thousands of Crudelis rose from the earth itself. Tom and Charlie fought side by side. Charlie's aim at the Crudelis was faultless, so many crumbled as he hurled stone after stone at them. Suddenly he felt a thud beside him and turning he saw that Andrew had fallen and was being dragged away by the creatures. Without any thought for his own safety he leapt onto the nearest one, hitting it hard with a rock. Others came forward in an effort to capture both boys, but they stood no chance, as Pitzic had seen the danger.

"Take your friend back to the church porch, Charlie," he shouted. "We'll deal with these."

Without speaking Charlie did as he was told. It was hard, he could tell from the weight that Andrew had passed out. It was difficult to drag him back but he did it.

Chapter Fifty-Two
The Bells are Tolling

Amazingly the storm, which was already ferocious, began to increase in its intensity. Never before had the villagers of Chepham experienced such savagery. The church itself began to creak and groan, and so it was that the bells began to toll.

"James." Mrs Thomas woke with a start.

"Mmmm," her husband shifted in bed.

"I heard a noise downstairs."

"It's the wind."

"No. Something fell over."

"The wind blew it over."

"No," insisted Mrs Thomas, who was now wide awake. She opened their bedroom door only to find Letty standing there.

"I was coming to find you," she said. "Andrew's not in his bed and listen… The church bells are tolling."

Mrs Thomas turned to her husband. "James!" she began.

"It's alright," he answered. "I can hear the bells, I'm coming." He flung on some clothes and rushed downstairs.

The church bells had summoned the villagers. They came armed with all sorts of weapons, from pitch forks to shovels and rolling pins. Letty and Mrs Robertson were there at the front, so were a couple of the teachers and Mr Philpott and friends. Although when they were asked about it afterwards many said they had no idea why they came so prepared.

It all ended with a violent crushing rush of lightning, and half of the damaged yew tree burst into flames and fell crashing down. The wind dropped and the rain slowly ceased. Tom lowered his sword and Charlie rushed to his side. The two boys were exhausted.

"I think we did it," said Tom softly as Charlie wiped away a tear. "How's Andrew?"

They both turned and couldn't help smiling. Andrew was sitting in a puddle looking very dazed, his face and hair was covered in mud.

"What was all that about?" he asked in a bewildered tone.

"We'll tell you later," replied Tom. "Uh-o. Here come your parents."

Mr and Mrs Thomas came running towards them from the vicarage.

"Even worse," muttered Charlie. "Here come Mum and Dad!"

Surprisingly, neither set of parents said anything. The storm had caused massive power cuts and Letty told them all to come back to the vicarage where she soon had hot drinks ready on the gas stove. It appeared that Mr and Mrs Ferriston had been locked in their car and could only be released when the bells stopped tolling.

Mr Thomas went back to the churchyard. The moon was now shining and bathing the wreckage of the night's storm in healing silver light. The old yew tree was still smouldering and some of the villagers had stayed to dowse it with water. What had happened here, he wondered? What had the boys witnessed? He stood in the South Porch and looked down at his feet. Little piles of stones and small rocks were everywhere. Then he glanced towards the open grave. Who had done this? He knew that they had left it closed the previous day. He was sure that the boys would not have attempted to open it themselves. As he walked closer he could make out a jumble of bones. It was a human skeleton.

Chapter Fifty-Three
Why?

There was an uncomfortable silence in the vicarage kitchen. Mrs Thomas had her arm around Andrew who was very quiet and pale, he couldn't stop his hands from shaking when handed a mug of hot chocolate. All three boys had been wrapped in blankets.

Mrs Ferriston looked at her two sons. "Why?" she asked. "What possessed you, Tom, to go to the churchyard in the dead of night on your bike? And in this dreadful storm? I don't understand." She hadn't touched the coffee which Letty had kindly handed her.

Tom was searching for an answer when Mrs Thomas suddenly said, "It was all my fault." The others looked at her in amazement.

"I unearthed all that information about your ancestor, Jonathan Ferriston, and I believe it has played upon Tom's mind. I'm so sorry, I didn't realise that Tom has not fully recovered from his earlier illness. I would never have told him all those things if I had realised."

"It's not your fault," said Charlie bravely. Tom agreed.

"No, it's not." Mr Ferriston shook his head. "It was a strange storm, most unusual for this time of the year, and none of this explains why we couldn't get out of our car. It was as if something or someone was deliberately keeping us there. Why?"

"And why did all those villagers suddenly turn up with spades and forks, just like weapons?" asked a bewildered Mrs Ferriston.

"They said it was to help with the yew tree and any damage in the churchyard," said Mrs Thomas.

"What with a rolling pin!" answered Mr Ferriston, taking a large gulp of his coffee.

Letty smiled.

It was four o'clock in the morning and everyone was tired. The Reverend Thomas suddenly appeared in the doorway.

"Well," he said. "The storm did do one good thing."

The others just stared at him, so he continued. "That terrible weed, the henbane, seems to have been destroyed and so it has revealed a grave. There is a skeleton and…" he added looking at Mr Ferriston, "it might well be your long-lost ancestor, Jonathan Ferriston."

It was all Tom could do to stop himself from punching the air. He grinned at Charlie. This did not go unnoticed by his father.

"Why, Tom?" he asked. "What makes you smile at that news?"

Before Tom could answer, Mrs Thomas said, "Oh dear, I knew it was all my fault. It must have played on their minds."

"How did you know, Charlie, that Tom would be round here at the churchyard?" asked his mother.

Charlie hesitated before saying. "I just guessed. I wasn't sure."

"You seemed very certain when you woke us up. You didn't sound as though you were guessing," said his father.

"We were talking about it before we went to sleep," said Tom. He looked at Andrew. "Thank you, Andrew, for coming when you did."

Andrew just nodded.

"Why are there so many little piles of stones around the South Porch?" asked the Reverend Thomas.

"Excuse me interrupting," said Letty suddenly. "But don't you think, Vicar, that it would be a good thing to get all these boys home and in bed. It's nearly breakfast time and they need to get some sleep first!"

All the adults agreed, especially when the Reverend Thomas offered to drive the Ferristons home. Mr Ferriston wanted his car checked over before he drove it again.

Chapter Fifty-Four
The Damage

Later that morning Mr Philpott stood gazing ruefully at what had once been his pride and joy. All his hard work, all his efforts in the churchyard over the past few weeks seemed to have been swept aside by the night's storm. Half of the scorched yew tree had fallen across some of the graves, a couple of which looked badly damaged. It appeared to him that most of the village rubbish had spiralled and threaded its way to rest amongst the tombstones, so adding to the picture of chaos which greeted him. Even part of the churchyard's south wall had crumbled and lay in ruins. What a mess! There were stones and small rocks scattered everywhere. He made his way towards his shed and as he did so he was joined by the Vicar.

"What a night, Vicar!" he called, as he struggled to release his wheelbarrow from the tangle of tools which had slid all over the place. The single shed window had been blown in and shards of glass lay everywhere.

"Indeed, Mr Philpott," answered the Vicar. "I think you may be surprised by what you find near your tool shed!"

Mr Philpott glanced in the direction of the Vicar's pointing finger and saw the jumble of bones.

"My goodness, have they been there all the time?" Without waiting for an answer, he frowned and added, "It looks to me as if there's been some strange goings-on here. You don't expect a storm, however big, to open up a grave on its own now, do you?"

"That's true," the Vicar replied. "On the other hand, look how the bushes and the stones around it have all been moved or uprooted. In normal circumstances I'd agree with you, but last night was no ordinary storm."

It was Mr Philpott's turn to say, "That's true."

"Anyway," continued the Vicar in a matter-of-fact voice, "I've phoned the police so that they can formally establish the date of these bones, though I sincerely believe them to be the bones of Jonathan Ferriston, an ancestor of Andrew's friend, Tom. They could be two hundred years old or more. Whatever the outcome, they will be laid to rest peacefully. I'll see that they have a proper burial service."

"At least one good thing has come out of the storm," he added. "Look around you."

"Where?" asked Mr Philpott, all he could see was weeks and weeks of clearing up all the debris.

"Weren't you worried about that weed, henbane, isn't it?"

"Good gracious!" Mr Philpott exclaimed as he began to examine the area more closely. Sure enough the henbane had been scorched and burnt, its leaves were brittle, brown and twisted, the whole plant had withered and shrivelled and now lay dead.

"It must have been struck by lightning," he said happily. "What a relief. I was always so worried that young children might come to pick the flowers. Whatever I tried, it would never die. Thank goodness it's gone."

The Vicar just smiled and returned to the vicarage.

Chapter Fifty-Five
Is this just a story?

Tom and Charlie looked at their father. He hadn't laughed at them, he hadn't even been cross, he had just let them tell their story.

They had told him that they believed the paintings to be valuable because Mr Rushforth had told them that Jonathan Ferriston had been a well-known artist. They didn't say that they had travelled into two of the paintings, nor that Tom had fought a dragon and won, nor that Charlie had been captured by the Crudelis. They didn't tell him anything about the land of Glencyndal, but they did agree that the visit of the possible burglars and Mrs Thomas's findings had probably influenced them that night. Why else would they have ventured out in that storm to the churchyard?

Mr Ferriston wasn't stupid. He knew that the boys were holding something back. Ever since he was a small boy this house, Green Willow, had been a mystery. So much had happened here in the past that none of the family could ever explain. Why did it sometimes seem to shiver? He felt it, their mother felt it, but what caused it to happen? And why couldn't they get out of their car when they reached the churchyard? It was only when Mr Philpott arrived with the other villagers that they seemed able to open the doors with ease. By this time Charlie had already rushed out to be with Tom. Who were these so-called burglars? Not normal ones that was certain.

"And you met this Mr Rushforth at Mrs Robertson's tea shop?" he asked.

They nodded.

"How do you know he's not in league with these burglars?"

"Oh no," Charlie gave a gasp of horror. "He's good, he really is. Why—"

Tom interrupted him, fearing that Charlie might give too much away. "He's a very nice man, Dad," he said. "He's a relation of Mrs Robertson, her cousin I think."

There was a long silence.

Then their father suddenly said, "Do you like it here? Would you rather go back to somewhere like West Lee? Back to your old school and friends? I know you were very upset, Tom at leaving West Lee. Would you like to return?"

The boys looked horrified.

"Why?" asked Tom.

"I don't want to go back," said Charlie. "I didn't like it here at first, but now I do. I want to stay."

Their mother gave them a hot chocolate as well as pouring out two coffees for herself and Mr Ferriston. She sat down at the table. "It may well be that we have to leave," she said quietly. "It's all proving far too expensive to complete, and that plus the problems with these strange burglars... well it's all becoming a bit too much."

"We need to talk to Coasters, the solicitors," said their father.

"Perhaps," said Tom, "we can sell some of the paintings. If Mr Rushforth is right, and I bet he is, we can raise a lot of money from these. Ask Mr Coaster if we can, Dad."

"We'll have a family get-together," said their father. "We'll see if in the circumstances we can perhaps sell some of the family items to raise money for the redevelopment of Green Willow. What do you think of that?"

The boys nodded.

Whilst Mr Ferriston was busy calling all his relations together, the Vicar and Mrs Thomas were following the mystery of the bones and making the necessary arrangements for a proper burial for Jonathan Ferriston. The police had readily agreed that the bones were undoubtedly centuries old and of no interest to them. A memorial service was arranged to coincide with the family gathering. In the meantime Tom and Charlie went to the tea shop and asked Mrs Robertson if she would organise a meeting with Mr Rushforth, which she agreed to do.

Chapter Fifty-Six
A Cup of Tea

Mandy and Andrew joined them at Mrs Robertson's tea shop. She had found them a quiet corner under an alcove that had once formed part of the tea shop's fireplace.

"Come in, come in, my dears," she said warmly. "Archie will be here any moment. He's had quite a difficult journey here today."

"I can't believe that you three had such an adventure," said Mandy. "Why didn't you wake me?" She looked accusingly at Andrew.

"There was no time," he replied. "Anyway, I could hardly go knocking on your door at that time of the morning. What would your mother have thought?"

Mrs Robertson brought them some orange juice and cakes. "These are on the house," she said grandly. "After what all you lads have done, you deserve it."

They thanked her and waited for Mr Rushforth.

"I still believe that those two in the churchyard were the burglars returning. Dad thinks that they imagined some of the treasures they were after, had been hidden in Jonathan Ferriston's grave," said Andrew.

"So why were you throwing the stones at the dark shapes?" asked Tom grinning.

Andrew didn't answer.

At that moment Mr Rushforth appeared, he shook their hands warmly before sitting down with them.

"You did well boys," he said smiling at them. "If you hadn't arrived when you did, Andrew, things would have been much harder for Tom. Charlie, you were fantastic.

You managed to get out of the car before Stincan locked it, and before the Crudelis arrived in great numbers."

"We've just been talking about it," said Tom. "What happened to Jonathan. I'm sure I saw him charge at Margar."

"You did," answered Mr Rushforth. "Margar and her cronies quickly disposed of poor Jonathan but that was always to be the way of things. He knew that in stepping out from his painting he would not have much time on this earth, however he managed to grapple with her just long enough to allow Kurz and his friends to arrive. They soon dealt with her!"

Andrew and Mandy listened in amazement.

"The Crudelis sprang up everywhere in answer to Stincan's call. They were a great hindrance, but when Stincan himself fell, they quickly turned tail and fled. The storm both helped and hindered us. With the rain lashing in my face, I missed the body of Margar and fell over it. The Crudelis might have had me then but for the bravery of Gioco and Pitzic. When I rose, Stincan swung round to send a bolt at my head, but I was able to thrust my sword in his chest. Then to my shame I lost consciousness."

Mandy let out a little "Oh my!" which caused some of the other customers to look their way.

Mr Rushforth gave a chuckle. "The death of Stincan brought the storm to an end and then we heard human voices approaching, so we all hastily left."

"But where were the bodies of Stincan and Margar?" asked Tom.

"The problem is that the Solanum will have ordered the Crudelis to retrieve them for later…" Mr Rushforth frowned.

"You mean they might come back?" Charlie looked worried.

"We will be ready," replied Mr Rushforth firmly.

"Did many of your friends die that night?" asked Tom.

Mr Rushforth nodded. "Yes, but they willingly did so because of all that you and Charlie have achieved for us. The Crudelis had grown in power and attacked our kingdom in many places. They gradually stretched my powers in many directions. Their aim was to find the paints and so dominate our worlds. Then you came, when all seemed lost, you saved us. I had forgotten that the paints could be used for good as well as evil."

Charlie muttered, "It was a great adventure."

Mr Rushforth smiled. "My powers were returned to me so that I might unravel the harm which Jonathan's ignorance and my negligence had unleashed into your world. If you had not defeated Bestim and helped me, then you and your family would have perished long ago with most of this village. Jonathan has paid his debt, but you and I," he looked at the children, "we will continue the battle against the darkness of evil for some time to come."

Mrs Robertson came to their table. "Archie it's time to leave now."

He nodded. "Until next time," he said, and disappeared into the back of the shop.

Tom looked at Mrs Robertson. "What did Ge… Mr Rushforth mean when he said that most of the village would have perished?"

Mrs Robertson glanced around her tea shop, it was empty so she drew up a chair and sat beside them.

"Long ago this village had a bad reputation," she whispered. "It was said that many witches, wizards and warlocks lived here. No one knew for certain whether they were good or bad. Strange things could happen here, like the flocks of birds which suddenly killed one of your ancestors and then disappeared." Tom and Charlie nodded.

"People would disappear and others, who came to take their place, would be odd, different." She continued, "Some said that they couldn't find our village, that it would sometimes disappear altogether."

"That's silly," said Andrew. Mandy shivered. "I mean, a whole village can't just disappear, it doesn't make sense. Sussex was famous for its muddy roads and potholes, no one liked riding through the lanes, but a whole village disappearing? Huh! The travellers probably just got lost."

Mrs Robertson raised her eyebrows. "I'm just saying what folk believed in those days," she answered. A customer came in. "I'd best be seeing to my tea shop," she said. "You take your time. There's no hurry."

The children thanked her but left shortly afterwards.

Chapter Fifty-Seven
Ends and Beginnings

A few days later they all attended the special memorial service arranged by the Vicar for Jonathan Ferriston. Great Uncle Arthur, Great Aunts Emma and Sara, even Uncle Thomas and Aunt Emily were there, in fact all the known members of the Ferriston family. It was just like Great-Grandfather's funeral all over again, only this time Tom and Charlie listened hard to all the conversations winging around the room. They remembered how they had missed that vital moment at Great-Grandfather's funeral when it was decided that they were going to move house. Their cousin Emma, who was five years older than Tom, was very envious of their large bedroom.

"Fancy having all this space, Charlie," she sighed sitting on his bed. "What I'd give to have a room as big as this all to myself. I bet you can't wait to decorate it!"

Charlie made a face, he was quite happy to wait for as long as need be. Other things were more important at the moment.

The local press had found out about the discovery of the skeleton and had decided to cover the story. They created quite an article about it; after all, as the reporter said, it's not every village that can boast a family tracing its ancestry back for over three hundred years and mainly occupying the same house. She told them it would be good publicity for their family venture into the hotel business, so they all agreed that she should print the article. She didn't realise how 'good for business' it was going to prove.

A London art dealer had a married sister who lived in a nearby village, and she sent her brother the cutting from the paper. When he read it he immediately contacted the Ferriston family and came down the very next day to meet them. Apparently, he had had dealings with one or two original portraits by a Jonathan Ferriston and wondered if it was the same artist. He muttered something about the 18th Century being an exciting time in English art and mentioned names such as, Wren, Reynolds and Hogarth. He could hardly conceal his delight when he realised that 'his' Jonathan Ferriston and theirs were one and the same artist, and he immediately asked permission to view all the paintings.

At this point Tom and Charlie asked if they could have a family conference.

"A family conference?" laughed their father.

"We'd like to talk to everyone before he comes back, and can Mandy and Andrew come as well?" they asked.

So, after the memorial service they all came back to Green Willow.

Mrs Ferriston had laid out a wonderful spread in the Long Room.

For a while a munching silence filled the room, and then the slightly overweight shape of Great Uncle Arthur shifted and he looked directly at the two brothers.

"Well, what is it that you wish to say to us?" His gruff voice was somewhat muffled by his mouthful of sausage roll.

"Don't frighten the boys," rebuked Aunt Emily. "You take your time, dears. I think you're very brave to ask to talk to all of us like this."

So, Tom began to tell the story of Jonathan Ferriston's gambling, even the finding of the 'special' paints with their 'almost magical colours'. He told them of the wickedness of Jonathan's so-called rich friends, who had caused Jonathan to go into hiding. He didn't say where.

Everyone just sat and looked at one another.

Uncle Thomas suddenly said, "I've heard about these 'friends' before. Mother used to tell us about them when we were very little. A sort of moral story about choosing friends wisely. I'd forgotten."

Great Aunt Sara just smiled.

"But boys," said Aunt Emily gently, "you haven't really spoken to Jonathan, have you? So how do you know all these things? You don't believe in magic, do you?"

Before either of them could answer, Great Aunt Sara said quietly in a matter-of-fact voice, "Father did."

All the adults stared at her, bar one.

Great Aunt Sara continued, "Father really believed that strange things were at work in this house. After Mother died, he used to talk to me about it. He believed that we, the whole family, had to guard 'Green Willow' as did all our ancestors. Something bad happened in Jonathan Ferriston's time. Little Joshua died, and then several of our ancestors died quite young. Even Father lost his two older brothers, and that's why he inherited."

"You're quite right, of course, Sara," said the tall man, who had been quietly standing in the doorway all this time. "We have been looking after your family estate for many years, and I can tell you in all seriousness that many of your ancestors felt a strong bond with this house," he turned to look at Tom and Charlie, "not least William Ferriston, your great-grandfather, boys."

"But, Mr Coaster," interrupted their father. "He had such a terrible time here, especially after the death of his wife, Mary. No one visited him here."

"Only your father left, Jack," Aunt Sara sighed. "The rest of us were very young. Emma was only fourteen, Arthur eleven, and I was just eight when Mother died. I was never sure, but I know that both Arthur and Emma believed, and still do as far as I know, that Mother was deliberately killed. They believed your father's version of events."

Great Uncle Arthur and Great Aunt Emma nodded sadly.

"So, I stayed until I met Francis," she patted the hand of the man sitting next to her. "And I did visit as often as I could. He was after all my father. He told me many things and that is why I believe quite a large part of the boys' story. If they say we should keep back some of the paintings, then that's what we should do."

"Go and fetch these special ones," said their father.

Tom and Charlie shot off to their room, Mandy and Andrew followed close behind.

"We'll carry one each," said Tom, as he carefully lifted the castle scene from the wall and handed it to Mandy.

"You're not going to say you've used these paintings as portals into another world, are you?" asked Andrew, clutching the garden scene.

"Of course not," replied Tom. He was holding the painting where Green Willow seemed partly in ruins. "I'm not daft y'know." He handed the picture of the ship at sea to Charlie. "Let's hope all the paintings stay in their frames when we go downstairs!"

"Oh dear," said Mandy, looking intently at the castle scene.

"I think Mr Coaster is on our side," whispered Charlie as they carried the paintings into the Long Room.

"They don't look particularly valuable," muttered Great Uncle Arthur. "They might fetch a bit though at an auction."

"Oh, I don't think they'd fetch that much," said Mr Coaster giving the boys a wink. "Who'd want a painting of a rotting tree, the ship isn't that well painted, and as for the castle…"

The others laughed. "We can see whose side you're on," said Great Uncle Arthur. "Very well, I think we should allow the boys to keep them, then we can have another cup of Sue's delicious tea, I'm parched!"

"I'm not sure—" began Uncle Thomas.

"Yes, you are!" interrupted his sister. She turned to Tom and Charlie. "You keep these paintings for us, boys. Then we'll know that they are in good hands and being well cared for."

Everyone nodded in agreement.

"Thank you, oh thank you," said Charlie.

"I'll put the kettle on," said their mother, and everyone relaxed.

As the boys made to leave the room, Great Aunt Sara leant forward in her chair and whispered, "Did you meet Geschwind?"

No one else heard, they were all too busy discussing the forthcoming meeting with the art dealer.

Tom didn't know what to say. He just stared in amazement at this very elderly lady whom he'd only met a few times. Charlie just gave a gasp. She smiled and her whole face lit up, her pale blue eyes sparkled as the little girl still within her saw their astonishment. She squeezed Charlie's hand gently. "Did you meet him?" she asked again.

Charlie nodded, and Tom gave a cough as though trying to drown an answer.

"Well done," she whispered. "I was too scared to accept his challenge and have regretted it all my life. I wonder if any of them," she nodded her head towards the rest of the family, "will ever understand the great debt we all owe you. Thank you, Tom, thank you Charlie." She gave them both a big hug.

"Come on," urged Andrew. "We should get these upstairs before the dealer comes."

So, they took the four paintings back to the relative safety of the boys' bedroom.

* * *

The art dealer's visit to Green Willow brought nothing but happiness for everyone, family and dealer alike. The Ferriston family owned a small fortune in original eighteenth-century paintings. Apparently, Jonathan had been something of an artistic giant and his works were much sought after. Dealers had known for years that there had to be other works by him but no one had discovered their whereabouts. Mr Coaster took over the negotiations and it soon became obvious that the family's future finances were well secured. They would be able to plan their hotel without any worries.

For Tom and Charlie it was a huge relief. They decided that they would have to make another visit to Mrs Robertson's tea rooms.

Chapter Fifty-Eight
Cream teas always help

Mrs Robertson was delighted to see them and suggested they came to her tea shop later that afternoon.

So, there they were again, sitting at the specially reserved table in the alcove.

"I don't want to go back to school," said Charlie as he munched his scone. "It's going to be so boring after all we've done this holiday."

Tom agreed.

"And what shall I write," he continued, complaining, "if the teacher asks me to write about my holidays?"

The others laughed.

"You'll just have to make something up," said Tom, giving all his attention to the strawberry jam which was delicious.

Mandy and Andrew agreed. "I always make something up," said Mandy. "It's much the best way to do it."

"You just have to be careful not to overdo it," said Andrew. "Just enough to keep the teachers happy."

Mr Rushforth chuckled. "Things won't be dull, I'm sure of it," he said. "Why we've only just begun!"

"You mean…" began Tom.

"Patience my dear young friend, patience," said Mr Rushforth, as he shook Tom's hand warmly. "There will be dangerous times ahead, of that I am sure. The Solanum are intent on finding the paints which are hidden somewhere in your home. With these, you know that they will be able to travel through many dimensions. Whilst the paints are lost, Green Willow and your family, in fact the whole village, is at risk. Do you understand?"

The boys nodded, but in truth they didn't really understand.

"Urthslean will help to protect you, Tom, as will Arula for you, Charlie."

Again they nodded.

"Now let us eat this delicious cream tea. I think we need more scones!" Mrs Robertson was only too pleased to bring them more.

* * *

Later that night, Tom and Charlie stood in front of the castle painting and just stared at it.

"Did all those things really happen, Tom?" asked Charlie.

"Yes, I think they did," said his older brother quietly.

There was the oak tree covered in green leaves, and there in the background rose the majestic towers of Campandella Castle. Just the sort of castle you might expect in a fairy tale, full of the promise of magic.

"What next, I wonder?" muttered Tom.

A shiver of excitement ran through Green Willow.

"Whatever it is," said Charlie. "We'll be ready for it."

Tom smiled and patted Urthslean.

About the Author

Jo lives and works in Sussex and from an early age she has written and told stories for children. She has written musical plays for schools and provided music for various local pantomimes. This is Jo's sixth published book. Her first children's book, *The Golden Shifter*, was published in 2014 and is the first in the Henrietta Trout series. It has been read and enjoyed by children and adults alike.

Lightning Source UK Ltd.
Milton Keynes UK
UKHW040709011218
333205UK00001B/60/P